WATERSMEET

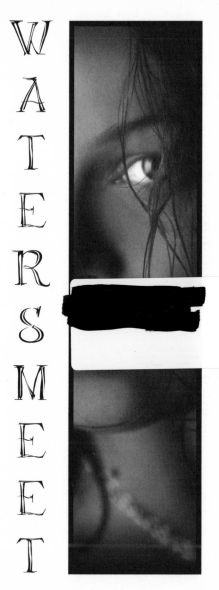

BY ELLEN JENSEN ABBOTT

MARSHALL CAVENDISH

Marshall Cavendish Corporation
99 White Plains Road
Tarrytown, NY 10591
www.marshallcavendish.us/kids

Library of Congress Cataloging-in-Publication Data
Abbott, Ellen Jensen.
Watersmeet / by Ellen Jensen Abbott. — 1st ed.
p. cm.
Summary: Fourteen-year-old Abisina escapes the escalating violence, prejudice, and religious fervor of her hometown, Vranille, and sets out with a dwarf, Haret, to seek the father she has never met in a place called Watersmeet.
ISBN 978-0-7614-5536-3
[1. Fantasy.] I. Title.
PZ7.A1473Wat 2009
[Fic]—dc22
2008000315

Book design by Alex Ferrari/ferraridesign.com
Map by Megan McNinch
Editor: Robin Benjamin

Printed in China
First edition
10 9 8 7 6 5 4 3 2

mc Marshall Cavendish

For Ferg, with all my love

Acknowledgments

Thank you to Robin Benjamin, whose insights and editing helped me get the book in my head onto the page.

And to all the people who believed in me, even before I believed in myself: Winslow and Montgomery Abbott, Susan Campbell Bartoletti, the class of 2k9, Elizabeth Cook, Margery Cuyler, Charlotte Feierman, Bridget Finnegan, Ginger Knowlton, Frederick Kurth, Leslie Goetsch, Margaret Haviland, Miriam Haviland, Alison Hicks, Jane Jaffin, Dicky Jensen, Kurt Jensen, Gail Carson Levine, Deanna Mayer, David Shenk, Barbara Shirvis, Suzanne Supplee, Nancy van Arkel, and my students and colleagues at the Westtown School.

Thank you especially to Ferg, William, and Janie, who shared me so generously with Rueshlan and Abisina.

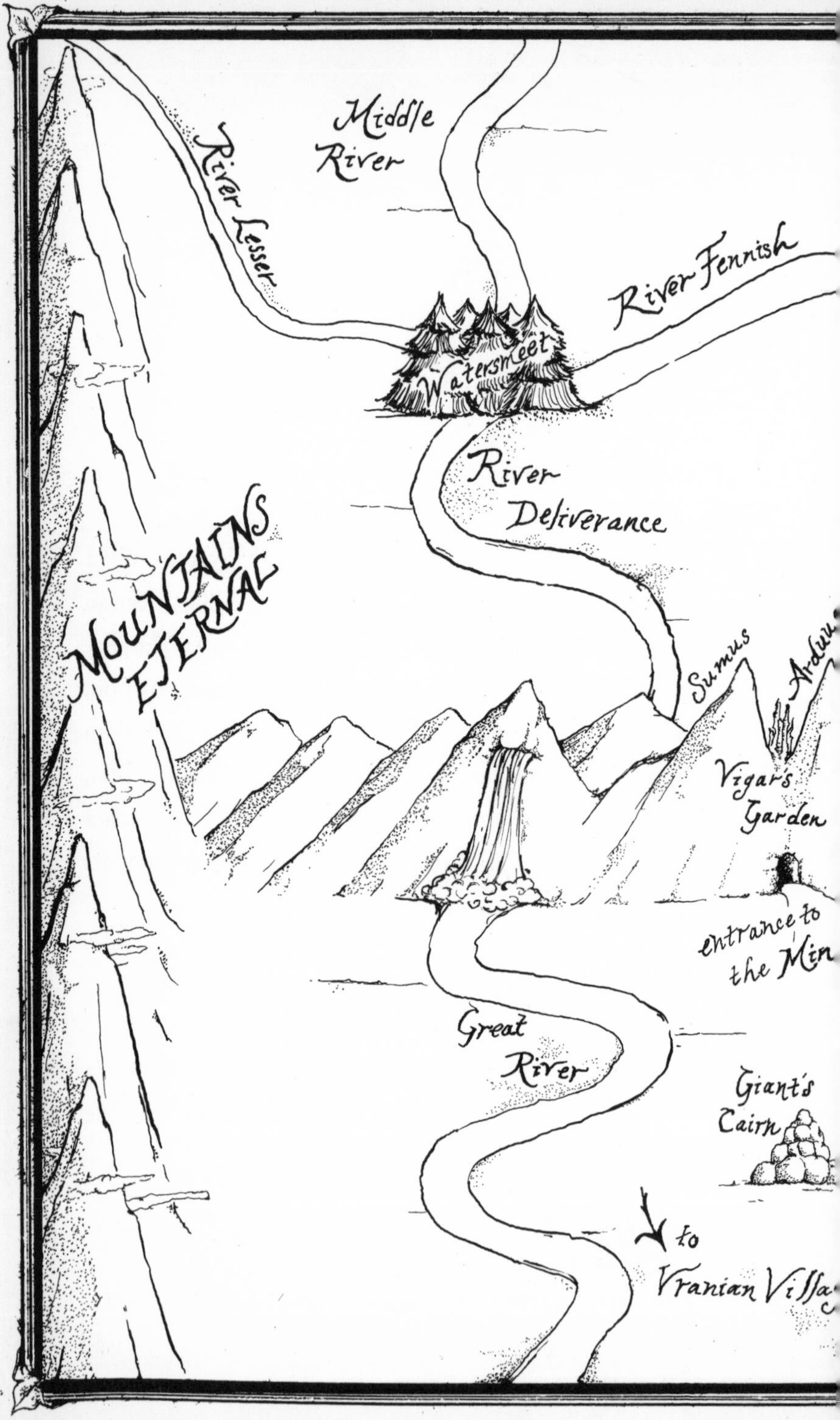

Middle River
River Lesser
River Fennish
Watersmeet
River Deliverance
MOUNTAINS ETERNAL
Sumus
Arduu
Vigar's Garden
entrance to the Min
Great River
Giant's Cairn
to Vranian Villa

Prologue

Long before the founding of Seldara—long even before the birth of the outcast Abisina—Vran, the Paragon of Man, led the people over the Mountains Eternal and into the land we now call the Southern Kingdom. His followers carved out an existence: building villages behind thick walls; clearing forest to plant grains and vegetables; battling the centaurs and the fauns and the dwarves who had already claimed the land for their own. Slowly, the settlements spread west until there were six— Vranham, Vranlyn, Vranberg, Vrandun, Vranhurst, and finally, Vranille. The settling of villages took generations and cost many lives, and still the Vranians had not realized Vran's vision of Men ruling the land. . . .

PART I

CHAPTER 1

ABISINA SCANNED THE CROWD THROUGH THE TANGLE OF her dark hair. *So many!* The widows and their children had all come, brought by the same rumor that brought her: the village Elders would be sharing out portions of cheese.

Abisina's empty stomach clenched. *Cheese!* She could feel its creaminess on her tongue, taste its sharpness. When was the last time she had tasted cheese?

I will be last, she thought, looking again at the crowd huddled against the thick-logged wall surrounding the village. That summer's centaur raids had swelled the number of widows more than the long drought and waves of disease. The gaunt faces, stooped shoulders, and swollen bellies told the story. Dirty, worn tunics hung on children like tents. Bony elbows poked through woolen under-shirts. Pockmarked faces. Chilblains. Open sores. All the women looked old. With their large eyes in wizened faces, even the children looked old.

A tiny child in front of Abisina clung to her mother's hand, whimpering. *She's never tasted cheese at all,* Abisina thought. *But no pity. They've never pitied you, And they'll get all the cheese before you get a morsel.* Abisina pulled her cloak around her tightly. The sun in the brilliant, late-autumn sky laughed down at the village, offering no warmth and no chance of rain.

"Move, Outcast!" Shoved aside, Abisina landed hard on the frozen ground. Footsteps circled her.

"Get up, demon!" a voice whispered close to her ear.

Lilas. Always Lilas.

"Get up, I said!"

Through her curtain of hair, Abisina could see Lilas's blonde braid dangling before her. That was all that saved Lilas. As an orphan and a girl, Lilas was worth little to the people of Vranille. But she was blonde, blue-eyed, and fair— too close to Vran's Paragon of Beauty to be an outcast.

"Dwarf-dirty!" Lilas taunted her.

Abisina bit her tongue and tasted blood. *Let it go,* she told herself, anger rising.

Lilas moved in closer. "Charach's coming," she mocked. "Coming to get rid of you and your freakish mother!"

Abisina fought the urge to throw herself at the girl. When would she learn how useless it was to fight back?

Then Lilas came in for the final blow.

"Bastard!" she hissed, and a fleck of spit fell on Abisina's hand.

In one motion, Abisina threw back her head and stared at

Lilas—a direct affront. An outcast could not meet the eyes of a villager.

A look of triumph came over Lilas's face, but as she opened her mouth to shout, a cry came from the widows. "Here he comes! Elder Theckis!"—and the scramble to be the first to get cheese drowned out Lilas's accusation.

"I'll get you for that!" Lilas threatened before cuffing Abisina on the head and disappearing among the widows.

Abisina was shaking as she got to her feet, the hate still bitter in her mouth. She tossed her hair forward to shroud her face again and turned to the crowd, an unbroken line of leather tunics and blonde braids.

Saved by Elder Theckis. She watched grimly as the Elder made his way to the storehouse. Like the rest of the villagers, he wore leather leggings and a tunic over an under-shirt, but the red sash tied across his chest, the iron pendant around his neck, and his full cheeks told his rank. *How disappointed he would be to know that he saved me from a good beating!*

A young man with a vacant stare and slight smile limped behind the Elder, shadowing his every step. He, too, wore a sash across his chest, but his was made of dirty rags; and the chain around his neck was made of bones. His name was Jorno, and like Abisina, he was outcast.

As the pair approached the crowd, the Elder called out— "Make way! Let me through!"—and Jorno mimicked his accent and tone exactly: "Make way!"

As the widows parted, Jorno's absent gaze rested on Abisina. For no more than an instant, recognition registered on his face. He *saw* her. But just as quickly, he resumed his empty stare.

Abisina gasped. *Did I imagine it?* Jorno had sixteen or seventeen winters, a few more than Abisina, but he had not grown up in Vranille as she had. Last summer, he had wandered into the village, his right foot toeless and half-severed, a sure sign he had been captured by centaurs. Abisina's mother, the village healer, had taken him into their hut. She brought down his fever, cured the infection in his foot, and repaired his wound as best she could. After his fever and delirium subsided, the Elders tried to find out where he came from, but he only repeated their questions back to them. His face remained blank. They let him stay in Vranille and Jorno had become a fixture in the village, wandering around, dragging his lame foot behind him, following the Elders, repeating the words and conversations he heard.

But that look was—intelligent. Abisina shook her head as she watched Elder Theckis disappear into the storehouse with Jorno on his heels.

"Get out of here, Outcast!" The Elder kicked him roughly.

"Out of here, Outcast!" Jorno echoed, his smile never flickering as he fell onto the dirt, then scrambled to his feet and stood at the door.

Elder Theckis emerged with a small wedge of cheese, and the crowd murmured in disappointment. Though she stood at the back of the line, Abisina could see green mold splayed across it. But the widows—rejected even by women because they had no men to hunt or farm for them—would accept whatever the Elders gave them. No one moved.

With a piece that small, I'll get nothing, Abisina thought, but she, too, stood her ground.

The Elder lifted the knife to cut the first piece—

"Theckis!" a raspy voice called. "Theckis!" Another man wearing a red sash and iron pendant hurried toward them, his gray beard blowing back in the wind. "It's true!" he cried. "The rumors are true! He'll be here for the Ritual!" Theckis stared at his fellow Elder while the villagers stirred. "He's coming, I tell you!" the bearded Elder insisted. "Charach is coming to Vranille!"

At his words, fear gripped Abisina. But the widows greeted the news with passionate cries:

"Blessings from Vran!"

"We're saved!"

"Our deliverer!"

Some knelt in the dirt, while others wept openly. A few laughed, the cold wind carrying the harsh sound from their lips.

Abisina hadn't noticed Jorno slip from the front of the line, but suddenly he was coming toward her, staring blankly as he bumped her with his shoulder.

"Get home!" a voice whispered in her ear as he rushed past, moving toward the village with his uneven gait.

Had Jorno spoken to her? Abisina looked to see if anyone heard, but the noise of the crowd had changed from joy to dismay as Theckis closed the storehouse door on the hope of food. The second Elder waited impatiently.

"We need our cheese!" someone cried.

Abisina raised her head. *Who would dare to speak so defiantly?*

A girl of about sixteen winters stood before Elder Theckis at the steps of the storehouse. Her chin was up, and she stared into the Elder's face.

Paleth. Abisina groaned inside.

When Abisina had five winters, her mother had been called to remove a centaur's arrow from the shoulder of Paleth's father. Unable to enter their hut as an outcast, Abisina settled in the dust outside to wait. After a time, she felt someone near her—standing still, waiting. She braced herself for the kick or blow that was sure to come. But whoever it was didn't move. Unable to stand the waiting, Abisina peeked toward her tormentor.

A girl stood there, smiling. Their eyes met. The girl held out her hand in offering, but Abisina could not make herself move. The girl had just taken a step toward Abisina when a sharp voice from inside the hut called: "Paleth!"

With a quick look over her shoulder, Paleth snatched Abisina's hand, put something in it, and fled back into her hut. Abisina sat stunned. A child, someone her age, had smiled at her, *touched* her. Then she remembered that the girl had given her something. She opened her palm to find a shiny white pebble winking up at her—the pebble that Abisina now carried in a scrap-pocket sewn in her waistband.

This same defiant Paleth now confronted Elder Theckis. He finally found his voice. "What did you say?"

"We need our cheese," Paleth repeated.

"Elder Theckis!" the girl's mother cried, shocked at her daughter's boldness. "She doesn't know what she's saying! She's had the fever!"

The ravages of fever were plain on Paleth's drawn face, but her eyes were clear and steady. "We've had nothing but moldy potatoes and rancid flour for weeks," she said, ignoring her mother. "My father died protecting this village. We deserve to be fed!"

The Elder's rage sputtered forth. "You—you will not speak to me like this!" he screamed. "Take the girl away!" A few women rushed to take Paleth's arms, but her mother threw herself at the Elder's feet.

"She doesn't know what she's doing! Take pity on her, in Vran's name!"

"How dare you, a woman, invoke Vran's name to *me*! Get out of my sight or you will suffer the same punishment," Theckis commanded, and another woman hurried to lead the mother back toward the village.

Paleth struggled as she was carried off, repeating, "We need to eat! We need to eat!"

Abisina tried to block out Paleth's fading shrieks and her

mother's sobs. Around her the crowd was breaking up, the talk returning to Charach. The echoes of that name intensified Abisina's dread. Jorno's whispered words came back to her: *Get home.*

Keeping her head down, she sought a way through the crowd, but every step was blocked by another clutch of women with the name Charach on their lips. Abisina dodged one group and then another. She broke free of the crowd and began to run, wanting only to put distance between herself and that name.

"Run, demon, run!" someone yelled after her, followed by a loud laugh.

Without looking back, Abisina ran through the dusty alleys of the village, dashing among the earthen huts that squatted under the merciless sun, cutting across little patches of garden now barren. She avoided the larger lanes that ran around the village in seven concentric circles and the six central roads that divided it like spokes of a wheel, each running from the outer wall to the common ground at the center. These roads and lanes would be especially busy today, clogged with villagers making preparation for tomorrow's Ritual.

Her hut stood on the outer ring, closest to the log wall. All the outcasts and the widows lived on this outer ring. In exchange for the small amount of food and protection they were given, these expendable villagers made the dangerous journey over the wall and into the surrounding forest to collect firewood. Although the location of her hut was supposed to be a symbol of her shame, Abisina liked being away from the activity of the village. She knew her mother could live closer to the center if it were not for her, but Sina always said that she preferred to be near the forest where she gathered the plants and roots she needed for her work. Of course, when Sina went into the forest, the village sent an armed guard to protect their only healer.

Abisina reached her hut and ducked inside. It was quiet and dusky; her mother was out tending to the sick. She sank down on the stool before the fire, where a few embers glowed from the morning's blaze. Paleth's shrieks still echoed in her ears.

As she had raced through the village, she'd noticed a change among the people, a churning of anticipation and hope unheard of on the eve of the Day of Penance. As the Elders were always reminding the villagers, they did not deserve to call themselves Children of Vran. He had brought their forefathers to this new land to be masters of it, but, generations later, they were still huddled behind the walls, living in squalid villages, barely eking out a living, and battling the beasts they should have dominated. Tomorrow, the Elders would grind penance out of them with grueling rituals and fasting.

But today, the people of Vranille had cast off the habit of submission. Clusters of women stood together talking in excited voices. Children played games of Kill-the-Dwarf, and no mother hurried to shush them. Men and guards, returning from prying the last of the blackened potatoes from the frozen ground, stood with their spades and bows over their shoulders, debating how Charach would lead them against the centaurs. The news of Charach had spread—and the villagers felt invincible.

Then Abisina heard Lilas again: *Charach's coming to get rid of you and your freakish mother!*

She shuddered. Would the village really turn on her mother? They needed her healing! And Sina was not truly outcast, not like Abisina with her black hair, copper skin, and unknown father. True, Abisina was not marked or deformed or deficient in her mind like some outcasts. And she had learned much of her mother's skill. In fact, her mother had said many times that Abisina had the gift of healing, perhaps greater than her own.

Abisina had once believed that the villagers would accept her when they knew how well she could heal. But now she knew better. *Stop your daydreaming*, she chided. *You are so far from Vran's Paragon of Beauty! You have the healer's green eyes and the gift, but what Vranian would allow you to lay your "dwarf-dirty" hands on him—even with death approaching?*

And now that Charach was coming, wouldn't it only get worse? Deliverer, they called him. Savior. Heir to Vran. Ever since rumors of Charach's arrival had filtered in from the other villages, the insults and violence Abisina lived with had taken on a sharper edge. When villagers spoke of defeating the evil in the land, Abisina caught their sidelong glances at her and the other outcasts.

She had always assumed that her mother's role in the village would shield her, but sitting now before the dying embers, Abisina began to wonder.

You didn't get left outside the walls. That was Mama's doing. Sina had delivered babies, set broken legs, brought down fevers—there was no family in Vranille untouched by her skill. They needed her and had let her keep her daughter. Could Charach, as a priest of Vran—some said a new *incarnation* of Vran!—could he change that?

"Stop shivering like an old woman!" Abisina burst out, standing up so quickly the stool fell over. The hut was dark and cold. Her mother would be home soon and would need supper. She grabbed a stick and began to stir the coals.

As the small hut warmed, the bunches of dried plants hanging from the roof released their individual perfumes: yarrow, lavender, feverfew, chamomile, elfwort, clover, and flax. Abisina breathed deeply, inhaling the smells that always clung to her mother's skin. The scents brought reassurance as surely as Sina's presence would. *My mother will know what to do.*

CHAPTER II

ABISINA HAD BROUGHT IN A FEW STICKS OF THE PRECIOUS firewood from the dwindling stack outside the cottage, shaken the sheepskins and animal pelts on the sleeping platforms, swept the dirt floor, and swung the cooking pot over the now crackling fire to warm the soup left from the morning meal. She was crushing some dried yarrow and chamomile into her mother's mug for tea when something on the table caught her attention: a few dried plants with faded yellow flowers, tied with a leather thong. Coltsfoot. Used to cure coughs, bring down fevers, and lessen swelling. It was her mother's gift for the Ritual of Penance.

The anger and fear of the afternoon seized Abisina again. Tomorrow, her mother would make this required gift to honor Vran—when it was Vran who caused all this misery; whose teachings made the widows beg for food rejected by the rest of the village; whose name would be invoked as Paleth was punished;

whose model of perfection rendered Abisina ugly and outcast. Abisina snatched up the coltsfoot, ready to throw it in the fire, when a gust of cold air announced her mother's return.

Sina smiled wanly at her daughter from the open doorway and headed to the fire, as Abisina hastily put the coltsfoot back on the table.

"If the Ritual day is as cold as this, I'll have to treat the whole village." Abisina's mother was tall and thin, though the three-year famine had made her skeletal. Even her penetrating green eyes were dulled. Without looking at her daughter, she said, "You heard about Paleth?"

"I was there."

Sina remained silent while Abisina laid out the bowls for the watery soup. Finally Sina spoke: "They beat her. She has at least four broken ribs."

Abisina gripped the handle of the kettle tightly as she poured boiling water over the herbs in her mother's cup. "She was already weak from the fever," she said.

As Abisina gave her the tea, Sina reached out and touched her daughter's hand. "There's more. Theckis insisted she be outcast."

Abisina turned away to hide the mix of emotions on her face. *If Paleth is outcast, I can speak to her!*

Abisina hated herself for the thought. How could she wish her life on anyone? Walking through the village with head down as children threw insults or rocks. Kicks from people like Lilas and others slightly better off than the outcasts, who flaunted their status by their cruelty.

Perhaps worst of all was the loneliness. Of all the outcasts, only Abisina had been born into her status. Flawed babies were simply left outside the walls to die, the village unwilling to feed and clothe them until they were useful as wood gatherers. The others were outcast as older children or adults, when hidden flaws were discovered: ominous birthmarks, missing digits, simplemindedness, excessive timidity or softness—any trait that moved them further from Vran's Paragon of beauty, intelligence, strength, and bravery. Even among the outcasts, Abisina was outcast; most of them had spent years despising her before their own defects were discovered, and they continued to shun her when they found themselves of her caste. In fact, the only happiness Abisina knew outside her own hut was in the forest. The freedom she found there was worth her constant fear of centaurs. And in the forest, she had her bow. Even outcasts were permitted to carry a bow beyond the village walls, and she spent hours practicing her shot, until she could hit a fist-sized target at seventy paces in a stiff wind. *If Paleth were outcast*, Abisina couldn't help thinking, *we could go to the forest together! I'd teach her to shoot, climb trees, read—*

Her mother broke into her thoughts. "You heard the other news, Abisina? About Charach?"

The tremor in her mother's voice startled Abisina. *Is Lilas right? Will the village turn on their healer?* She turned back to Sina, searching her face for reassurance. "What will it mean, Mama?"

Again, Sina's voice betrayed her: "I don't know."

No! The anger at Lilas's taunts rose again, claws and teeth bared. "We can't let them do this, Mama! We have to fight— like Paleth!" Abisina snatched the coltsfoot and flung it into the fire, watching in triumph as it blazed up in a brilliant flame.

But as mother and daughter looked on, the flame dimmed, leaving sprigs of white ash that crumbled and disappeared.

Abisina's fury crumbled with it.

Sina said nothing, and Abisina mumbled, "I'm sorry, Mama."

"I felt the same when I was your age," Sina said.

"Mama?"

Sina looked at her daughter. "There is something that I should have told you earlier. I was afraid. But I should have seen that you're ready. Vran . . . for all his strength and power . . . was only a man."

Abisina expected the door to fly open and the Elders to come pounding in. "Mama! You can't say that!"

"What I'm saying is true, Abisina. The villagers have forgotten. When Vran, the man, died, his legend lived on until he became some sort of god. Yes, he led the people over the Mountains Eternal, and that is miraculous. But miracles—they come from somewhere else, somewhere beyond human power. It wasn't Vran alone who led the people. And we can be sure of that because, later, he went so wrong. . . ."

Abisina shook her head, the blasphemy ringing in her ears, and with another glance at the door, she whispered, "I don't understand."

"I know, dear heart. The story I have to tell begins— well, it begins when Vran first came over the mountains, but I will start in Vranhurst, where I lived before Vranille existed."

Abisina sank onto a stool by the fire while Sina sat in her chair, the soup forgotten on the table. Sina's hand went to her throat, to the necklace that she wore hidden inside her tunic. The necklace was made of a white, glowing metal. A pendant hung from the delicate chain—ribbons of metal, thin but strong—each weaving among the others until they merged into a single twisting strand. Abisina knew the neck- lace was a gift from her father, although Sina had never told her this. On the rare occasions when her mother spoke of him, her hand went to this necklace.

"I know you have wanted to learn more about your father. It never seemed safe. Now that Charach—"

"Charach? I don't understand."

Sina began again. "Growing up in Vranhurst, I felt as you do now. We weren't outcast. My mother was the healer, and my sister and I had the green eyes, so we would be healers, too. But I saw the same wretchedness you see: my mother coming home distraught when she had to surrender a new- born to the Elders for a supposed flaw. She did what she could—covered birthmarks with chalk, stripped color out of darker hair. She couldn't save them all. Three of her own children had been left outside the village walls."

"Why?"

"Green eyes," Sina replied bitterly. "They let me live because people were convinced that the healing gift came with green eyes. They let my younger sister live, so that if something happened to me, she could fill my place. But the Elders said, 'No more.' I saw what my mother and father went through with each child—the months of hoping and worrying. They didn't care if the baby was a girl—as long as it had blue eyes!

"Then the Elders called for volunteers to found a new village, and I knew I would be forced to go. They would need a healer, and my sister was too young. I didn't know how I could leave my family. But then one night, a man named Filian came to see me. I hardly knew him. But Abisina, he opened a new world!" A smile lit Sina's face. "He put into words all the wrongness I had been feeling—the wrongness you feel now. Vran was a man, he said, a man who could be as wrong as any other man. Why did we continue to follow his teachings when they brought such suffering? Filian said we are afraid. We have to fight so hard to survive! It makes us feel better to believe that we are following a god's commands—not a man's. It gives reason to our misery."

Abisina broke in: "Even if Vran were just a man—" and then dropped her voice. "How does that change anything?"

"It changes everything, Abisina! You know it's wrong that

babies are abandoned and that Paleth was punished for speaking the truth. All of this is based on Vran's teachings! If he were wrong, all the rules that govern us are wrong, too." Sina clasped her hands together. "After talking to Filian, I felt light! The sense of injustice I'd been carrying was gone! He told me about his vision for Vranille. There were others who believed as he did, and all of them had volunteered to go. Vranhurst wasn't sending any Elders at first—too dangerous—so Filian thought he had a good chance of leading the settlers away from Vran's law. And once the other villages knew what life could be like, they, too, would follow Filian."

Sina's face darkened, and she sank back into her chair.

"Filian was so sure, so powerful in his vision. I would have followed him anywhere. But right from the start there were problems. You've heard of those hardships again and again on Founding Day. Filian made little progress in opening others' eyes. We spent most of the summer clearing the land, building shelters and a fence, planting and combing the forest for anything that might sustain us through the winter. It was then that I met your father."

Abisina gripped her seat. Had the time come at last? She'd long since given up asking. Mentioning him brought too much pain to her mother's face. Abisina didn't even know his name.

"I was off collecting herbs." Sina paused, and when she spoke again, her voice had a different quality—breathy and wistful. "I can remember the first time I saw him, standing in a ray of light that reached all the way to the forest floor. I know I've never really described him to you. He—he was beautiful." Sina sighed, while Abisina waited anxiously. "You have his coloring. Hair the color of the raven, skin like copper."

"What?" Abisina leapt to her feet. "He was outcast?"

"Where he comes from, there are no outcasts."

Abisina tried to take in her mother's words. "He—he wasn't Vranian?"

"He came from beyond the northern mountains—the Obrun Mountains, he called them."

"It's true? Those stories about creatures from beyond the mountains? But—but—they're devils!"

"No!" Sina grasped her daughter's clenched hands. "They're human, as we are." She pulled Abisina to her. "We've been taught so well," she said, "taught to hate any creature different from us. And you must understand. I had come here to escape that. To reject Vran and his teachings. Filian said that we needed to work *with* the dwarves, the fauns—even the centaurs."

"But the centaurs—what they do to us! They're our enemies!" How many times had she hidden from centaurs in the forest—under an overhang or up a tree? She shuddered at the image of their malevolent faces as they thundered past her hiding spots. Without thinking, she felt for the bow she always wore outside the walls.

"Filian believed we brought their hatred on ourselves. We moved into their land with one thought in mind: build a homeland for Man. We didn't care that there were creatures already here. But have you ever wondered why we speak the same tongue—centaurs, dwarves, and humans? Filian believed that long ago we all shared this land—that Vran's ancestors must have come from this side of the Mountains Eternal. And your father said that all of us—all creatures—are united by the same spirit."

Abisina tried to make sense of what her mother was saying. *I look like my father. His hair is black like mine.* "I—I always imagined him—like Vran." As she said it, the bands around her chest tightened more.

"Oh, Abisina!" Sina hugged her again. Her mother's necklace pressed into Abisina's chest, and suddenly her father was there, too—this new father from beyond the mountains.

"You've always told me I have gifts, Mama. And I've tried to believe you. But it gets harder and harder. All my life I've heard them say I'm a demon sent as a punishment to Vranille." Abisina's voice broke.

"It was Elder Theckis who told the village that." Sina released Abisina. "He was both your savior and your tormentor. This is part of the story, too. Theckis saved your life."

Abisina moved back to her stool, braced for Sina's next words.

"When you were born at the beginning of the second summer, we were just getting back on our feet from fever, the centaur raid, and the starvation of winter. Much of the settlement had been wiped out. Filian was dead. . . . Two men had left for Vranhurst to bring an Elder and more people. Once the Elder arrived, I knew you would be left outside the wall. You were only a few days old, but you already had a head of hair as black as your father's and skin that I knew would darken. I brought you to Theckis and showed him.

"Though he is an Elder now, Theckis had been a follower of Filian, his right hand. But like so many, Theckis believed that our settlement had been cursed for straying from Vran's laws. Or that's what he said. As our dreams fell to tatters, he may simply have decided to save himself by professing the beliefs of those now in power. He turned to the way of Vran.

"I threatened to expose his support for Filian if he didn't save you. I had saved him from the fever, and he owed me his life! So when the Elder from Vranhurst arrived, Theckis told him that some had strayed, and the raid and the fever were Vran's punishment. He had decided to let you live as a reminder of Vran's curse on us for our weak loyalty. The Elder believed him. You were saved—but outcast."

Sina stopped speaking as Abisina absorbed her words. She had been saved by Theckis when hundreds of other babies had died. The women had always been particularly cruel. Abisina had been spared when their own children had perished, their cries getting weaker and weaker from the other side of the wall.

But is life as an outcast really better than the release of death? Especially death as an infant? In the rituals, in the ceremonies, in the talk along the lanes and in the storehouse lines, Abisina had learned that the world was divided between the Children of Vran and the creatures who hated Vran. Centaurs, dwarves, the devils beyond the mountains—they were man's enemies: unnatural and evil. Like her. *I might have been better off with those other babies. . . .*

No! I did not deserve to die, any more than they did. I'm not a demon! Didn't Mama say that my father, who is dark like me, is beautiful? That beyond the mountains I would not be outcast?

A new thought came to her. "Why—why did my father leave us?"

The fire, sunk now to a bed of coals, cast shadows on Sina's wasted face. Her words were dragged from deep inside her: "I made him. I was sure that Filian would accept your father as I did. But when I told him about your father, Filian flew into a rage. He said I was putting all that we had worked for at risk. That the people would turn against us, and drive us from Vranille. He forbade me to meet your father again. But I had to say good-bye. So one night, I slipped out. Your father was waiting for me at the edge of the trees. He knew. Without my saying a word.

"'Come with me,' he said. 'You will be welcome in my home.' But we both knew I wouldn't go."

"He asked you to go with him? To leave Vranille?"

Sina nodded, eyes on her daughter's anguished face.

"And you said no?"

"I couldn't leave, Abisina! I still believed in Filian's vision. And I couldn't leave the people here without a healer."

"We could have lived where I would not be outcast! I

could have been accepted! I might have had *friends*!"

"I did what I thought was best, Abisina! You must believe—"

"You don't know what it's like for me here, Mama. You say you're like an outcast—but people *talk* to you! Touch you! You can go into their houses and walk the streets without wondering when you will be hit or kicked or spit on!" She was yelling now, not caring who heard her. Let the Elders come! So what if it was the Eve of Penance! What more could they do to her? There was the door right in front of her, and every instinct in Abisina wanted to fly out of it. To run into the night and away to this place beyond the mountains that offered her a future.

"Abisina!" her mother pleaded. "When I told him to go—I didn't know about you. I realized a few days after he left—when it was too late. For a while I hoped he would come for me. But he had been so angry. He swore he never would." She stopped and her next words were barely audible. "And he didn't."

Silence stretched between them until Abisina could hear the wail of the wind beneath the fire's hiss.

Sina spoke again, her voice flat: "When Filian guessed my secret, he threatened to send me back to Vranhurst. But then the centaurs struck and he, along with so many others, died in the raid. We had unknowingly built Vranille on their sacred winter grounds and when the herd returned—well, you know the story. Filian had hoped to make peace with the centaurs"—she laughed bitterly—"and then he helped build a settlement on one of their most sacred places."

Abisina stared into the coals, her rage cooling in the face of her mother's sadness. *It has been hard for her, too—this life in Vranille.*

"My hope died in that raid. Filian's other followers—those who survived—began to doubt his plan and turned back to Vran's ideals. It would have been easy to join them, and I thought about it, but then you were born. If I were to act as a follower of Vran," Sina said, her voice stronger, "I would have had to deny you, and that will never happen."

Abisina still said nothing.

"I must believe I've done good here—in healing—and in other small ways. The oppression has driven others to question Vran. There are only a few of us. Some were there today: Magen, the woman who led Paleth's mother away before she got beaten. She began to doubt when her mother hung herself after her third child was left outside the wall. And Robia. She gave Paleth some valerian so she wouldn't feel the beating as much. Her son was sent to fight the centaurs when he had only eight winters. Jorno, too, does what he can to fight the Elders."

Abisina stared at her mother. "Robia and Magen risked the wrath of the Elders?" She didn't think it was possible. Of all the villagers, women suffered the most. And Jorno— she recalled his look that morning, the whispered warning. She hadn't imagined it. "Even Jorno?" she said.

"Jorno's tricked everyone since he arrived. Because they think he's a half-wit, people talk freely in front of him. He came to tell me the news of Charach and later about Paleth. He spends his days following the Elders and collecting tidbits of gossip that might give some protection to those who need it."

"But Mama, why have you never told me all this?"

"I was afraid," Sina said quietly. "Theckis's power has grown; no one would believe that he was once a dissenter. And he has always watched me. If he suspected me in any way, our lives would be worth nothing."

"But you're the healer! They *need* you!"

"Perhaps. But my sister has children. They could send to Vranhurst for another healer. I couldn't risk your life, so I told you nothing." Sina's hand went to her necklace again. "Still, I may have been wrong. When I hear that you think yourself a demon—" She broke off, and Abisina watched her mother control her emotions. "I should have spoken sooner. I've meant to ever since the rumors of Charach started." At the mention of his name, Sina's face hardened. "Charach has already been to the other Vranian villages. They say he has come to lead us against the 'monsters' that surround us. I fear—I fear that it will be even more difficult for the out-casts." She gripped Abisina's hand. "We have to leave Vranille. Your father told me how to find him—if I ever changed my mind. We must find him now."

"He told you?" The anger flared again. "You knew how to find him—and we stayed?"

"He lives so far from here—I didn't think we could do it alone. And before, you were too young to try. Now, he's our only chance."

"But where is he?"

"He's in a place called Watersmeet."

"Watersmeet," Abisina repeated, the word like a drop of cool water on her tongue.

"I don't know much more than that—except that we can go there and be welcomed."

Deep in Abisina, something stirred. *We will leave Vranille. I will know my father, and find a new home.*

"We cannot put it off," Sina said. "They might notice if we're not at the Ritual. But tomorrow night, when it's over, we will leave for Watersmeet."

CHAPTER III

ABISINA WAS SURE SHE WOULD LIE AWAKE ALL NIGHT, running through her mother's story again and again, always returning to that final, mysterious word: *Watersmeet*. In the end, she must have slept, because she opened her eyes in the early light of dawn and found her mother's bed empty.

On countless nights, a hurried knock awakened Sina, calling her to tend the sick. Abisina had long ago learned to sleep through these knocks, waking alone as the sun rose. This morning her mother's absence unsettled her.

It's nothing, she thought, kicking off her warm bedskins and pulling on her leggings stiff with cold. *You're just nervous.*

Once dressed, Abisina could barely contain her worry. She cast about for anything to keep her hands busy. But the law for the Day of Penance permitted no work; she could not even build a fire or eat a bite of food.

Why bother? she wondered, enjoying the feeling of

rebellion. *Why observe the fast today, when by nightfall we will have left Vranille?*

Reaching for the cold soup left on the table, she remembered the coltsfoot that had lain there the night before. The gift for the Ritual! She had burned it!

With sudden inspiration, Abisina grabbed her old work tunic hanging by the door. She tore a bit of leather from the frayed bottom and fished a piece of charred wood out of the fire. She hastily scrawled something on the leather and then sat back on her heels to study her work with satisfaction.

Abisina arrived at the center of the village just before the Ritual was to begin. The Elders' large huts ringed the common area, glowering down on the gathered people. The sheep and goats, which had been pastured in the common during the most recent round of centaur raids, bleated in a makeshift pen at the far end. Most of the villagers had already taken their places, forming ever increasing half circles around the huge stone altar: first men, then boys, then women, girls, widows—and finally, outcasts.

From behind her loose hair, Abisina checked the crowd for any sign of Charach. The Elders huddled together to the right of the altar. Surely, he would be with them? But the faces were all familiar. She could feel the anticipation in the air, but as she watched Theckis break from the other Elders to squint down the lane toward the village entrance, she knew Charach had not come.

She frowned. *If he doesn't come, will we still leave?* How strange to *want* him to come—this man she had feared since the first rumor of him was discussed in the streets. Would her mother agree to go if Charach did not arrive?

"Where is your wife?" A loud voice startled Abisina.

"She is laboring, Elder, bringing forth a boy!" a man near her answered. The men of the village always spoke of their unborn babies as sons. Abisina glanced at the expectant father—Hain, Bryla's husband. He already had four girls. "The healer's with her."

Abisina's frown deepened. Bryla was a long laborer. *This baby better come before nightfall!*

"You there! Outcast!" The Elder scrutinized Abisina. "Make your gift!"

Abisina hurried to the altar. The offerings from the meager harvest looked pitiful on the stone slab: bug-ridden turnips, slices of coarse brown bread, wormy onions, stunted squash, a few sheaves of grain, a dusty cask of beer left from last year's brew, skeins of wool, bits of thatch, a cheese rind, a few bows and arrows. *Even the Elders will not eat well this winter.* The only plentiful item on the altar was a pile of coarse hair—black, brown, white, gray. Centaur tails, cut from the bodies of the slain creatures. Later, they would be hung on the village walls. The centaurs, too, collected prizes from their victims—toes and feet—after mangling every other part of the bodies. *And Filian thought we should befriend them?*

"Outcast!"

Abisina spun around to find the same Elder standing over her. He was tall and broad with meaty hands. "Make your gift!" he commanded.

She reached for the bit of leather tucked into the sash of her tunic but froze as she thought of what was written there. She couldn't take it out now! Not with the Elder watching her!

"Make your gift!" The Elder's voice grew louder, and the noise of the crowd fell. Shaking, Abisina tugged the gift from her belt and tucked it under a piece of thatch.

She turned away, but the Elder stopped her. "Not so fast, Outcast!"

He reached toward the little leather scroll and picked it up. With nerves as tight as a drawn bow, she watched him unfurl it. And there it was, scrawled in black:

Watersmeet

She thought of running, but the whole village was watching. And they were supposed to leave tonight! How could she have been so stupid?

But after looking briefly at the leather, the Elder threw it back on the table. "Hand!" he barked.

Abisina's relief left her limp as she held out her right hand, palm up. The Elder drew a short switch from his own waist cord. *Whack! Whack!* His blows left a red, stinging stripe across her hand. "Don't make me speak to you again, Out-cast!" He turned his back on her before Abisina mumbled the required—"In the name of Vran."

She scurried through the crowd toward the spot farthest from the altar, nursing her palm but stifling a grin. She had gotten away with it! The Elder couldn't read!

But I must be more careful! Women—and all but a few men—were forbidden from learning to read, though Sina had convinced the Elders that reading was one of the healing arts. If this Elder could recognize script, as some could, he would now know that she had taught Abisina. *Any risk is dangerous today!*

Reaching the crowd of outcasts, Abisina threw herself on the ground as the Elder at the altar called out, "Prostrate!"

The crowd folded on itself, kneeling with their hands and foreheads in the dirt.

"Come to us, O Vran!" a weak voice cried, starting the Ritual. It was Elder Kayn, the oldest of them, clinging to a stick for support. The horizontal bar of iron on the chain around his neck seemed to pull him toward the earth; he was bent with his face almost on the altar. "Come to us in our need!" he croaked, then stopped, interrupted by a spasm of coughing. "Great Vran," Kayn continued, "fill us now with the awe of your presence that we can honor and glorify you, O Paragon of Man!"

As the Elder wheezed out the final words of the invoca-tion, the crowd lifted their foreheads from the ground and sat back on their heels, heads bowed. Abisina shifted her weight off her right knee where a sharp stone stabbed her. She risked a glance to her left and spotted Eagan, a boy about her age guilty of one of the most heinous crimes: when face-to-face with a young centaur, he had hesitated to kill it. Next to him knelt Delvyn, who had tried to hide her son when the Elders called for a raiding party; farther on she saw Colbart, whose dark birthmark—called a "dwarf patch"—had been discovered when the chalk that covered it washed off in a rainstorm; and Jorno, his face impassive. What was he thinking?

Abisina glanced to her right where more outcasts hunched: Urya, Garm, Ain, Cadrin—all guilty of some crime against Vran in their actions, their words, or just their skin and hair. What was the number up to now? A quarter of the village? More?

Someone groaned near her, and Abisina lifted her head slightly to see who it was. She bit back a cry. Paleth—the side of her face covered with purple-green bruises, a line of dried blood snaking from the corner of her mouth. The white pebble tied into Abisina's waist cord pressed into her belly. Paleth looked toward her. Their eyes met briefly before something whistled through the air, and Paleth crumpled to the ground. "Eyes down, Outcasts!" a voice growled and Abisina, too, felt a hard knock on her head. Lights exploded before her as she stared back at the ground.

The Elders patrolled the crowd with long sticks topped by iron bars like the ones around their necks. If they spotted anyone drooping or drifting from the required position, they brought the bar down on the offender's head, a reminder of what Vran expected of his people.

After the Elder moved on, Abisina risked another glance at Paleth. She lay in a heap, arms wrapped around her rib cage, her breath rasping. But Abisina could not move from her own position to help. She remembered Paleth's defiance the day before. She had faced Theckis and not backed down. And this is what it got her. Abisina swallowed hard. *I may leave tonight, but Paleth will be outcast for the rest of her life.*

"Confession!" A new, stronger voice called. *Theckis.*

With the rest of the villagers, Abisina lay flat on the ground, her nose in the dirt. Paleth did not stir.

Theckis took up the chant of confession: "O Vran, Paragon of Man! We are unworthy of your example, unworthy of your gifts! You led us to the Land of our Destiny, but we have been unable to make it ours. Have we worked as hard as you worked for us?"

"No!" the villagers cried into the dirt.

"Have we pushed our bodies as hard as you pushed yours?"

"No!"

"Have we denied ourselves as you denied yourself?"

"No!"

"Have we thirsted?"

"No!"

"Have we hungered?"

Abisina spat quietly to get the dirt out of her mouth. It was a battle she would fight through the rest of the confession. The outcasts lay where the goats and sheep had recently been pastured. Her moist breath warmed the rutted earth, and at each "No!" her lips grew blacker. When Theckis began the list of general transgressions, the filth began to move into her mouth.

"Meekness!" he bellowed.

"We beg your forgiveness, Proud Vran," the crowd murmured.

"Weakness!"

"We beg your forgiveness, Strong Vran."

"Trembling!"

"We beg your forgiveness, Courageous Vran."

Theckis's voice was like a hammer, beating them into the ground.

As the Ritual moved into individual confessions, the Elders paced among the prostrate forms, listening closely. Confessors who seemed insincere or who offered trivial confessions were rewarded with a knock on the head or a kick to the ribs. But confessing anything too heinous would be more severely punished. Two years ago, the Elders had overheard a father confess that he loved his daughter more than his sons, and he had been outcast ever since.

Confessing brought greater danger for women. If the Elders judged a woman's confession incomplete, they asked her father, husband, or son to stand and list her offenses. The village still discussed, in awed but excited tones, the year a husband accused his wife of "sympathizing with centaurs." In the middle of the Ritual, the village—including the woman's five children—rose up and drove her into the forest. She had not been seen again.

The Elders ignored the outcasts during the rite of Confession—they were unredeemable, their every breath an offense to those who followed Vran. As Abisina pushed the dirt and gravel from her mouth, she tried to block out the murmurs, accusations, and prescribed punishments.

Only a few more hours. Never again would she be subjected to this harrowing day with its humiliation and pain. But a groan from Paleth recalled her mother's words: *You know it's wrong that Paleth was punished for speaking the truth.*

"Supplication!" an Elder cried.

As Abisina pulled her stiff body into the correct position—on her knees again, hands cupped before her—she noticed that Paleth was not the only villager crumpled on the ground. Older women, widows, and a few men had fallen and could not be roused by the prodding of the Elders. One Elder tried to kick Paleth awake, but she did not rise. And after a few more kicks, he gave up and moved on.

The sun was setting behind the fence, and the cold wind gained new strength as Abisina and the rest of the villagers assumed the final position: Adoration—sitting back on their heels, arms extended toward the sky, palms up, heads raised. Abisina felt her anger rise at the cruelty of the ritual: more villagers had collapsed, including a small girl a few feet from her. Paleth had curled into a ball, and Abisina could no longer hear her labored breath.

Charach had not come.

Abisina's left leg cramped painfully. She tried switching her weight to her right, but her knee pressed into the sharp rock that had bedeviled her all day. She had no idea where the Elders were and took the chance of sliding slightly backward. She braced herself, but no blow came.

The chanter was singing the story of Vran—his miraculous descent down the Mountains Eternal with a small band of followers. Like everyone in the Vranian villages, Abisina knew the story as well as the Elders did. At every ritual, every funeral, every wedding, some version of the story was sung. Today they would chant the longest, but even this Abisina could recite herself.

She let her focus drift—the scene blurring to a swath of browns and grays. She tried to blur sensation, too, losing her pain in the haze, but a stirring in the crowd claimed her attention. She blinked a few times and realized that the Elder's rough voice had been replaced by a clear, musical one.

A tall young man stood behind the altar now, a wreath of golden curls crowning his head. High cheekbones and a strong jaw gave his face dignity and power. His shoulders were broad, his waist thin. He was dressed in the same simple clothes as the villagers, but his were made of a rich fabric that contrasted sharply with the rough wool and soiled leather of the suppliants in the dirt. He stood in the posture of Adoration, eyes closed, the setting sun making a nimbus of his golden curls.

Is this—Vran?

Many villagers had dropped their arms in amazement, while the Elders stared and held their rods still. The young man continued to chant, but his melodic tones brought Vran's story to life in a new way. Warmth radiated from Abisina's chest to her stiff limbs. She wanted to pull the stranger's words into her, make them part of her.

His voice changed as he described what Vran and his followers found when they descended from the mountains: "The land teemed with bestial centaurs, lustful and licentious! And as your people spread east, O Vran, we met demonic fauns, vile and depraved! And the dirty ground-dwellers— the dwarves—repugnant perversions of Man's beauty!" The youth's high forehead was furrowed as he spoke, his voice shaking with disgust. Abisina had never seen dwarves or fauns; though she had heard these descriptions at all of the Rituals, she felt them now more vividly than ever before. At the stranger's words, Abisina's stomach churned and she thought she might vomit into the dirt.

"But, you, O Vran," the stranger sang, his tone now high and ethereal, lifting Abisina out of her disgust, "your beauty and perfection remind us of what we can be, what we must be, with you as our ideal and guide."

As he sang, Abisina soared to heights beyond the Mountains

Eternal. Gone were the pain and stiffness. She could kneel through the night and into the next day, if only the stranger kept singing!

For almost the whole of his chant, the young man stood motionless and reverent. *How does so much music come from his still body?* Abisina wondered. But as he began the final phrases of the Adoration, he lowered his arms until his hands rested on the stone table. And at the last word, he opened his eyes.

As the stranger looked toward where Abisina knelt in the dirt, the beauty he had woven with his words fell to shreds and darkness threatened to swallow her. The handsome young man was gone. In his place stood a grotesque figure: a White Worm, propped up on two thick limbs with razor claws. Its mouth gaped, dripping a viscous fluid. But the eyes were what revealed its evil heart, a ring of black pits circling the creature's head.

Charach!

CHAPTER IV

THE WHITE WORM'S EYES RESTED ON ABISINA FOR A LONG moment, then moved across the crowd. The darkness receded. The golden youth again stood behind the altar.

The silence of the Ritual broke, and throughout the crowd, people were getting to their feet, crying out, jockeying to get closer to Charach. Abisina rose unsteadily. In the rush, she glimpsed a prone old woman stepped on as if she were a hillock of grass.

Paleth! No one was watching the outcasts now. Abisina ran to where Paleth lay in the dirt and took the girl in her arms. "Paleth!" She tried to rouse her, but her eyelids didn't even flutter.

Shouts came from throughout the crowd: "Deliverer!" "Come to save us!"

Abisina laid Paleth gently back on the ground and got to her feet. She needed her mother! If Bryla had her baby already, Sina would have come to the Ritual. But as Abisina searched the crowd, she saw no sign of her mother. The people were looking hungrily toward the altar, hoping for Charach's gaze to fall on them. *Didn't they see the Worm?* Even the outcasts had joined the growing chant, "Charach, Charach!"

She bent back to Paleth. If she couldn't wake her, she'd have to carry her to Sina. She worked her arms under the girl's back and was just starting to lift her when Jorno appeared, taking the burden from her.

"I've got her," he said, settling the limp form on his own shoulder.

"My mother—she's with Hain's Bryla. I'll go with you."

"No, you stay here!" Jorno glanced toward the Elders, who had joined the chanting. "If we both leave, they might notice." Jorno took off, barely slowed by Paleth's added weight. He disappeared among the village huts.

Abisina looked back toward Charach. He stood now on the altar, his cloak pulled from him in the frenzy, and reached out to the hysterical villagers—taking the dirty, work-worn hands in his own strong fingers. His face, lit with a smile and the blush of health, beamed on the sallow faces lifted to him.

He straightened and called to the crowd. "My friends! My friends! You do me too much honor!" The people tried to drown his humility with their roar, but he held up his hands and said, "Please! Let me speak!" and the shouts died to a murmur.

"We have sung today the story of our Deliverer. Vran brought us here so many generations ago, and we have repaid him with our humbleness and adoration. He is our Paragon, and we offer him our hearts. I see the love on your faces."

"Vran! Vran!" the crowd chanted.

"But I see something else, too: Hunger. Disease. Suffering." Charach paused as if overcome with their pain. "We have come far, but we have labored hard."

"He speaks as if he is one of us!" someone cried and the shouts resumed.

"For years"—Charach spoke over the tumult—"our crops have been plagued by rains that wash away the seeds sown with our sweat. Or the summer's heat beats down on the tender seedlings, killing them in the inferno."

A groaning cry rose from the throng.

"And the beasts set upon us! We must keep our flocks inside our walls"—he gestured toward the sheep and goats— "while they grow thin and listless on this barren common. We cower behind our walls, afraid to harvest what we have sown. Is this what Vran wanted for his people?"

"No!" the crowd cried in unison.

"Is this why Vran led us over the treacherous mountains?"

"No!"

Abisina fought the urge to cover her ears.

Charach let the people vent their fury before raising his hand for silence.

He spoke just above a whisper at first, but his voice grew

louder and louder. "We offer our voices in song to Vran. We confess our transgressions and beg forgiveness. We offer sacrifices." Charach picked up a handful of onions from the altar and held them toward the crowd as he thundered, "It's not much, but we have so little!"

A few shouted, "Yes," but other villagers hesitated. Could they have given more? The Elders shifted uneasily.

"Maybe we do not quite deserve what Vran gave us." Charach's words sent a tremor through the crowd. "Maybe we are too weak. Maybe we hold to our small comforts because we cannot seize his great reward. Look at these gifts." His voice echoed off the village walls. "Is this what our Lord Vran deserves?"

"No!" called a lone voice, and immediately the rest of the crowd bellowed, "NO!"

Jorno appeared beside Abisina, panting slightly. "Is she safe?" Abisina had to shout to be heard.

Jorno nodded, but before he could say more, Charach began to speak again.

"We stand on the brink of realizing Lord Vran's vision! Right now, in the other Vranian villages, men and boys, even women and girls, are hard at work: training to be soldiers, fletching arrows, stringing bows. Will Vranille join them? Will Vranille follow me against the beasts who have kept us down far too long?"

The response of the crowd was deafening. Across the common, people screamed, hands in the air, fire in their eyes.

"Then you must show Vran your love—as the rest of the Vranians have done!" Charach screamed. "Show him that you deserve what he foresaw for you: defeat of the beasts and the dominion of Man!"

Abisina remembered her churning stomach when Charach had first spoken of the beasts. But this time, as his eyes flicked toward her, it was his gaze that brought a sick fear.

"There is pollution here, within these very walls! You have grown soft in enforcing Vran's law! How can you expect to conquer the monsters that plague your land, when you cannot conquer yourselves? You must wipe out all that is weak in you! You must atone!" The crowd was again on the move, pushing harder to get close to Charach. The outcasts joined the press, drawn by his rousing words.

"It is time for the rise of Man! It is time to take our rightful place. But first, we must rid ourselves of all that is not worthy!"

The crowd went mad—a woman in front of Abisina tore at her arms until they bled. Men ripped off their tunics and beat their chests. The outcast Delvyn fell to her knees and dashed her head against the ground. Through the crush of bodies, Abisina could make out Elder Theckis standing back, arms crossed, watching.

Next to her, Jorno put a warning hand on her arm. "Be ready to run."

Abisina spotted a large man throwing himself through the crowd like a fish swimming against the current. "The outcasts!" he screamed. "The cursed outcasts!"

His cry spread, and the crowd rounded on the outcasts. Without a second thought, Abisina was running—vaulting a fence, rushing down a lane. Jorno matched her stride for stride. She glanced back only once as the surging crowd trampled two outcasts who had fallen. She turned and ran for her life.

Abisina ran blindly, slipping behind huts, leaping short garden fences, switching direction with no plan for where she was going. Jorno was no longer with her, but she didn't know when or how they got separated.

Eventually her mind caught up with her feet. She had to run *somewhere*.

The cries of the mob became fractured as their quarry scattered. Abisina paused for a minute against a hut, thankful that the sun was now behind the wall, leaving the village in twilight.

I have to find Mama!

Abisina tried to get her bearings. Bryla lived on the northeast side, in one of the outer rings of huts. Luckily, she had run north. It was not far.

She took a step out of the shadows, intending to cross the lane and lose herself in the huts beyond, when a figure came around the corner of a hut twenty paces from where she stood. She leapt back and held her breath. The figure stopped a few feet away, and Abisina recognized the familiar blonde braid. *Lilas.*

Lilas tilted her head as if listening for something. Abisina waited one moment, two, but Lilas showed no sign of moving on. Abisina fumbled at her tunic belt, pulling out Paleth's pebble. Holding the stone in her hand, she thought of Paleth—unconscious and hidden somewhere in the village. *Let her be safe!* she thought fervently. And then, she drew her hand back and threw the pebble as hard as she could down the lane behind Lilas. The plunk of the pebble on the packed dirt made Lilas spin around just as a knot of villagers entered the lane, carrying torches.

"They're headed toward the gate!" someone in the gang cried.

Lilas took one last look around her and raced toward the villagers, leaving Abisina in the silent shadows.

Thank you, Paleth! Abisina set off in the opposite direction.

She stayed next to the huts, glancing down each lane or alley before she crossed.

As she got farther away from the village center, the cries of "Die for Charach and Vran!" grew fainter. But a few alleyways before Bryla's hut, she ran into six or seven boys about her age, carrying sticks and rocks, also headed toward the gate. The gang stopped as the lead boy called out, "Someone's there!" He scanned the lane in front of him. Abisina slid farther into the shadows, but she tripped and landed hard against a hut's mud wall. At the sound of her fall, one boy looked right at her.

She knew him. His name was Corlin. She'd been to his

hut once when his mother had the fever. Sina had wrapped the sleeping Abisina in plenty of skins against the bitter cold outside while she tended Corlin's mother. But his father had found her and carried her in. Abisina still had the vague memory of waking up in the strong arms of Corlin's father and being laid gently by the fire.

But his father wasn't here now. She braced herself for Corlin's shout.

"It's nothing!" he cried. "The outcasts are at the gate!"

She knew Corlin saw her. *Is he protecting me? Is it possible?*

The leader of the gang started to run toward the gate, followed by the rest, but one older boy hesitated. "No, someone's there!"

He took a step forward, but Corlin got ahead of him, reaching the edge of the lane and peering into the darkness where Abisina held her breath. "There's no one here," Corlin said.

"I saw someone," the boy insisted.

"If there was someone, he's gone now."

Abisina longed to run, but hesitated. *Can I trust him?*

"Go!" Corlin breathed.

It was all she needed. She slipped down the alley as Corlin yelled, "Is that fire by the gate?" She kept moving, gaining speed until she was again at a full run. No one chased her.

Tears filled her eyes as she spotted Bryla's hut and her mother ducking under the low lintel. "Mama!" she cried.

Sina looked up in surprise. "Abisina! I just finished—"

"Charach! They're after me—after the outcasts!"

In a glance, Sina took in her daughter's pale face, the shouts, and the glow of flames to the south. She grabbed Abisina, pulled her around the corner, and began to run along the lane between the back row of huts and the village wall. They stopped at a ladder propped against the wall, used by outcasts to get to the forest for firewood. A second ladder for getting down the other side lay on the ground, pulled in for safety.

"Climb," Sina whispered. "I will lower you from the top, and you can drop to the ground."

"But what about you?"

"I'll jump. It will be all right." But she pulled Abisina back before she could go. "Listen to me, Abisina! To get to Watersmeet—"

"Mama! We have to go! Now!"

"If we get separated—" Sina gripped her daughter's wrist. "There is a pass between Mount Sumus and Mount Arduus, at the entrance of the Obrun Mines."

"Mama—"

"Listen!" Sina clutched Abisina's wrist tighter. "Your father said I would find Watersmeet at the meeting of three rivers. And Abisina—this is very important. He can help us. Tell him about Charach. Tell your father what happened here!"

"Why are you doing this?" Abisina cried. "We'll be together!"

"Yes—we will be together, but I feel better now." Sina

hugged her daughter and then checked the lane. It was empty. "Go! I'll be right behind you."

But now Abisina clung to her mother's hand.

"Go!" Sina repeated, and Abisina did.

She was halfway up before the ladder shuddered from her mother's weight. She almost lost her balance but kept climbing, the top of the wall three rungs away.

"Outcasts!" The cry came from nearby.

"Keep going!" Sina shouted.

Abisina climbed faster. Feet ran from different directions, drawing closer.

"There's no time. Jump!" Sina commanded as Abisina reached the top of the wall. She swung her leg over and looked down at the hard ground. The wall had never seemed so high. The ladder lurched beneath her. "Now!" her mother cried, and Abisina put her other leg into the air, held the top of the wall for an instant, and dropped.

She landed with a teeth-jarring thud and fell against the rough logs of the wall. Her ankles screamed from the impact and she tasted blood in her mouth, but she stumbled away, clearing a place for her mother to land.

She looked up and saw her mother's head silhouetted against the flame-lit sky. Suddenly, it jerked out of sight.

A cry rose from the crowd.

It must have been the middle of the night when Abisina heard the Great Gate opening on the far side of the village wall. She crouched in the brush at the edge of the trees where she had been waiting since the moon rose. Fire glowed above the walls of Vranille, and the village still rang with hateful cries. *They're burning outcasts' huts. Is one of them ours? Is my mother—*

She refused to finish her thought. The village would not harm their healer. *Mama will come to me once the village is calmer.*

But what about Paleth, Jorno, the other outcasts? She imagined Paleth found by the mob, Jorno run down as he fled. She heard again the whoops of triumph as her mother had disappeared from the top of the wall. And she couldn't close her eyes without recalling the terrifying darkness of Charach's gaze.

Now the Great Gate was opening. Months had passed since the village last raised it, fear of raids forcing them to use the Lesser Gate to get to the fields and river. What was making them open it now, in the waning hours of the night?

Abisina couldn't see the gate from where she hid, but soon a bobbing light appeared from around the side of the village. Then another. And another. A silent snake of torches grew longer and longer until Abisina was sure the entire village had left its walls. Were they going to burn the village, too?

The line bent toward a point on the edge of the forest about half a league east of where Abisina hid. They were going to the village burial ground!

But burials are never held at night. She strained her eyes in the darkness, seeing nothing except the bobbing torches. The wind blew away any voices that might have reached her.

Abisina began to creep closer to the burial ground. *What can it mean?*

The light of the torches was swallowed up by the tall pines standing sentinel. She hurried forward, but she was stopped by a sound that chilled her—an otherworldly scream. Then a finger of red and purple flame shot from the clearing inside the circle of pines.

Abisina stared at the flame growing higher and brighter, but she willed herself to keep moving. In the lurid light, she could pick her way among the trees more quickly, and soon she ducked under the branches of one of the enormous pines. Next to the trunk, she had room to kneel while still concealed by a curtain of boughs.

Through the mesh of branches, Abisina watched the strange fire on the altar at the top of the clearing; its jagged peaks seemed to reach higher than the tops of the ancient trees. The villagers circled around, their features twisted by the eerie light, their mouths open in harsh shrieks. In front of the altar stood a figure Abisina immediately recognized, though his golden hair now reflected the redder hues of the fire. In the leaping flames, the figure of Charach, the man, alternated with images of the White Worm. And still no one else seemed to see him for what he was.

He was directing the activity around the fire as the villagers fed the flames with large loads of some kind of fuel.

Abisina inched closer, peeking through the low boughs to get a clearer view.

Bodies!

That was what the villagers were throwing on the inferno. *Bodies of outcasts!*

Instinctively, she reached for the bow that should have been hanging on her back—even as she knew that it wasn't there. If only she could get a shot off! One arrow, and she could end this, end Charach. Who cared what happened to her after that? But she was powerless, trapped under that tree, with no way to stop the gruesome scene.

She closed her eyes and thought about running into the darkness and silence of the woods.

But she couldn't leave. She had to know.

She forced her eyes open.

Dawn came slowly, the sun obscured by the billows of smoke that still poured from the smoldering fire. Sometime before dawn Charach disappeared, though Abisina didn't see him go. He had been there one moment, gone the next, his absence draining the scene of color, the dying flames pale and feeble. Without Charach to hold them there, a few dark figures began to straggle away from the burial ground. They looked broken, huddled in their smoke-stained cloaks. A few more followed them. And a few more.

From her hiding place, Abisina searched and searched the dispersing crowd. But she saw no sign of her mother.

Abisina!

Her eyes flew open at the sound of her mother's voice. The dappled light coming through the pine branches told her it was now midmorning.

"Mama?" she whispered.

Abisina crawled from under the trees into the burial ground, ready to fall into her mother's arms and sob out her relief.

But the burial ground was empty.

The pines reached toward the sky, their boughs streaked with soot, their needles singed. The usually neat graves were trampled; the iron bars marking the Elders' graves were kicked over or knocked askew. The smooth, white stone of the burial altar was stained black, a deep pile of ash smothering the few glowing embers. From the ash, currents of heat rose shimmering in the air.

"Mama?" she said, louder.

Silence.

Abisina walked toward the altar, recalling the White Worm next to the cruel fire, the silhouettes of the villagers carrying the bodies.

"Mama?" she cried desperately. She walked with halting steps, afraid of what she might find yet drawn forward.

Suddenly, the sun was obscured by a bank of heavy

clouds—the first in months. The wind picked up and the air became so thick with fat snowflakes, she couldn't see the altar in front of her.

She stood still, letting the wind whip her hair and drive the snow against her face. The wail of the wind was her own voice, the snow melting against her cheeks, her tears.

And then, as quickly as it came, the wind died. The snow settled on Abisina's hair, her hands, her shoulders. The altar stood before her, swept clean.

Except for a ribbon of silver glittering against the blackened altar stone.

Her mother's necklace.

PART II

CHAPTER V

AN INSISTENT HUMMING PULLED ABISINA FROM SLEEP, BUT she didn't want to wake up. She tried to draw the bedskins over her head, but her right arm wouldn't move. With great effort, she heaved her arm away from her body and was met with searing pain. She groaned, and the humming stopped.

"Awake then?" A raspy voice was followed by the sound of shuffling feet.

Abisina cracked an eye open to find a figure bent over her. She could not focus on the face. Lines of pain crisscrossed her forehead.

"Mustn't wiggle," the raspy voice said. "Had a nasty bump. You've been asleep these three days. Fixed those gashes in the shake of a mole's tail, with you so sleepy. But you must eat now. 'Get that soup. Stop your tongue wagging,' as Haret would say. 'Get to business. . . .'"

The voice faded away.

Abisina tried to clear her head, to make sense of the rock-hewn ceiling lit a dull red.

Where am I? What's happened to me?

Gingerly she pushed herself into a sitting position, but pain shot into her right shoulder and stopped her. She managed to sit up by using her left arm. Her head swam, but then the room righted itself.

She was in some kind of cave. The red light of a fire glowed through an archway opposite her, casting deep shadows on the rough walls. She lay on the ground on a mattress made of something soft and fibrous, and an animal-pelt quilt covered her.

The right sleeve of her woolen under-shirt had been cut away and her arm bound to her body with strips of cloth. Above her elbow, she saw a lumpy bandage with a line of pink running down her arm from the wound to her wrist. *Infection*, she thought instinctively. The smell of flaxseed came from the bandage, and as she inhaled the odor, she felt inexplicably sad.

Pushing back the animal pelts, she carefully moved her bare feet to the dusty floor. Though she hardly knew if she could walk, Abisina had to get out of that bed, to look around this cave for some clue as to what was happening to her.

As she stood, the leggings she wore fell to the floor. She tried to bend over, but the movement made the floor tilt, and she fell back onto the bed with a cry. The room spun and Abisina thought she might throw up. At last, the spinning slowed, the roaring in her ears quieted, and she heard feet shuffling closer.

A lumpy figure stood silhouetted against the fire's glow. At this image, fear gripped Abisina, but before she could search her memory to discover its origin, the figure trundled forward, rolling as it walked, and the image was gone.

"Sitting up! Don't try too much, dearie. Got more healing to do. I've your soup here—" It fumbled with a sconce on the wall, and the white light of a candle flared.

Abisina bit her tongue to keep from screaming.

The creature in the candlelight couldn't be human. It had arms, legs, and a neckless head perched on a torso. Long, dirty hair fell in a tangle of gray and yellow, hiding its face in shadow. The creature was short—almost as big around as it was tall—and it wore clothes made of small animal pelts like the ones from Abisina's bedding: a tunic belted at its middle—you really couldn't call it a waist—and a skirt that fell to its knees, exposing two thick legs swathed in woolen leggings and animal-pelt boots.

It clicked its tongue, unaware of Abisina's fearful stare. "These are a bit too wide in the waist for a waif like you!" The creature reached a gnarled, brown hand toward the floor, where the leggings had fallen at Abisina's feet. "Need a belt." It chuckled, pulling up the leggings. Abisina trembled as a claw-like fingernail brushed her skin.

"Lay back down, dearie," the creature cooed and tucked Abisina's legs under the covers.

It perched on a low, three-legged stool that looked ready to splinter under its bulk and picked up an iron bowl from the dusty floor. It dipped into the soup and held a spoon up to Abisina, the creature shaking its hair off its face as it did so. Abisina shrank back.

A mouth bent in a lipless grin, exposing four broken teeth. A bulbous nose dotted with warts. Leathery skin streaked with dirt. Grimy hair hanging across a strangely bumpy skull. Curious brown eyes staring at Abisina.

Before she could move or cry out, the creature leapt forward with unexpected speed and popped a bite of soup into Abisina's gaping mouth. She gagged as a thick broth slipped down her throat, leaving the taste of mud.

The creature chuckled at Abisina's expression. "My Haret hates this soup, too. But the mushrooms and roots thicken the blood, make you strong. Another bite now." And a second spoonful of the putrid soup was dished into her mouth. "That's right!" it crowed. "You'll be up and about in no time!"

The insistent spoon hovered again near Abisina's lips. She turned her head away, sending the room into a spin and bringing another chuckle. "Must be feeling better if you can fight."

What are you? Where am I? As she opened her mouth to speak, the spoon found its target. Abisina spluttered. She tried to sit up higher in her bed, but the scene before her slipped sideways and she felt as if she were falling from a great height.

"Whoops!" the creature cried and strong hands lifted Abisina.

She struggled but stopped at the shrieking pain. "My arm!"

The creature nodded. "Broke it. In the ravine. That's where Haret found you. You must have fallen. Had a good gash in your head. I've sewn up both, your head and your arm where the bone broke the skin. Will be fine once we fatten you up. So thin!"

The spoon swooped in, and Abisina gagged again. "What—who are you?" she managed between bites.

"I'm Hoysta, dearie, and Haret is around here somewhere, though he may have gone scouting again."

"But—but—" Somehow these answers didn't get at what Abisina wanted to know. She couldn't remember being in a ravine. She couldn't seem to remember anything before waking in this cave—and there was something—something *important*—she had to remember.

"Don't worry yourself now. You're still weak. Give yourself time—and more soup!"

"Grandmother!" A deep voice spoke from the archway. Another creature appeared—as short as the first, but more finely formed: barrel-chested, muscular, a definite neck. It, too, wore an animal-skin tunic and kilt, but its powerful legs were bare and covered by black, wiry hair, matching that on its head and chin. This one looked younger and healthier than the one on the stool, but it had the same dark eyes and dirty skin.

Crossing the room, the second figure stared coldly at Abisina. "Has she said anything of Watersmeet?"

That word. She knew it—but how? Her head was growing fuzzier the longer she sat up.

The bearded creature leaned closer to Abisina. "Human! Your folk and mine are not friends, but I saved you. Now I want you to do something for me. Tell me about Watersmeet."

Watersmeet—is this what I need to remember?

"Speak, human!"

"Haret, you're frightening her! She's not ready to talk!"

Haret glared at Abisina but did not repeat his question.

"Leave us," Hoysta rasped. "She needs to eat and rest. Talk to her later."

After another hard stare, Haret began to leave but then faced Abisina again to threaten: "You *will* tell me." Abisina slumped against the wall.

Hoysta watched him go and shook her head, a crease of worry deepening her brow. "No patience. Feels the Obrium." Turning her attention back to Abisina, she exclaimed, "All worn out!" She moved Abisina away from the wall and laid her on the spongy bed. "Sleep now," Hoysta said and began to make that throbbing hum again, a kind of lullaby.

Abisina didn't know how long she slept in the cave, waking up from dreams of snow and fire, with Hoysta hovering nearby holding the detestable soup bowl. Each time she woke, her head was clearer, though memory of anything before this cave still evaded her.

With Hoysta's urging, Abisina began to stand and take a few wobbly steps, most of her weight on the creature's broad back. Haret was present for several of these strolls, leaning against the archway, frowning, but he never tried to question her again. Abisina held the word *Watersmeet* in her mind like a talisman, without understanding its meaning.

And then one night, she woke alone. She could tell by the low glow of embers that the fire in the other room was banked—the cave was asleep. She felt restless for the first time since she had been here. Sitting up, she waited for the familiar roll of nausea, but it didn't come. She swung her bare feet over the side of the bed and, with her good arm, pushed herself to stand. Hoysta had removed the stitches from her wounds that morning, but her right arm was still bound to her body. Weak but excited, she took a few steps. Hoysta's enormous leggings were now securely tied around her waist with a piece of rawhide. Sliding her feet through the dust, Abisina managed a few more steps.

She crossed the room and stopped at the archway to catch her breath. Looking into the room beyond her own, she could see little in the darkness except the long swath of glowing embers from the fireplace. On either side of the fire, deeper darkness suggested tunnels or doorways leading farther into the cave. She stepped into the room. A slight breeze touched her ankles, flowing from the left and holding an edge of cold. *A way out,* she thought, breathing in the fresher air. Abisina moved toward it, but caught a familiar scent coming from the darkness to the right of the fire. Her steps turned toward it, the scent growing stronger.

She reached the doorway of another cave and entered into the darkness beyond. The odor was thick here and she inhaled deeply, hungrily, pulling the smell into her lungs. Then the words came: *elfwort, feverfew, clover, chamomile, yarrow....*

Mama!

Images burst into her head: her mother silhouetted against flames, the angry mob, the black stare of the White Worm....

Abisina cried out and fell to the floor, crushed by the flood of memories. "No! No!" She covered her head with her good arm, trying to ward off the painful images that rained down on her.

And then Hoysta was there, pulling Abisina to her feet with her strong, capable hands. "Dearie, dearie," she cooed as she half dragged, half carried Abisina back to her own room and soft bed.

Tears ran down Abisina's face as Hoysta smoothed her hair and forehead. "There, there, my pet," she murmured. "Safe now, you're safe."

"I remember," Abisina choked, "I remember."

"Then it's time she told her story." Haret stood in the middle of the room carrying a torch. His stony voice checked Abisina's tears.

"Haret, please," Hoysta said. "Not now!"

Haret put his torch in a bracket on the wall. "You've coddled her too long, Grandmother. Have you forgotten that she is a human—and all that the humans have done to the dwarves?"

Dwarves! Abisina had never seen one, but she knew the tales: Perverse half-men. Filthy mud-dwellers. Monsters. Fear blotted out her despair and strengthened her. She had to be on guard. They had killed thousands at Vrandun. And now, she was their prisoner. "What are you going to do to me?"

"We *saved* you, dearie!" Hoysta said, sounding hurt.

"*She* saved you out of goodness, human!" Haret snarled. "But let me show you why *I* saved you." He stood over Abisina, fumbling at his throat. "This!" he cried. "This is why I brought a human to my home!"

He dangled something before her, and she knew it at once: her mother's necklace. The ribbons of metal gathered the low light from the torch and reflected it off the stone walls. She saw again the unnatural fire in Vranille's burial ground and stood before the blackened and windswept altar, snow stinging her cheeks, as she found the silver necklace.

"Dwarf workmanship!" Haret said. "I've never seen its like. It's made of Obrium, human, and I want to know where you got it."

"It was my—my father's. He gave it to my mother."

"Where does a Vranian get something like this?" Haret

said viciously. He pulled his hand back, as if ready to strike her. "Don't lie to me, human!"

Watersmeet. The word was there with the answer she had been searching for.

"My father was from Watersmeet."

Her words had an immediate effect on Haret. He'd been leaning over the bed, his nose inches from Abisina's face, but now he pulled back and grabbed Hoysta's hand. "Oh, the Earth," he breathed. "She's the one, Grandmother! After so many years, this girl comes—with Obrium and Watersmeet! It's finally happened!"

"Haret, you can't mean it," Hoysta pleaded. "You can't mean to try again!"

"I must know, Grandmother. I must put this legend behind me. I was beginning to think we were mad—and our fathers and mothers before us—to keep believing and hoping."

"You're the last one. No, I will not lose you to the same madness. And the human may know nothing about the Mines!"

At Hoysta's words, Haret rounded on Abisina again.

"Tell me how to get to Watersmeet," he commanded, the wistfulness gone from his voice. "It will do no good to lie."

Abisina had been prepared to do just that—anything to get away from these dwarves. But then she recalled the moment right before she and her mother had climbed the village wall. *If we get separated,* Sina had said, and Abisina again felt her mother's grip on her wrist, *there is a pass between Mount Sumus and Mount Arduus . . .*

The barest outline of a plan began to form in her head, and at Haret's words, Abisina leapt at the tiny hope it offered. "You must begin at the Obrun Mines. Do you know them?"

"Don't insult me, human," Haret said. "They are *our* Mines!"

"Then that's where we start."

"*We?*"

Abisina willed her voice to stay firm. "I'm going with you. To Watersmeet."

CHAPTER VI

ABISINA BEGAN TO DOUBT HER PLAN AS SOON AS SHE LAY down on her pallet and tried to sleep. She had claimed she knew how to get to Watersmeet, but did she? She ran over and over her mother's instructions, and each time they seemed flimsier. Haret knew the Obrun Mines, but her mother hadn't said how to find the pass once they were at the Mines. *And what about the meeting of three rivers? What if the land beyond the mountains is crawling with rivers?*

And the centaurs.

She flopped onto her belly. At first, Haret had refused to take Abisina, saying that she would "draw centaurs like a bear to bait." Just that fall, a boy from Vranille had been snatched by the centaurs while getting water. A raiding party had gone after him, returning a few days later with the boy's broken body and another centaur tail for Vranille's wall. Abisina would never forget the boy's sightless stare, his footless ankles.

She had to stand by while her mother cleaned the body and buried him in the woods. Violated by centaurs, he was outcast in death and could not be buried in the village's burial ground. She had assumed the dwarves and centaurs were allies, joined together by their beastliness and hatred of humans. But the way Haret had talked, the dwarves hated the centaurs, too. . . .

How could she think of putting herself at the mercy of a dwarf? Stories of Vrandun, the fourth of the six Vranian villages, haunted her. Cunning dwarves had tunneled underneath the village, bringing down the walls and huts, burying most of the inhabitants alive. Now she was heading out into the wilderness with one of the vile half-men who'd brought about their deaths!

And even if they got to Watersmeet, would her father be there? Would he want to see her?

I have no choice. Abisina tried to bring back the flame of courage that had fueled her. *And if I go with this dwarf, I will stay close to Mama's necklace.* She closed her eyes, aware of the emptiness around her neck. The necklace was all she had left of her mother.

She did not sleep much that night—or any of the other nights as they prepared for their journey and waited for winter to release her grip. When sleep did come, purple flames, razor claws, death-dark eyes, and shouts of hate filled Abisina's dreams.

Days were no better. She couldn't let Haret see her worry, but trying to appear strong exhausted her. And Haret wanted to "toughen her up." She woke to him standing over her bed yelling, "Get up, human!" As soon as she was on her feet, he led her to the great room where Hoysta was getting breakfast and made her walk in circles until she was drenched in sweat. Stroking his beard, he would mutter things like, "We have a difficult journey, and you are puny and weak like all of your kind." With a cold look at Haret, Abisina would pick up her pace.

Hoysta clicked her tongue at Haret when she heard him speak like this to Abisina. "Don't wear her out!" she repri-manded as she fixed another bowl of her foul soup. "You saw how skinny she was when we first found her. And her journey here through the snow!" Hoysta had explained to Abisina that the closest human village was a four-day journey.

"That's four *human* days," Haret had interjected. "A dwarf can do it in two days and a night."

But Abisina had never remembered anything from those four days, though other memories of her last day in Vranille returned. Did she sleep in the snow? Did she find anything to eat? Did she bother to look? The fact that she still had her feet, not to mention her life, told Abisina that she hadn't encountered any centaurs. But how had she broken her arm or cut her head?

As Abisina grew stronger, she helped Hoysta with her work. In the far reaches of the cave, Hoysta bred moles, mice, badgers, and rabbits for food and fur. Now Abisina and Hoysta culled the flocks—smoking what seemed like hundreds of moles in a hollow log; knitting silky rabbit fur into hats, mittens, leggings, and under-shirts; piecing various skins into snug sleeping rolls. They baked batch after batch of flatbread made of root flour, and they mended cloaks—including the one Abisina was wearing when Haret found her. Hoysta chewed leather to a supple softness to make Abisina a new pair of boots.

Abisina saw plenty of evidence of the "dirty and repugnant" dwarf habits she had heard so much of in Vranille. It was hard for her to watch Hoysta's warty hands immersed in root flour or her filthy fingers straining pans of badgers' milk. The voices of the Elders rang through her head: *The foul mud-dwellers wallow in their own filth, hiding their ugliness in the ground.* It was true that their food tasted of mud, each bite gritty on her teeth; Hoysta's hands and face were black with dirt; and Abisina had watched both Haret and Hoysta rub their hands in an urn of dirt before eating.

But after a few weeks, Abisina could not deny that she had more flesh on her bones than she ever did in Vranille, and she was getting stronger. The Elders would not have given the widows half this much food, to say nothing of the outcasts. And the Elders had seen Abisina herself as no better than a dwarf—hadn't the villagers called her "dwarf-dirty" for as long as she could remember? And eventually, Abisina realized that Hoysta and Haret's skin was not as dirty as she thought; it was darker. Like *hers*. And they weren't washing in that urn of earth before eating; they were thanking the Earth for the gift of roots and animals that sustained them.

But Abisina still avoided Hoysta's comforting pats and pulled away from her frequent hugs. She told herself it was because of the dwarf's musty odor, but she knew she was lying, and her conscience pricked her. *Hoysta healed and cared for me, while the people of Vranille refused even to touch me,* she berated herself. *Only my mother would have cared more for me.*

There were other things Hoysta did for Abisina that reminded her of her mother—and each memory brought a grief that blotted out other thoughts. Several times the old dwarf tried to get Abisina to drink a cup of cool feverfew tea. "Been through a lot, dearie. Drink this and you'll feel better," she said, patting Abisina's hand. But Abisina couldn't swallow the bitter infusion. As a small child, before she learned to hide her feelings, Abisina had returned to her hut to weep out the pain of the other children's taunts and tricks. Sina, too, had comforted her with a cool cup of feverfew tea.

Hoysta's feverfew did make Abisina feel better, but not in the way Hoysta expected. One day, the old dwarf returned from tending her flocks with a nasty badger bite on one of her fingers. Abisina sat by the fire sewing pelts into a sleeping roll and watched as Hoysta put some cobwebs on the wound to staunch the bleeding before she returned to sewing.

"I'd put some feverfew on that," Abisina suggested as Hoysta picked up her needle with her injured hand and winced.

"On a badger bite?"

"It'll bring down the swelling and ease the pain."

"A tea will do that?" Hoysta said doubtfully.

"Not a tea. A tincture." Abisina sewed a few stitches and added, "I'll make one for you, if you like."

"Where would you learn something like that?"

"I'm the daughter of a healer," Abisina answered, her chest aching. But later, as she collected the dried feverfew from Hoysta's herbs, she recalled the bunches hung from the eaves in the hut in Vranille—and she felt the tiniest easing of her pain. Through her, someone would benefit from her mother's gift.

Abisina enjoyed the work she did with Hoysta. The dwarf's constant stream of conversation kept her thoughts busy, and through Hoysta's stories, Abisina began to understand Haret's intense interest in Watersmeet. Hoysta spoke of the dwarves' ancestors living in a vast city built into the roots of the Obrun Mountains—the same mountains Sina had mentioned that last night in Vranille. The Obrun City was rich and cultured, complete with palaces and plazas, underground rivers, broad avenues, spacious halls, canals, tier upon tier of dwellings, and libraries.

"Libraries?" Abisina asked incredulously. "Dwarves can *read*?"

"Of course, dearie! Can't you?"

"Well, yes, but we had to hide that my mother was teaching

me. Women aren't allowed to read in Vranille, and most men can't either."

"Women can't—? Humans!" Hoysta shook her head and gave Abisina a pitying look before resuming her story.

The wealth of the Obrun City came from the Obrium Lode—a vein of the wondrous metal that Sina's necklace was made of. The Lode ran through the earth right underneath the city, giving it and the mountains their name. "Dwarves never name mountains! We've no use for them—poking into the sky." Hoysta chuckled. "But other creatures do."

The stories of Obrium astounded Abisina almost as much as the libraries—a metal as flexible as gold but stronger than diamond. According to Hoysta, even a thin sheet could protect the wearer from an axe blow or an arrow shot by a centaur's longbow. The only known source was the Obrium Lode, and dwarves alone knew how to mine the metal and work it.

Abisina presumed that most of what Hoysta told her about the Obrun City was legend. Dwarves, who now lived in holes in the earth, covered in dirt, used to live in luxury beyond what the Elders enjoyed? But Hoysta spoke with such detail, such reverence, that Abisina got caught up in the stories, just as she got caught up in the fanciful stories of long ago that her mother used to tell.

"You haven't told me what happened to the city," she said one day, as they sat by the fire sewing skins into a cloak for Haret.

Hoysta's face changed; her voice became raspier and

lower. "The city was destroyed by the Great Earthquake. Till that time, the Obrun Mountains were nothing but hills. Dwarves and other creatures moved easily over them to the north and the south. Even the Mountains Eternal were smaller. My grandfather spoke of seeing the summit of one of the lower ones!" Hoysta shivered at the thought. "But after the Earthquake, all that changed. The Mountains Eternal shot up into the clouds. And the Obrun Mountains doubled in size. The Obrun City was destroyed. Only a handful made it out. Tried to tunnel back to see if anyone or any part of the city survived, but met a wall of rock that they couldn't break without their Obrium tools buried behind it. Couldn't find a way to cross the mountains either. Wanted to see if there were any other Obrun dwarves who had made it out on the northern side. Heard they did. Somehow the word 'Watersmeet' reached them. They began to believe that this was where the survivors had fled to. But they gave up trying to cross. Had to. Set up their own communities. Mixed with the woodsy dwarves living south of the mountains.

"So much lost!" Hoysta lamented. "Riches, know-how, city-building. Most of the dwarves think it's a legend, a tale to tell the young by the fire of an evening. But my son and his bride, Haret's parents, believed the stories. And my father, and his mother." Hoysta sighed. "Went off to find the Mines, all of them. Obriumlust, it's called, this maddening desire to dig for the metal. Done all I can to hammer it out of Haret. Won't lose another! Then you came—with Obrium and the word 'Watersmeet' on your lips—and the madness is building in him."

Abisina thought of Haret pacing the great room after supper—and the sound of his feet tramping, tramping as she lay awake on her cot.

Hoysta plucked her needle out of a pelt in agitation. "I was beginning to think Watersmeet was a legend myself, till we met you. But now the Mines pull Haret like a lodestone—like they pulled his parents." She looked up at Abisina. "All these years, we've searched. Can anything be worth the suffering?"

As time passed, the cave became more and more suffocating to Abisina—the air stale, hot, and heavy with the smell of smoked mole. With no sunrise or sunset, she lost track of day and night. She longed for one breath of fresh air. And finally, she got her wish.

Hoysta had just finished untying her arm, carefully flexing the elbow to work out the stiffness. Then she led Abisina to the tunnel at the far end of the main room—the way out! A heavy curtain of animal pelts covered the tunnel to keep the warm air of the room from escaping. Abisina had longed to lift it and breathe the fresher air of the tunnel, but the first time she put out a hand to the curtain, Haret's bellow told her that he was sure she would run away if given the chance.

Now Hoysta, torch in one hand, basket in the other, told Abisina to pull it back. "We're off to collect some roots!" she said with a grin.

Abisina stepped into the tunnel and drew in her first breath of fresh air in months. She followed Hoysta up the steep incline, brushing her head on the low ceiling. Within twenty paces, they came to a fork, and Hoysta went right, onto the steeper of the two pathways. They continued to climb another two hundred paces before the tunnel leveled off and opened into a long, low room. Abisina entered, stooping, and walked into Hoysta, who had stopped and set down the basket.

"Now let's see." Hoysta leaned back to survey the roof of the cave.

Abisina twisted her neck to look along the ceiling. In the torchlight, veins of white fretted the dark earth, some more slender than strands of hair. Hoysta reached up and probed the ceiling with her sharp fingernails until she found what she was looking for. She dug farther in, clumps of dirt falling onto her head, and then she pulled something out and held it up to Abisina.

"Supper!" Hoysta held a gnarled white root, caked in soil, between her thumb and forefinger.

"Aren't we—aren't we going—out?" Abisina stammered, dread tickling her scalp.

Hoysta shivered. "Out? My, no! This is close enough for me! Give me walls of Earth above, below, and around. Don't see how Haret stands it, crawling on the surface of things. You don't mind it, of course, being a creature of the surface. But not me. I was made to be underground."

"But I must go out! I must see the sun, even for a moment! Please, Hoysta!" Abisina grabbed the dwarf by the shoulders.

"Don't hurt me!" Hoysta cried.

Startled, Abisina let go. Hoysta's frightened face reminded Abisina of her own reaction when she realized Haret and Hoysta were dwarves: *What are you going to do to me?* she had cried. Did she look as terrifying to Hoysta now as Hoysta had looked to her then? What kinds of stories had the dwarves heard about humans?

"I won't hurt you," Abisina promised, trying to sound calm and soothing. "It's as you said, I'm a creature of the surface, and I need the sun, the wind. Anything."

"But there is no way to the surface from here. This is our rootfield— Wait, I've got an idea!" Hoysta studied the ceiling again and prodded it with a crooked finger. "No," she murmured, moving to another spot. "Try this one." She poked again and then in a third spot. "Ah!" Hoysta raised both hands to the roof, pulling so hard that for a moment she hung from the ceiling, kicking her short legs and grunting until whatever it was gave way. She tumbled to the floor in a shower of earth and snow, with a root the size of a pumpkin on her chest. "Hee, hee, hee!" came her wheezy laugh as she stood up and wiped her eyes. "There!" she said, pointing toward the ceiling.

Abisina glanced up, not knowing what she was supposed to find, and saw only the dirt roof. Then, looking closer, she realized that the loamy black was broken by the thinner darkness of night. She stood up and held her face to the opening left by the root, letting the air rain its coolness on her. She smelled the sharp odor of firs and felt the stab of frost in her nose. "It's night," she murmured.

"Sorry, dearie," Hoysta said, "I can't sense when it's day and night like Haret can."

"No, it's fine." Abisina fixed her gaze on the small patch of sky. The darkness shifted above her, and she recognized tree branches moving in strong wind. And as she stared upward, a pinprick of light twinkled and was gone, was there, then gone, then there again. "A star," she said, afraid to blink in case she lost the tiny spark.

Hoysta let her stand there while she gathered more roots. Abisina didn't know how much time passed before the dwarf said, "Dearie, must go now," laying a hand on her arm. "Haret will be wanting his supper. Don't know day and night, but I know supper and breakfast," and she chuckled.

I'll be up there soon, traveling toward Watersmeet, Abisina thought, her worry eclipsed by the freedom of seeing the outside world again. She followed Hoysta to the entrance of the rootfield and touched the old dwarf's shoulder. "Thank you," Abisina said softly.

Hoysta smiled, exposing her few teeth, the skin crinkling around her eyes. There was no fear in them now. "Have to think of something to tell Haret about *this*." She raised her basket laden with the root she'd pulled down to expose the sky. It was four times larger than any of the other roots.

Abisina answered Hoysta's smile with her own, and they trooped back to the cave.

Haret said nothing about the root. He just raised his eyebrows as Hoysta tried to hack into it with a large knife, and then he regarded Abisina suspiciously. But Abisina didn't care. That pinprick of starlight gave her new energy. Every stitch she sewed in a sleeping roll, every loaf of flatbread she formed, every smoked mole she stowed in the leather travel bags got her closer to the outside. Still, her stomach clenched the night she overheard Haret say, "We leave tomorrow."

She had been lying in bed, waiting for sleep. She knew Hoysta and Haret were sitting by the fire in the great room. She could hear the soft tap of Hoysta's knitting needles and see Haret's shadow as he paced.

His words brought a cry of protest from Hoysta. "Not yet, Grandson! She's still weak! And she's just a child."

"She is not as young as you think. I would guess fourteen or fifteen winters."

"A baby!"

"They don't live as long as we do. It's as if she had more than twenty winters!"

"Still! Not *so* old," Hoysta said grudgingly.

"She is not your pet, Grandmother." Haret's voice was hard. "Have you forgotten your sister's children hunted down while they fished along the Great River? And what of Siedra, who went to *talk* to the humans and never returned? And

Stonedun—or *Vran*dun, as they call it! The humans built their village on top of our own city until it collapsed on itself."

The dwarves destroyed Vrandun! But Abisina knew the Vranians were capable of hunting down dwarves—even dwarf children. *Could it have been the humans' fault?*

"And now the humans talk of another war," Haret continued. "A new leader is stirring the villages. I have it from a scout who returned yesterday. He's called Charach, this leader,"—darkness reached toward Abisina at the name—"and he plans to finish what they started so long ago, to 'subdue the monstrosities.' That's how they speak about us, Grandmother. Do you think they would offer you one pebble of the care you've given *her*?"

Hoysta was silent, and Abisina crept out of her bed. Staying in the shadows, she peeked into the great room. Haret stood with his back to her. Despite the low light, she could see the pain on Hoysta's face.

"The snow is all but gone. The human is ready," he said.

"A few more weeks would make her stronger."

"We don't need a few more weeks, Grandmother. We leave tomorrow."

"But, Haret, think of your parents! Your uncle! Your grandfather! Digging till their tools broke. Digging with their fingers till they bled. Digging their own graves. I am trying to spare you!"

"I'm different, Grandmother. I don't have the Obrium-lust."

"I can see it. You've grown thin with pacing. Your temper! You are not the boy I raised."

"It's for my parents—for all of them—that I'm doing this! We've never had a chance like this before. To turn my back now would be to turn my back on all that we are as dwarves!" Haret's voice rung with finality. "I am going to the Mines to face this demon, once and for all."

Hoysta lowered her head and said nothing. When she looked up, the skin around her eyes and along her jaw had gone slack. She seemed ancient. But her voice was firm. "You think I'm a foolish old woman. Maybe you're right. But I have lost too much to this quest."

"Grandmother." Abisina had never heard Haret's voice so gentle. "I will return. I give you my word. And—and I will take care of the human."

Hoysta reached out and touched her grandson's face with her gnarled hand. "I have dreamed of this metal, too. It's in our blood. But at my age, the metal has tarnished. News of our kin, dwarves who escaped to the other side of the mountains—that is all I want now. Bring this news to me, Haret. Leave the Mines. Find our kin and come home."

The old dwarf and the young one looked at each other for a long moment before Hoysta rose to go to sleep. Abisina crept back to her own bed, leaving Haret to resume his pacing.

Abisina woke to Hoysta's voice: "Don't forget to feed her the soup once a day. Needs the strength!"

She sat up. *Today we leave for Watersmeet!* The skin on her arms turned to gooseflesh despite the cave's heat.

Next to her pallet, Abisina found her new clothes laid out: knitted mittens and hat, a pair of leggings, a tunic made of rabbit pelts, and the fur-lined leather boots she had watched Hoysta soften with her own teeth. Her throat tightened as she began to dress.

She stepped through the archway into the great room, where the dwarves stooped over two sacks set by the fire.

Glancing up, Hoysta cried "Leaving today!" and pulled Abisina to her. The smell of earth hung about her, but it did not make Abisina cringe. And the quiver in the old dwarf's voice made Abisina's throat tighten again.

Hoysta, eyes wet, led her over to a stump-stool and thrust a bowl of root porridge at her. Abisina tried to eat, but her stomach rebelled and she put her bowl aside after a few bites.

"Eat more!" Hoysta urged. "You need strength!"

Abisina choked down two more bites before Haret grunted, "It's time to go." He picked up one of the bags at his feet and held it out to Abisina without a word. She braced herself for its heaviness but found it light. As Haret lifted his own bag bulging with provisions, Abisina realized she'd been given a fraction of the gear. She pushed aside her pang of guilt, reminding herself that Haret would have let her die in the snow if not for the Obrium necklace, her mother's necklace, which was around *his* neck. She settled the weight of the bag on her left shoulder, the leather strap across her chest. She added a water skin over her other shoulder.

Haret buckled a belt with a long dagger around his waist, tucked a small hatchet into the belt, and set a bow and quiver across his back.

Abisina was ready for this moment. "I need a weapon."

Haret narrowed his eyes. "You think I'll arm you, human?"

"I need to protect myself, like you. A bow and arrows. I learned to shoot when I was a small child—we never left the village without them."

"I'll protect you," Haret said.

"You would have left me for dead—"

"We have no other bow," Hoysta said quickly.

"Then I'll make one on the trail," Abisina replied with a defiant look at Haret, though she had no sinew to string it.

Hoysta hurried to tie the mended Vranian cloak around Abisina's neck. It fell several inches shorter against her legs. *Have I grown taller?* Abisina wondered. *Eating that horrible soup?*

Walking stoop-shouldered up the tunnel, excitement tingled down to her fingertips. In a moment she would be outside in the sun and the air! The three of them came to the fork—and this time went left. The farther they moved along the tunnel, the cooler and lighter the air felt in Abisina's chest.

Haret suddenly threw himself on the ground. Abisina hesitated.

"On your belly, dearie," Hoysta said behind her and pushed her gently to the ground. "Small tunnel. Looks like a badger hole."

Abisina crawled forward, pushing her bag around to her back. But the bag snagged on the low ceiling, forcing her to return to a wider point in the tunnel, remove her bag, and start in again.

"Human!" came Haret's growl.

As Haret left the tunnel, Abisina saw a circle of daylight and felt a rush of cold, clean air. She wriggled on her belly until, at last, she poked her head out into brilliant daylight. Haret knelt next to the hole, holding back the branches that covered the entrance. Abisina got to her knees. Patches of snow still lingered under the tree, drifts of blinding white. Abisina followed Haret as he crawled under the tree's branches and into a small clearing.

The light made her squint, her eyes watering. She peered upward, where she expected to find the sun's golden face burning down through the overlapping branches. Instead, she saw only a few patches of cloud-covered sky.

Hoysta, who had followed them out of the hole, also looked skyward, but warily, as if expecting something to swoop down on her. As she helped Abisina put her bag over her shoulder, Hoysta's movements were awkward and rushed.

Only Haret's eyes were wide open.

"Have everything?" Hoysta asked Haret, her words clipped.

"Yes, Grandmother."

"Well then—" Her voice caught. She took Abisina's hand and held onto it tightly, like someone drowning. "Dearie, maybe you will hear what I am trying to say. Haret believes that humans and dwarves are not friends. You haven't always wanted my care"—Abisina looked down—"but no good has come from our hate. Perhaps, some good will come of our friendship. You can trust my Haret."

Hoysta hugged Abisina to her hard, and Abisina could feel her shaking.

"Thank you," Abisina whispered. "I'll never forget you." As she hugged Hoysta back, she realized what she said was true.

Hoysta pulled away, wiping her eyes. "And you, Grandson. Be careful. For both of you."

Haret took her hand. "I will. Good-bye, Grandmother."

Hoysta embraced her grandson, her tears falling openly, and scuttled back under the branches, her sobs fading as she disappeared down the tunnel.

CHAPTER VII

As they set off, Abisina gloried in the air on her face, the spicy smell of pines, the cacophony of bird calls, and the hazy green of budding leaves covering the maples, oaks, and beeches. The drought was over. All over the forest, water gurgled underground and dripped from the trees. The pine needles beneath her feet were slippery with melting snow.

"How much snow did we get?" Abisina wondered aloud.

"Twice the size of you," Haret grunted.

Even Haret couldn't bother her now. Abisina sighed happily. Everywhere she looked, Spring asserted herself, and Abisina drank it in.

But this euphoria did not last. They followed a trail north, threading through tall groves mercifully clear of undergrowth. As the day progressed, however, the path narrowed and then faded away altogether, while the undergrowth grew thicker. Soon they had to pick their way among saplings, brambles, and brush that pulled at Abisina's clothes, slapped her in the face, and pricked her hands until they bled. Clouds of gnats clustered around her eyes and whined in her ears.

These irritations were nothing new—she had worked hard in Vranille and in the forests surrounding it. But after her injuries, followed by months of confinement in the cave, Abisina had lost her hardness. And Haret set an infuriating pace. Although her legs were longer than his, she had to jog to keep up. For six hours they climbed uphill without rest— except for the times she slipped on pine needles and fell, once landing on an exposed root. The spot on her hip still throbbed, and she knew a purple bruise was hidden underneath her leggings. After this fall, Haret paused long enough for Abisina to get back on her feet and then set off.

Abisina vowed that she would not ask Haret for a rest. But as the shadows of the trees lengthened, she could go no farther. They had not eaten since they left the cave. She had sipped from her water skin, but her mouth was dry and her head ached. Though walking kept her body warm, her hands and feet were ice.

"Haret!" His pace did not slacken. "Haret!" Louder.

Still nothing.

"Haret!" she yelled, and he spun around.

"Quiet, human! You've now alerted all the centaurs to our presence."

"I have to rest. And eat," she said, lowering her voice and casting a fearful glance around her.

"Not here." Haret kept moving.

"Haret, please." Abisina hated herself for sounding pitiful, but he merely ducked under some branches and disappeared. Abisina had no choice but to follow his back under more boughs. When he stopped, they were beneath a squat bush just putting forth its leaves. Haret crouched on the ground and opened his bag. Abisina sank onto the damp earth beside him, not meeting his eye when he handed her something dark and stiff.

She recognized it immediately—one of Hoysta's smoked moles. It was bound to be nasty, but she had to eat it. She wiped her hair from her face and put the whole thing in her mouth, almost breaking a tooth on the tough, sinewy meat. It tasted mostly of smoke, but she could detect a little of the familiar muddiness. She was still chewing the meat into a softness she could swallow, when Haret put his bag back on his shoulder.

Not yet, Abisina thought. "I need more food." Her voice was firm.

"More?"

Abisina got four moles out of him and four long drinks, Haret looking on in disgust.

As Abisina rose to her feet, she saw that Haret had pulled her mother's necklace from under his cloak and was caressing it.

Abisina gasped, startling Haret. He turned away and stuffed the necklace back into his tunic.

It was all Abisina could do to command her emotions—remembering her mother with a hand at her throat. *We were supposed to go on this journey together!* How different it would have been standing here with Sina. Abisina pushed the thought away. She couldn't afford to be weak now.

She lifted her pack to her shoulder and faced Haret. "I may not be as fast as you, but I'm strong. Let me carry my own moles. I will slow us down less if I eat more frequently."

"Typical human," Haret sneered, but he dug into his pack for the moles. And when they started walking, Abisina could keep up without jogging. Her head and muscles still ached and she was tired within moments, but she gritted her teeth and trudged on.

Abisina assumed that they would stop when it got dark, but the sun sank, the stars and the waning sliver of moon peeked between the branches of the trees, and except for pausing to cover their tracks in muddy areas, Haret showed no signs of slowing. For what seemed like hours, Abisina had told herself, *Any moment now, he'll have to stop. . . . Just up that rise. . . . He's looking for a safe place.* When she realized he would *not* stop, she did. She sat on the ground without uttering a word, forcing Haret to circle back when he noticed that she was not behind him; he returned, stamping his feet in anger. She could just discern his solid figure in the darkness. "I have to sleep," she told him.

"Not yet," he growled. "We will travel till dawn, sleep during the day, and walk again at dusk."

"I cannot walk all night!" Abisina insisted.

"You must, human. We're in the thick of centaur territory."

Thoughts of those cruel faces and their footless victims filled her head. *And I have no bow!* There was nothing for her to do but get to her feet and walk.

Before long, they lost even the paltry light of the moon. After the sun had gone down, Abisina tripped so often that she started lifting her knees to step over the rocks or roots. But now, she was blind. She walked into branches and trees and slowed down so much that Haret made her put her hands on his shoulders. It was humiliating to be led through the dark completely dependent on Haret's sharper night vision, and their feet got tangled more than once, sending them both into a pile on the ground. Invariably this brought curses of "Human!"

When he stopped again, Abisina sank to the ground, beyond caring what Haret thought of her as long as she could sit for a few moments before they continued this grueling march. The trunks of the trees around her were just visible against the night sky. Dawn could not be far away.

"It should be right here," Haret muttered to himself and took a few steps. Abisina was too tired to ask what he meant or to follow.

"Ah!" he cried and he was back, dragging her to her feet and pulling her forward. "Bend down," he barked as he pushed her head toward the ground. Abisina staggered, her nose filling with the smell of dust and damp, and she knew she was in a cave. She fell to her knees and crawled, but before she'd moved the length of her body, she bumped into the rough rear wall. She lay down right there and didn't move. Haret squeezed in behind her and slid over to the side.

"You can sleep here," he said. She heard him fumbling in his bag, but still she did not move. "We can sleep now," Haret repeated irritably. When she did not answer, he reached over, yanked Abisina's bag off her shoulder, and pulled out her sleeping pelts. Abisina wanted to refuse his help but couldn't summon the energy even to lift her head. She fell asleep before Haret had laid the pelts over her.

Haret shook Abisina awake at twilight, the last rays of the sun visible through the cave's entrance. He handed her a few pieces of dried mole, a wedge of badger cheese, some flatbread, and her water skin. Abisina pulled herself into a sitting position, every muscle crying out in pain, while Haret gathered up her sleeping pelts, stowed them in her bag, and then stood impatiently clenching and unclenching a handful of dirt.

As soon as Abisina had choked down the last bite, he crawled out of the cave. She followed, groaning as she got to her feet in the sharp, cold air. Haret had already pulled his heavy bag over his shoulder, thrown some dried leaves over their footprints to the cave, and begun to walk. With a sigh, Abisina lifted her own bag, but she yelped when it hit her hip and shoulder. Haret stopped and looked at her. Abisina tried to adjust her under-shirt, but it stuck to her shoulder. She yanked harder and the shirt ripped away from her skin. The spot where her bag had rested was rubbed raw and now bled afresh.

Haret came closer and glanced at the wound. "Ready to give up?" he asked, arms folded.

Abisina shook her head without looking at him.

"Look at yourself, human! You're bruised, bleeding. I know every skinny muscle in your body is screaming. Admit it. You can't do this. Tell me how to get to Watersmeet. I'll take you back to my grandmother—at an easy pace."

In answer, Abisina returned her bag to her shoulder, gritting her teeth against the pain. She stared at Haret defiantly.

"Give me the bag," he said finally.

"What?"

Instead of answering, he grabbed the strap, tugged it off her shoulder, and started walking.

She stumbled after him, head low, cheeks red with anger.

Abisina passed the next few days in a numb stupor. At dusk, Haret would shake her awake and wait as she ate a few mouthfuls of bread. And before they set out, always the same question: "Ready to give up?" These were the last words either would speak until the next evening when he asked the question again: "Ready to give up?"

The farther they got from Hoysta's, the more often Haret stopped to bend down and examine the ground, grabbing a fistful of dirt and sniffing or tasting it, running his hand over a tree trunk as if reading the bark. Begrudgingly, Abisina admired his skill. She had taught herself to track and hunt in the woods of Vranille, but her skills were clumsy compared to his—and that was in daylight! As dawn softened the blackness in the east, they would stumble into a cave, under an overhang, or into a clump of trees to sleep away the day huddled under their pelts until Haret shook her awake again.

They continued to head northwest, through forests and low mountains no Vranian had ever seen before. Abisina saw little herself. At dusk and dawn she glimpsed variegated-green forests, a mix of the lighter broad leaves and the sharp needles of firs and pines. Now and then, she heard the distant chatter of water flowing over rocks. Owls hooted, wolves cried, and animals scurried in the undergrowth. A few terrifying times, she spotted the leaping flames of centaurs' fires and heard their raucous singing. Her hand would reach for her absent bow, and Haret would strike out on a new course away from the danger. Nothing else broke her walking-trance and the realities of tired feet, cold hands, and sore thighs.

A couple of weeks into their journey, Abisina woke without Haret shaking her. She knew that something was different. In the mouth of the cave, snowflakes fell thick in the twilight. Haret sat before a small fire, twisting the Obrium necklace, its light dancing on the ceiling.

Abisina shut her eyes and felt the wash of loneliness brought on each time she saw the necklace. Haret was silent as she got to her feet and tried to stretch her taut, aching muscles. But when she bent down to roll up her bed, he grunted, "We're not traveling today. Too much snow."

Abisina stopped rolling and stood where she was. She relished the idea of sitting by the fire wrapped in warmth or getting some extra sleep, but she did not relish being in a small cave with Haret, who still sat holding Sina's necklace.

"I—I need you to put it away," she said.

"What?" He looked up at her with a frown.

"The necklace—my *mother's* necklace."

Did he see her tears? *Would he care if he did?*

But he stuffed the necklace back into his tunic with a—*Is it even possible?*—guilty look. "I've made some soup," he said gruffly and pointed to a small earthenware pot on the edge of the fire.

Abisina moved to the fire as Haret reached for his pack, retrieving another wooden spoon. He picked up the pot and placed it before her. "Don't touch the pot!" he said as she bent to pick up the soup.

"You touched it."

"I'm a dwarf, born to work hot metal." Abisina bristled at his superior tone. "I've added some comfrey for your muscles," he continued, handing her the spoon. Abisina's temper flared. *Comfrey—he's had it all the time! I could have made a poultice, which is much better for soreness than comfrey in soup.*

But the heat of the soup felt nice in her belly, and the comfrey added a flavor that softened the usual taste of mud. As she sipped, Haret gathered a few more logs from the rear of the cave. Abisina wondered where they came from, but refused to ask.

"I saw signs of the snow coming. Got the logs while you slept," he said, anticipating her question.

"Don't you ever sleep?" she asked. It came out like an accusation.

"Not as much as you, human," Haret shot back.

After she finished her soup, Abisina announced, "Well this *human* is going back to sleep" and crawled into her sleeping roll. She drifted off, lulled by the soft snap of the fire and the whine of wind underneath it.

She woke with a start. Looking around, she took in the dull red coals of the dying fire, the mouth of the cave almost filled with snow . . . and the silence.

Haret was gone.

Abisina fought her rising panic. *He's gone to get wood*, she tried to convince herself, even as she noticed the stack at the far end of the cave. She stirred the fire and sat near it, watching the shadows leap on the walls. The flames sank low and she added more wood and stirred again. And again. Still, Haret did not come.

"He's left me." She spoke the words that had threatened her since she woke. She knew he would. Hadn't she learned about the treachery of dwarves all her life?

She stood up quickly. She had to act—do something to save herself. She grabbed Haret's abandoned bag and ripped through it. The bowls, mugs, and spoons; the cooking pot; two flints; sacks of moles, flatbread, badger cheese; a packet of herbs—she recognized yarrow, coltsfoot, comfrey, and ginger root; a bone needle and few feet of sinew (she could make a bow!); and her own bag folded at the bottom. *I'll take what I need and set off on my own. Head north toward the Obruns and figure out the rest from there.*

She set her bag, Haret's bowl, mug, and spoon aside and stuffed her sleeping pelts into his bag. Spying Haret's pelts, she stuffed them in, too, a tight fit.

When she had the bag packed, Abisina paused. *Now what?*

She glanced toward the mouth of the cave, trying to gauge the narrow slit of darkness. *Is it the middle of the night? Closer to dawn? How long have I slept?* The panic closed in.

She couldn't travel at night like Haret. In the day, she might be spotted by centaurs. She had no bow yet. And if she got to the Obruns, she needed Haret to show her the Mines. Abisina threw the bag down hopelessly, disgusted with her fear.

Something moved behind her. She spun around.

There was Haret's head, poking into the cave, his dark beard flecked with snow. He held two dead rabbits in his mittened hand.

"Going somewhere?" he spat, eyeing the stuffed bag.

Abisina looked away, hiding the relief on her face.

"I should have known, human," he said as he crawled into the cave. "After all I've done for you."

"All *you've* done?" Anger wiped away her relief.

"If not for me, you would have died bleeding and frozen at the bottom of the ravine. Or any number of times on this journey." He turned his back on her.

"You've kept me alive because I'm worth something to you! It was Hoysta who saved me, not you! And the stolen necklace you wear is proof."

"Stolen!" He reeled around.

"It belonged to my mother! And my father before her!"

"This is dwarf work! Dwarf metal! Consider it a very small payment for all your people have stolen from us."

"They're not my people!"

"You're human, aren't you? All the same."

"I'm not the same! I *hate* the Vranians."

Haret snorted.

"And I wasn't leaving," Abisina added. "I thought *you* had left *me*."

Haret fixed her with a glare. "And left my food and sleeping pelts?"

Abisina said nothing. *Why had it made so much sense before?*

"You're either very stupid or lying. Probably both. I gave my grandmother my word that I would keep you safe. But what would a human understand of honor?" Haret threw his rabbits on the floor and brushed past Abisina to get his bag.

She stood still as her anger ebbed away.

Haret fished out the pot. "It's almost dawn. The snow is deep, but a warm wind is blowing from the south. We'll stay here tonight and tomorrow while the snow melts. Leave tomorrow night. If you still insist on coming." He picked up a rabbit and began to skin it with sharp strokes.

"I wasn't leaving," Abisina said again.

Haret gutted the rabbit in silence.

That night, Abisina was startled awake again. She didn't know why until she heard—

"The Obrium! The Obrium!"

In the dim glow of the fire's coals, Abisina could just make out Haret writhing under his pelts. "Eee-aaah!" he screamed, an eerie, panicked cry.

"Haret!" she said, but the writhing continued.

"No, I'll get it! I'm almost there! Just a little farther!"

"Haret!" Abisina yelled as she crawled out of bed. "Wake up!" She tried to pull the pelts off him, but he hung on.

"No! Just a little bit more! I can *feel* it! On the other side of this wall!"

"Haret! It's Abisina!" She yanked at the pelts again and heard leather ripping.

He flipped the pelts off his head. His hand was caught between his neck and Sina's chain. He hastily pulled it out and hunched his shoulders to keep her from the necklace. "Get away!" His voice was high, his eyes blank.

Abisina reached forward to shake him out of the dream that still possessed him, but he shrieked as her hand neared him.

"You can't have it!"

"You're sleeping, Haret! It's a dream!"

Her words finally seemed to reach him and he shivered, focusing on her for the first time. "Wh—what is it?" He sounded like a frightened child.

"You were dreaming," Abisina said gently. "About the Mines."

"Oh," he said, his fearful eyes hardening against her. Without another word, he wrapped himself in his pelts, lay down, and turned his back to her.

Abisina crawled into her sleeping roll, and her flying heartbeat slowed. Across the room, Haret's breathing continued quick and shallow as if he, too, couldn't settle back into sleep. Once, Abisina sat up to speak to him, groping for words of comfort. But what could she say to Haret? He must have sensed her movement, because he pulled the skins more tightly around him and rolled farther away from her. She lay down and forced herself to sleep.

As Haret had predicted, the next morning the sun's bright rays, coupled with the warm wind, had melted most of the snow. Abisina spent part of the morning sitting in the mouth of the cave, the sun on her face, while Haret sewed up the rent in his pelts, studiously avoiding her gaze. After lunch, Abisina took a nap and by the time Haret woke her, there were only patches of wet snow left on the ground.

"It's time," he said. He had already packed his bag and was waiting.

As Abisina rolled her pelts, she surprised herself as much as him by saying, "I can take my bag again."

Haret raised an eyebrow but dug it out. He handed it to Abisina, his eyes on hers. She returned his stare without flinching. Stowing away her pelts, she placed the bag on her shoulder as nonchalantly as possible. She worried that she would cry out in pain when it came to rest on her sore, but it had healed enough.

"Ready," she said and followed Haret out of the cave.

Each evening after that, Abisina asked Haret for more to carry—first her mug, then her spoon and bowl, then a portion of moles and cheese. By switching her bag from shoulder to shoulder, she managed to keep both from being rubbed raw. Over the next week, she asked Haret for a rest less and less often, and to slow down, almost never. She usually woke before he had to shake her.

And there was one other difference: Haret stopped asking if she were going to give up.

When the light afforded a view, Abisina was awed by the beauty of the country they traveled through: hillsides carpeted in every shade of green; deep, icy lakes reflecting the rising moon; streams leaping over rocks into mossy pools; meadows dotted with white and yellow wildflowers; and rocky slabs covered with gray lichen. She had no idea the land could offer such variety. One clear morning, just before they found their cave, Abisina climbed a rise and stared back at the sweep of the land below her feet. Somewhere down there, far in the hazy distance, Hoysta tended her rabbits and badgers. And beyond that stood Vranille, Vranhurst, and the other Vranian villages. What was happening there now? Had Charach convinced the people to form an army? Or had they seen his true nature? She thought of her mother's final words to her: *Tell him about Charach. Tell your father what happened here.*

Abisina turned away. Without realizing it, she had made a decision during the months with Hoysta and on this journey with Haret. *That world doesn't concern me now.* She faced north. Toward Watersmeet. And life free from Charach and Vran.

One night Abisina noticed that Haret had relaxed his vigilance in covering their tracks. "We're in dwarf territory," he explained. Abisina waited to be taken to another cave like Hoysta's—she even looked forward to it, eating anything besides smoked mole and badger cheese, sleeping in a bed—but Haret never brought her near the other dwarves. One evening she woke to find him drinking from a new water skin, and she knew he had visited the local dwarves while she slept. She tried to ignore the sting of being excluded—reminding herself that she would hate being stuck in a cave with a bunch of strange, dirty dwarves.

Before they set out, Haret had a warning for Abisina: "A rough band of centaurs has started raiding these parts, according to my cousins. Between here and a place called Giant's Cairn. They particularly like *humans*."

Now their pace really slowed as Haret took great care to keep their trek hidden. They built no fires, walked through streams when they could, and crisscrossed their own tracks to confuse any pursuers. Sometimes Haret paused to study tracks that were invisible to Abisina. Some, she couldn't miss. A few times they came upon clearings trampled flat around the remains of huge fires, the bones of large animals strewn about. "Cannibals!" Haret cried once, staring at the bones. At Abisina's questioning look, he explained, "Centaurs can communicate with hoofed animals: deer, moose—even wild pig. But these centaurs are *eating* deer." He spat in disgust, before moving on.

Haret would often yank Abisina behind a cluster of trees when his acute hearing told him something was coming. Most often it was a bear, a wolf, or a stag, but once, when there was little ground cover to hide in, Haret insisted that a large group of centaurs was heading their way before Abisina could hear anything.

"We have to hide!" He scanned the brush for anything big enough to cover even one of them. Abisina's instincts took over, and instead of looking down, she began studying the trees. Branches, knots, even slight swellings in the trunk were all she needed to climb into the canopy above the sightline of the centaurs.

There! Straight ahead was a pine with enough bulges to get her to the first branch. Just in time. Now even she could hear the rustling of branches and the thud of hooves.

"Human!" Haret was at her elbow. "I think there's cover enough for you there!" He pointed to some brush.

"You take it! I'll go up!" And she scrambled up the trunk before Haret could react. As she reached the first row of branches, she saw Haret slip into the brush just as a centaur came into sight. She risked one more swing upward to give her a little more shelter. She wasn't as high as she'd like to be, but any more movement would catch the centaurs' attention. From her perch she watched the herd canter past, only a pace from Haret's hiding spot. She stared at their powerful haunches and broad shoulders thick with muscle, their tangled tails, matted winter coats, the women's bare breasts, and the men's snarled beards. Their foreheads were heavy, their eyes deep-set. They didn't speak but there was a menace about them, their heads swinging from side to side, searching for signs of prey.

I need a bow! Abisina reminded herself to badger Haret for the sinew she knew he had in his bag.

After the centaurs passed, Abisina let out her breath. But neither she nor Haret moved for a long time. When she climbed back down, Haret was waiting for her, an amazed expression on his face. "Going up! I never would have thought of it! And it's a good thing you did, human, because you would have stuck out like a gem in coals down here. None of this cover was enough for someone as poor at blending in as you are!"

Abisina decided to take the compliment and ignore the insult.

Haret refused to give Abisina the sinew to make a bow, however. "I swore I would protect you, human!" seemed to be his only real argument. And it was true that whenever they were on the move, Haret stayed within several feet of her. But one evening, as they broke camp, a rabbit dashed past the entrance to the cave and Haret went after it. "Stay where you are," he shouted over his shoulder as he drew an arrow from his quiver. "I'll have this one in the shake of a mole's tail!"

Abisina sighed and sank to the ground. *I could have it in less than "the shake of a mole's tail,"* she thought.

She sat watching the full moon rise over the darkening trees, but then something thrashed in the underbrush opposite where Haret had disappeared. She scrambled to her feet. *Centaurs?* Grabbing their bags, Abisina darted back into the mouth of the cave. She needed a weapon! A dead branch lay nearby. It wouldn't do much, but it was all she had. She grabbed it and crouched in the cave's shadows, ready to use her club on anything that moved.

She had never seen anything like the three figures that lumbered into the small clearing before the cave. Horns longer than her arm protruded from heavy, bony brows over wide-set eyes. Their faces were all nose, ending in fat, wet nostrils that belched steam in the cold air. The moonlight gleamed off hulking shoulders, massive legs, and thick arms. They had the heads of bulls and the bodies of men, their limbs and chests covered with thick hair. Abisina could hear their teeth grinding as their malicious eyes raked their surroundings.

"Why have you stopped?" a thin, grating voice said from the darkness behind the creatures. A smaller figure stepped into the moonlight—a human woman, stooped with age, carrying a gnarled staff. She looked tiny, frail, with strings of tangled hair, but she spoke to the bull-headed men as if they were her inferiors.

"Smell," one of them grunted.

"Ignore it. Keep moving." She prodded the back of one of the beasts with her staff, and it snorted and ran a few steps. The other two followed, herded by the threat of the staff, and crashed into the forest.

When Haret returned, he found Abisina studying the tracks, trying to make sense of what she had seen. He dropped the rabbit that he'd been holding up in triumph. "What is it? What did you see?"

"I don't know." Abisina shook her head to dislodge the image. "They had heads like bulls—horns and wide noses. Tiny eyes."

"Men with bulls' heads? Minotaurs?" Haret whispered the last word. "My grandmother told me stories, but I thought— they were just stories." He stared at the tracks, noticing the prints of the hag. "And the human?"

"An old woman. She controlled them somehow, driving them before her with a staff, off to the south. Haret," she added, "I *need* a bow."

For once, he seemed to think about it. Then he picked up a handful of dirt and muttered, "Minotaurs!" Then louder: "Well, our way lies to the north, and I'll thank the Earth if we see no more of those beasts!" He rubbed the dirt over his hands before letting it filter through his fingers.

For days after seeing the minotaurs, they slogged through a steady rain. Remembering Vranille's searing drought, Abisina relished the water running down her face, into her ears, and down her neck. But as the rain continued day after day, she thought she would go mad from the wet. Her feet and hands were wrinkled and pale; at night, her sleeping pelts were sodden; her under-shirt and leggings clung to her uncomfortably; the dried moles became stringy and glistened with a white sheen.

On the night the rain stopped, the dripping leaves prevented Abisina from drying out. After coming through a particularly squelchy part of the woods, she paused at the edge of a clearing to empty out her boots. Before she could pull the first one off, Haret looked at her urgently, pressing his finger to his lips.

Centaurs? she wondered. *Or minotaurs?*

She saw nothing. But then the clouds moved off the face of the full moon. The wet grass of the clearing shone like silver, and shadows flitted at the edge of the trees. Haret grabbed her wrist and pulled her toward a huge oak, his finger remaining sternly on his lips. Abisina followed him behind the tree and crouched down in the waves of roots rippling from the trunk.

He leaned around the tree, trying to get a better view of the clearing. Abisina did not move.

Haret glanced back at her and pointed to the other side of the tree. "Fauns! Over there. Watch! Even you might learn something of beauty."

Beauty? Images of fauns ran through her head, fed to her by the Elders: diabolical creatures, perversions with cloven hooves and goat horns.

But she, too, peered around the side of the tree. A whistle came from the right of the clearing. A whistle from the left answered. Suddenly, the whistling swelled from all sides and the clearing filled with dancing shapes. For the first few moments, Abisina saw only a blur of bodies, but soon she began to pick out individual fauns with sinewy arms, hairy legs, and horned, curly heads. Some were as fair as an ideal Vranian, while others were darker than Abisina or Haret. The women wore garlands of flowers in their hair; the men wore them as sashes across their chests. A few blew into wooden pipes while others sang in high-pitched, melodious voices, tracing intricate harmonies that made her skin tingle, though she didn't understand the words. And their feet never stopped moving—they wove in and out of one another in choreography with no beginning or end.

Abisina caught her breath. The wood itself seemed to be closing in on the dance, trees moving with the music, although no wind touched Abisina's face. Haret turned to her, face shining, a half-smile pulling at his lips. She looked back at the swaying—*dancing*—trees and imagined great faces in theirtrunks—deep-set eyes, crooked mouths, knobby noses. Their branches looked like spikes of hair sprouting from their foreheads.

She sat transfixed, unaware of the rough bark biting into her shins. The fauns' song spiraled higher and higher until Abisina thought her heart would break with joy. Then, the ritual stopped. The fauns disappeared and the trees stood still again. A deafening silence filled the clearing. Blinking as if just awakening, Abisina realized that the sun had peeked over the tops of the trees. She sank back onto her heels.

Haret's eyes were moist, his cheeks flushed.

Abisina had no words to describe her feelings, and a look at Haret's face told her he felt the same way. They both sat for several moments, joined in awed silence.

He finally shook himself and broke the spell. Abisina got stiffly to her feet while Haret shouldered his bag.

"Day is here, but we must go farther before we can stop. Hurry," he said gruffly. But the hunger around his eyes—appearing deepest when he stroked Sina's necklace—had eased. He looked more whole.

Abisina lifted her own bag, and with one last glance at the empty clearing, followed Haret into the trees.

CHAPTER VIII

IT FELT STRANGE TO BE WALKING IN DAYLIGHT, THOUGH Haret stuck to deeply shaded places where the trees grew very close together. It was also warmer, and after half an hour, Abisina took off her cloak and draped it over her bag. The fauns' music still played in her head as she walked.

Haret stopped in front of her, squinting up toward the sun, touching the mossy side of a tree. Abisina glanced around. Behind them lay forest as thick as any they had moved through, but ahead there was more space between the trees, mounds of rock jutting from the earth, and boulders dotting the forest floor. Patches of sunlight now reached a carpet of fallen leaves, dotted with wildflowers. She noticed that the land sloped upward more steeply, and she was wondering if this might be the foothills of the Obrun Mountains when the woods filled with shouts and the snaps of breaking branches.

Something grabbed her around her waist and yanked her off her feet. She heard Haret shout, but then the world turned upside down. Abisina's head flopped toward the ground, which was rushing by below her. The thick, muscled legs of a horse flashed in and out of view.

She had been captured by a centaur!

Abisina pulled and struggled, but her bag and cloak hung around her head, tangling her arms. She shook them off and fought like a wild thing, twisting, clawing at the strong arm that held her, trying to sink her teeth into any body part she could. But the arm pinned her tighter, the drum of the hooves never faltering.

Abisina hung there, trying to collect herself. To her left, she saw the centaur's muscular human abdomen, flecked with mud and sweat, disappearing into the gray hips of a horse. Gathering her strength, she tried to fight again, but the centaur swung her away from its body and shook her hard. Her teeth clattered together and her bones grated in their joints. She went limp, and it held her again by its side.

She had to think! Had to get away! Clenching her teeth, she reached out a third time to scratch its belly or kick at its sides. But it shook her again, and Abisina's neck snapped, and all went black.

A hard smack against her cheek woke her.

She opened her eyes to find the cold, blue stare of a female centaur on her. Matted gray hair hung over the creature's breasts, her mouth twisted in a cruel grin. Abisina sat on a high tree branch, arms pinned to her sides, as the centaur held her waist.

"What's this?" the centaur mocked, examining her up and down. "A human takin' up with mudmen?"

Abisina tried to get her bearings, but her head pounded and moving her neck sent a stabbing pain through her shoulders.

"And what kind of human are you? You're as brown as the mudman! And this hair!" She yanked down the braid Abisina had taken to wearing and stepped closer so that Abisina could see her broken teeth and smell her foul breath. "Are you *all* human, girlie?"

Abisina swallowed hard and tried to look past the leering face.

"Lookin' for your friend? Don't worry. My brother has him, and you'll soon be together!"

A brown centaur galloped up in a rush of hooves. He was shorter and stockier than the female, his eyes dull, his features thick.

"Where's the mudman?" the gray centaur asked sharply.

"Surl, don't be mad!" The brown one put his hands up to defend his chest. "He kicked me in the face—look!" He pointed to his lip, split and bleeding. "I dropped him, and he was duckin' under trees before I knew what'd happened. I chased him for leagues, but he got away," he finished, taking a step back.

"For leagues, you chased him," Surl sneered.

"Well, far, but—but he's quick and stuck to low places."

"I should've known you'd lose him, Drolf. But I thought even you could handle a mudman." She released Abisina with her right hand as if ready to strike her brother, and Drolf cringed.

"I told you—he kicked me!" he pleaded. "And we got the human."

Surl appraised Abisina. "But will she please?"

"She looks, er, different," Drolf noted, with a wary glance toward his sister's free hand. "Was the mudman her *sire*?" he asked, impressed with his cleverness.

The blow came. Surl struck Drolf's chin, without looking in his direction. "Don't be thick. Look at the fine bones in her face and hands." She leaned in closer. "And the eyes. Green." Surl paused, thinking. "It's a risk. . . . If he doesn't like her—remember what he did to Lachlin?" Drolf, massaging his jaw, shuddered. Surl reached down and removed the boots Hoysta had made and flung them aside. She took Abisina's bare feet in her rough hands and stroked them. "We'll do it," she murmured as she straightened up. "We'll tell him she's rare, not like the yellow-haired ones. Better."

Drolf had been waiting for his sister's decision. "If they let us in the herd," he said eagerly, "we'll have all the meat we can eat. And the mead."

"Stop thinkin' about your belly!" Surl reached out to cuff her brother again, but, ready this time, he dodged the blow.

"Now shut up so I can think how to present her. . . . I'll do it in front of the whole herd," she said slowly. "Murklern and his guard'll try and stop me from gettin' to Icksyon. But I'll tell them I've a gift. The herd'll come back to camp just before nightfall. But all they'll be thinkin' about is meat and mead. I'll come after their bellies're full and—"

"But if we get there early, we can eat, too!" Drolf licked his lips.

Surl ignored him. "You'll have to hold her while I talk to the herd."

"Yeah, I'll hold the human," Drolf agreed.

"But can I trust you with her?" Surl turned on her brother.

"Surl, I can hold a human!"

"Like you held the mudman?"

"He was strong!" Drolf protested. "Not like this puny one."

With Surl distracted by Drolf, Abisina tried to gather her scattered thoughts. They were taking her to Icksyon, a herd leader. And *they* were afraid of him. She had to get away!

She stole a glance into the branches above her, but the next one was at least two body lengths away along a smooth trunk. The ground was a similar distance below—but that was her only hope. If she dropped to the ground, she could run.

But where? They'll be right after me. Twenty-five paces away was a tree she thought she could climb. If she could get up it, she'd be safe. *And trapped like a raccoon with wolves on his tail!* Still, it was her one chance. She got ready to drop the instant Surl relaxed her grip.

"That's right, teach *me* a lesson!" Surl was mocking her brother. Drolf's face was red with fury, his fists clenched. Surl looked at ease, but one of her back legs pawed the ground. "Come on!" she taunted until Drolf rushed her. Surl jumped aside, releasing her hold on Abisina.

Seizing her chance, Abisina dropped to the ground.

But as she took her first running step, her feet slipped from under her. Pushing herself up, she tried again to run, but something slammed into her. She felt a sharp pain in her head and another in her nose as she rolled over and over.

"The human!" Surl cried above her, and the buffeting blows stopped. "You clumsy bastard! You almost killed her! Icksyon'll want her alive."

"She was runnin' away!"

Surl snatched Abisina off the ground. Abisina could feel the bruises growing under the centaur's fingers. Surl shook her, hard.

"Tryin' to run!" she spat. "Drolf, get some vine to tie her up." Surl slammed Abisina back onto the branch but did not release her grip. "You won't try that again, girlie!"

It seemed to take hours for Drolf to get back with the vine. Abisina sat silently, the centaur's blue eyes boring into hers. When Drolf returned at last, Surl ordered, "Tie her tight." Drolf passed lengths of vine around Abisina's chest and arms, pulling it so that the vine cut into her skin through her under-shirt.

"Turn 'round," Surl barked at her brother when Abisina

was tied. Despite Abisina's struggle, Surl forced her onto Drolf—her legs uncomfortably straddling his wide back—and lashed her to Drolf's torso, her cheek pressed against his back, the smell of his body in her nose.

Abisina now faced the tree where she had been held, where she'd thought she might escape. On the ground, she saw a patch of mushrooms, red caps flecked with white; a swath through the middle of the patch was crushed where she had slipped.

She knew those mushrooms! Her mother had warned her about them. Eating even a tiny bit would bring sickness, horrifying visions, and finally death-like sleep. Eat too much, and you would never awake. *If only I had one of them now.* Anything—even death—had to be better than what the centaurs had planned for her.

"You've cost me time," Surl told her brother. "We're goin' hard to Giant's Cairn. And you'd better hold the human."

Drolf's body lurched below Abisina as he began to gallop, taking her to Icksyon.

Abisina endured the next hours in a haze of pain and fear as the centaurs cantered on—sometimes among scattered trees, other times on open, rocky hilltops—but never with any sign of stopping. Her thighs ached; the vines cut into her arms so that her hands tingled and then went numb; her face and chest ran with the centaur's sweat; her head throbbed where Drolf had kicked her, and sticky blood dripped from her nose. But the terror of what lay ahead was worse than any pain.

The sun had gone beneath the horizon and the air was cool by the time the centaurs slowed to a trot and then a walk.

"Get over here!" Surl barked. "I'm goin' to cut her off."

"Why?" Drolf's words rumbled against Abisina's cheek.

"Do it!"

Drolf took a few steps, and some of the vines around her tightened and then released. She was lifted off and again faced Surl.

"Did we have a nice ride, girlie?" Surl asked.

Abisina could barely hold her head up.

"Why're we stoppin', Surl?"

"I told you to shut up and follow orders!" Then, after a pause, "The Cairn's just up there. I'm goin' to check that the herd's finished the meat. I'll come back when I want you."

Drolf's huge hands gripped Abisina's waist, and she was pressed against his chest in a strange mockery of a mother holding a baby.

As they waited, the blood rushed back into Abisina's arms with a thousand pinpricks, and she realized that Surl, while cutting the vines that lashed her to Drolf, had also cut one of the bands that bound her arms. Overlapping vines still held her arms to her body, but there was enough slack to wiggle her aching arms and hands. As the feeling returned, she noticed that her right hand was coated in something sticky. *Blood?* Drolf took a few steps forward, peering into the trees for Surl, and the moon, just past full, washed over Abisina. She glanced at her hand and found not blood, but flecks of something white dotting her open palm.

Mushroom!

When she had pushed herself up after falling, she must have put her hand into the patch of them—and now, a few broken bits still clung to her. *There might be enough!* Death-like sleep, her mother had said. And if she didn't wake up, well . . . Without hesitation, she bent her head and started licking her hand.

"Stop jigglin', human!" Drolf grunted, tossing her against his arm. But Abisina didn't stop: licking her palm and between her fingers, picking up pieces of dirt and leaves, and, she hoped desperately, some bits of mushroom.

Drolf tossed her again. "What's wrong with you, human?" he cried, holding her before him.

"My—my nose," Abisina stammered. "I was wiping the blood."

"Let it bleed!" he said roughly, but then he took her weight in his right arm and wiped her nose with his left.

"What're you doin'?" came Surl's voice.

"Just—just givin' the human a shake to stop her wigglin'!" Drolf demonstrated and Abisina's teeth clattered together.

"Get over here!" yelled Surl. "They're done with the meat. He wants to see her."

As they trotted toward a hulking darkness split by a line of red light, Abisina willed something to happen inside her.

But she felt only the emptiness of her belly, saw only the moon and stars clear against the velvet sky.

Surl stopped a few paces from the dark mass: a pile of huge rock slabs jumbled together in a mound many times taller than the wall around Vranille. Giant's Cairn—it made sense now. A pile of rocks so big only a giant could have built it. The light glowed from a passageway into the center. Shouts and laughter rang out.

"Give me the human." Surl pinned Abisina under her arm so tightly she could barely breathe. They entered the passage. Tall, sheer faces of rock towered above them, disappearing into the blackness. Abisina listened to every pore in her body, waiting for some sign of the poison working.

But there was nothing.

This is the end, she thought. *It wasn't enough mushroom.*

The passage turned abruptly to the left, and the walls widened into a circular den, open at the top to show the distant sky. Around a blazing bonfire stood some thirty centaurs, most of them larger than either of Abisina's captors, but with the same matted hair, their bodies streaked with mud, their tails knotted and burred. Many of them had scars on their faces and chests. Some had been in the herd that had passed Abisina while she hid in the tree. A few bled from fresh wounds and did nothing to staunch the blood. Despite the open roof, the room reeked of horseflesh, sweat, and manure.

On the opposite side of the fire stood the largest centaur

Abisina had ever seen—two heads taller than any other, with a chest so wide the others looked scrawny by comparison. But instead of being muscular, his chest hung with fat—rolls falling over his horse hips, belly bulging. The hair on his body and head was dirty-white, his beard long and grimy, his eyes red-rimmed.

Icksyon.

In one motion, Surl swung Abisina up to show the gathering their prize. Though Abisina desperately wanted to close her eyes, they were locked on Icksyon's mad ones.

"Ah, the human. You're right, Surl. She's *unusual.*" Icksyon's voice caressed the word. "Bring her closer." The centaurs moved back to let Surl pass.

As she changed hands, Abisina gave a fierce twist, but Icksyon's grip closed around her waist even before Surl had let her go. He held her before him. Half crazed with fear, she beat and kicked at his chest, but her swats only made him raise his thick brow.

"You want something?" A slow smile pulled at his fleshy lips, and the room rumbled with laughter. "Maybe she wants to get down. What do you think, my friends?"

And he put her down. Abisina took a few running steps, but the legs and chest of another centaur barred her way. She spun around and ran in another direction only to be blocked by a pair of muddy legs. She knew it was useless but ran again, this time toward an opening between the flanks of a roan and a black, but they leapt together as she reached them, the rock walls echoing with laughter. She reeled back and rough hands seized her and lifted her into the air.

A centaur with a heavy black beard and blacker teeth leered down at her. "She's a fighter, Lord Icksyon!" he shouted. "More fun than that last one! And much more fun than those babies they leave us outside their walls."

"Send her back to me, Murklern. I want my prize."

Murklern handed Abisina to the centaur next to him, who held her by the heels over the fire, her hair hanging just out of reach of the hungry flames. The laughter rose as she writhed away from the heat.

Not to be outdone, the next centaur held Abisina above his head, wagging his tongue at her, bringing new shouts of laughter.

The next pushed Abisina's hair off her neck and bent his head as if to bite her.

But worse was the female right next to Icksyon who fondled Abisina's bare feet before showing them to her master. "Look m'Lord. How'll these add to your collection?"

Icksyon held something in his fist, which he shook like dice. "Let's see, shall we?" he purred, and he opened his hand.

Several shriveled nuts lay in his palm. Abisina didn't understand—until he held one of them up to her.

"Toes," he whispered to her. "I can't get enough. So *different*. And yours will add a new flavor to my collection—rich and brown."

Suddenly, she saw toes everywhere—many of the centaurs

wore necklaces of them, a few had them dangling from ear-lobes, Icksyon had a chain of them belted around his waist.

As Icksyon bent over her foot, teeth bared, Abisina went limp. She felt as if she were floating somewhere above the fire in the cool darkness. From this safe vantage, she looked down, heard the harsh laughter, saw but did not feel Icksyon biting her smallest toe.

It was the pain that pulled her back.

Not just her foot. Her entire body.

Icksyon lifted his head, her toe gripped in his bloody teeth, bringing cries of triumph from the watching centaurs. But Abisina gave no thought to them now. Something rippled under her skin like a fish swimming close to the surface. She groaned, and the fish rippled again. Pain seized her com-pletely. On—no, *in*—her back, her belly, her calves, fingers pressed, prodded from the inside out, wading through muscle, burrowing into tissue, squeezing her heart into new rhythms. She tried to scream, but as she opened her mouth, the fingers scurried to pluck her vocal chords, probe her nose, clog her throat.

She struggled for air. Stuffed with earth, buried alive, her lungs filled slowly, and every breath pulled the earth deeper until it ran in her veins, damming her blood to a sluggish trickle. The heat followed. From the center of her chest, it spread to her shoulders and neck, down her arms to her fin-gertips. Her blood flowed again, carrying the heat to her hips, to her thighs, down her legs, and to her injured foot. Her body softened. Pleasant at first, the heat intensified. Her flaccid muscles continued to soften until they felt like liquid seeping away. As the heat increased, so did her fear. Her skin seemed to be melting from her face, her fingers dripping off her hands.

Fire danced on the screen of her closed eyelids. Her hair dissolved, her bones floated in pools. She would seep into the earth, leaving nothing but bone to mark her existence.

A figure stood in the flames, blurred by the shimmering heat, but growing clearer and larger.

The White Worm, his maw open in a triumphant laugh, the void of his gaze closing in on her, as his clawed arms reached for Abisina.

So this is death, she thought, as the darkness enveloped her. But before the last pinprick of light died, hooves rushed toward her. The pinprick flared up and revealed, not the hideous Worm but a man, with skin like burnished copper and hair the color of a raven. He gestured to Abisina. "Come," he said.

She had eaten enough mushroom.

CHAPTER IX

"HUMAN!" THE HOARSE WHISPER PULLED ABISINA OUT OF the darkness. But she fought it. There was pain that way. And fear.

"Human!" It came again, nearer now, and Abisina heard a low groan.

Finally, right next to her: "Abisina."

She opened her eyes.

Rock was inches from her face. Pain defined her body, acute at her ribs, her neck, her shoulders, and her thighs—searing on one of her feet. Her mouth was dry and swollen. She thought of her fingers, and a stab of pain answered. She thought of her feet. Another shock of pain with a strange emptiness at its center. She moved her head to see who had spoken her name, and a flood of agony threatened to knock her out again.

A familiar face hung next to hers. Dull light made it hard to see the features.

"Human, we have to go now. Can you move?"

It wanted something from her, this face, but what?

"Human, are you with me? Can you hear me? We have to go! Oh, the Earth! Can't you hear me?"

Abisina closed her eyes. Let the face go away. She would stay here. Quiet. It was better than—somewhere else.

"Abisina!"

She opened her eyes again. But this time the face was gone. Light filled the space around her, painting the rocks with brilliance.

She tried to find the light's source. And then she saw it— ribbons intertwining into one twisting strand—*my mother's necklace.*

Someone lifted her head, placed the thin chain over it. She could feel the weight against her chest.

Haret. He was here, and now she heard the desperation in his voice. "We need to move somewhere safer!"

"Where are we?" she croaked through cracked lips.

"Giant's Cairn. The centaurs are gone, but they'll be back soon. We need to move. Now."

The Cairn.

Fear throttled her into action. She was wedged under a shelf of rock. Haret lay on his belly, his face next to hers. She lifted her shoulder to roll over and crawl toward him, but she hit the rock shelf above her hard. "No room," she moaned.

A rustle, and Haret's hands grasped her under the arms. She cried out as he began to pull her body over the rough rock.

"Can you help me at all, human?" he grunted near her ear.

Despite the sickening pain, Abisina bent her knees, managed to get her heels flat on the ground, and gave a push. The muscles in her legs cramped, her right foot throbbed in agony as her toes curled with the effort, but Haret murmured, "That's it! Again, and I think I can pull you the rest of the way."

Abisina couldn't straighten her legs, but she pushed again, and Haret scrambled to his feet behind her. She still saw only rock above her, but now Haret's pull had more power, and she found herself blinking up at a gray sky. Once her shoulders and chest cleared the rock, Haret pushed her to a sitting position, and she rested her head on the stone in front of her.

She was surrounded by rocks, some several times taller than she, others no bigger than her fist.

"Now, on your feet," he said.

Abisina gritted her teeth and dragged her legs from under the rock. Grasping a small ledge higher up the stone face, she pulled herself to her feet, unsteady until Haret draped her arm over his shoulder. As she regained her balance, she glanced through a gap between two boulders and stifled a scream.

Below her, not fifty paces away, gaped the entrance to the Cairn.

"It's right there! It's right there!" she sobbed, gripping Haret's shoulder.

"They're gone now." Haret tried to speak calmly. "But there's only an hour of daylight left; they could come back at any moment." He pulled her face around to his. "Human, pull yourself together. I'll help you get down. There are trees—cover—not far from here, and I've found a small cave. You'll be safe there."

Abisina fought her rising terror. She gripped Haret's shoulder harder; he felt solid beneath her hand. Looking down, she saw the pendant around her neck and her fear receded slightly. "I'm ready," she said.

Haret set off, half-dragging Abisina as she hobbled over stones and between boulders. Her feet, bare except for a bandage around her right toes, got scraped and bruised. In a few paces, they came to a series of ledges leading down to the ground. Abisina had to jump from the last ledge, supported in part by Haret, daggers shooting up from her injured foot as she landed.

The trees Haret spoke of were half a league away, but between their current spot and the scrubby pines was nothing but barren ground, dotted here and there with tufts of dried grass.

"I can't do it," she moaned, her legs buckling.

"You can, human. You must. You have survived this far. You must do this one last thing—get to the pines."

Abisina tried to look back toward the Cairn entrance, which she could feel threatening behind her, ready to swallow her whole, but Haret held her firm against him. "Don't look back. Just go. I'm looking for both of us."

They limped across the open ground, Abisina straining to

hear the thunder of hoofbeats at every step. She felt like a mouse waiting for an owl to dive from the sky and grasp her in its talons. Once, she looked back at the Cairn, sure they were coming for her, but it remained a silent, sinister pile of rock rising from the desolate plain.

"Keep going, human!" Haret urged through clenched teeth.

Abisina willed herself to take step after step. Her mother's necklace bumped against her chest at each footfall, and she let this rhythm guide her feet. Step, bump, step bump.

But a few paces before the edge of the forest, Haret stumbled and Abisina cried out, hitting the ground with a jarring thud. She crawled forward before Haret had time to help her to her feet. She reached the first trees, crawled a few more paces, and collapsed. Haret threw himself down beside her, panting heavily.

They didn't move for several moments, but finally Haret stirred. "We must go farther—to the cave. Can you stand?"

Abisina got onto hands and knees. "I think so."

Haret, standing, offered his hand, which Abisina grasped. When she got to her feet, she put her arm around his shoulders again. She looked at Haret, taking in his face for the first time. His right eye was swollen shut. A long scratch festered on his left cheek. His nose was crooked, his lower lip split.

"I don't want to meet the centaurs again any more than you do, human," he said, with a half-smile. "Let's get to the cave."

Somehow, they did. Abisina's strength gave out just after darkness, and Haret had to carry her inside, laying her on the rough floor. Barely conscious, she felt him change the bandage on her foot with gentle hands. She tried to murmur her thanks, but she wasn't sure if she made a sound.

Abisina woke several times in the night, jerking up with a scream, sure she would see Icksyon's mad eyes staring into hers, his hands on her feet. But each time, she woke to Haret's voice telling her she was safe, they were in the cave, she could sleep.

The last time she bolted awake, a wan sunlight filled the low, wide mouth of the cave. She lay on a bed of pine boughs with heaps of leaves piled on top of her. Abisina sank back onto the bed and placed her hand on her heaving chest. She found her mother's necklace, cool to the touch, and held it for a moment before putting it back inside her tunic. Haret was not there. *Probably out finding breakfast.* She knew he would be back.

Haret returned, his arms full of firewood, a bunch of greens clutched in one fist. His face was worse than the night before—his eye and lip more swollen, the festering cut on his cheek weeping yellow tears.

Haret touched her forehead. "No fever," he said, relieved. He held the greens out to her, and Abisina sat up. As she took them, he reached into his pocket to retrieve a few brown mushrooms. "Eat these, human. A few nibbles of greens, then the mushrooms, then wait before doing it again."

Abisina groaned. "No mushrooms."

"You haven't eaten in two days, and you lost a lot of blood. To heal, you must eat." He sounded like Hoysta.

"I'll eat the greens. Not the mushrooms."

"You need the mushrooms for strength!"

"I can't," she insisted. "I ate one before. . . . It was poison."

"What kind of mushroom?" Haret asked.

"A red cap with white flecks."

"Red cap? White—oh, the Earth! How much did they give you?"

"Not the centaurs. I ate it myself."

Haret put his head in his hands. "You can't eat any mushroom you find, human! You're lucky you're alive."

"Lucky? I saved myself by eating that mushroom!" Abisina's indignation gave her new energy. She sat up straighter. "My mother showed it to me. She's a—she was a healer: Sina, the healer of Vranille." It felt good to say her mother's name out loud. "I knew if I ate a little, I would appear dead. If I ate too much, I would *be* dead. Either way, I'd be better off."

Haret was silent, then said, "Still, you're lucky I came along when I did."

Abisina didn't reply. She could hear the respect in his voice. She started nibbling at the greens. "How did you find me?"

"I found you because I'm a dwarf," Haret said matter-of-factly. "I tracked you. The centaurs left a trail I could have tracked next winter. But then I ran into them coming back. A few of them came galloping by me—hard. They never move like that after dark. Vision like humans—useless at night. One called out not six paces from where I hid: 'Surl! Herd-traitor—we'll find you! Offering rotten flesh! We'll teach you to insult Lord Icksyon!'"

Abisina felt a grim satisfaction at these words.

Haret continued, "When they called you 'rotten,' I thought they meant your coloring—but now I understand. You were sick! That's what broke up their little party."

She shuddered.

"I found you at the back of the Cairn—curled in a ball. They must have thrown you aside. I thought you were dead." Haret's voice shook slightly. "But then I found a weak heart-beat. I had to climb into the Cairn, hide you, and find a cave. I came back to get you before evening, but it took much longer to wake you than I thought."

"That's when you gave me this," she said, pulling out the necklace. Wearing it, she felt like a piece of herself had been restored.

Haret swallowed hard and looked down. "Please—put it away." Thinking how many times she had said the same to Haret, Abisina tucked the necklace into her tunic. Haret went on: "I couldn't save our bags. When the brown one got me, I couldn't reach my knife, and I had to fight with my hands. He collided with a tree. Stupid brute. Got me, too." Haret pointed to a cut on his forehead. "He didn't try to follow me after that. From there, I followed his trail to the one who had you."

They lapsed into silence.

"I'll replace the gear we lost," Haret said at last. "But now we need water. You need to flush out what's left of the poison. And your foot needs to heal."

Abisina refused to look at the empty space on her right foot. Was Icksyon wearing her toe on his belt even now? Her voice was steady: "It won't slow me down."

"You're not going to give up." It was not a question.

"I'm going to Watersmeet."

"Suit yourself, human," Haret said, but as Abisina got to her feet, he offered her his hand. And a smile.

CHAPTER X

ABISINA AND HARET SPENT MORE THAN A WEEK IN THE cave recovering and replenishing their supplies. Her foot still wrapped and painful, Abisina was limited in what she could do, but Haret worked untiringly. He taught Abisina how to make a cooking pot by digging a hole, lining it with clay, and building a fire on top to harden the clay. He set traps near a stream for rabbits and squirrels, but the most important trap he set was a spring trap for deer.

He whittled down a few saplings into deadly points, attached these spears to a flexible branch near the stream, and set up a trip line using creeper vine. The first night, he returned with a doe; the night after that, he got a buck. The stomachs and bladders became new water carriers; the hide was stretched on a frame, dried over the fire, rubbed with wood ash, soaked, rubbed with a nauseating mixture of deer brains and fat, dried again, then sewn with a bone needle and sinew to become sacks and new boots for Abisina; more bone was sharpened into arrowheads; and a veritable feast of venison was prepared with plenty left over to smoke on a tepee of sticks.

Haret was his usual gruff self, barking "Human!" when Abisina let the drying deer hide get too close to the fire, when she asked too many questions about how dwarf snares worked, and when she washed the greens instead of leaving the "good, clean" dirt.

Still, Abisina knew their relationship had shifted. Haret let her apply her poultice of slippery elm to the cuts on his face and nodded his curt approval when he found her making ointment of elder leaves to help with bruises and sprains. He may have saved her because she could lead him to Watersmeet, but he had endangered his own life to do it. By eating that mushroom—and surviving—she'd shown him that she was made of stronger stuff than he'd thought.

And he had returned her mother's necklace. She knew that cost him. Several times she noticed him staring at her tunic where the pendant hung hidden from view. Once, when she was leaning over the fire, the necklace had swung loose and Haret groaned as the light reflected off it.

She quickly put it away, and he let out a shaky breath. After that, she took more care to keep the necklace out of sight.

For Abisina, the worst part about their time in the cave was the closeness of the Cairn. Whenever she left their hideout, she felt like Hoysta, terrified of the surface world. Even with the new bow and arrows that Haret had made her, she was nervous. She would have insisted they have no fires, but they needed them to smoke the meat and dry the clay and hides. Every morning before dawn, Haret stole back to the trees near the Cairn to watch the herd ride away. Then he would come back to the cave and stoke the fire for the work of the day, putting it out well before nightfall and the centaurs' return.

By the time they were ready to continue on their journey north, Abisina's injuries were almost healed; she still had fingermarks on her upper arms and bruises on her back and sides where she had been stepped on or kicked, but even these were fading. Her foot ached where she had lost her toe, and she limped as she walked, but there was no infection, thanks to Haret's careful cleaning and her poultices. Haret's cuts would leave scars, but they were no longer inflamed.

They set out one evening, the waning moon obscured by clouds. Haret crept to the Cairn and waited until the centaurs' mead-fueled songs and arguments rang out before returning to the cave for Abisina. As she stepped out into the cold night, she knew she wouldn't stop listening for hoofbeats until they were leagues and leagues away from Giant's Cairn.

They went northwest into the foothills of the Obruns, and the terrain grew rockier and steeper, with fewer tall trees, more underbrush to wade through, and less shelter. It would take them several days to reach the Mines, "especially at this pace," Haret groused, more out of habit than irritation.

On the fifth night of walking, Abisina realized that Haret was heading toward a ribbon of gray threading its way through the trees. She trotted to catch up and ask what it was, but he reached the ribbon first. When she got there, she found the ruin of a road paved with enormous stones. The stones were cracked and broken, and trees grew through fissures in places, but even in its dilapidated state, there was no mistaking the grandness of this road. The paving stones were great slabs of rock several body lengths long and one or two wide. Ten broad-shouldered men could walk down it abreast. Haret picked up the pace, and Abisina had to hurry to keep up.

"Haret!"

"What?" He sounded truly irritated this time, but he stopped.

"This road! Where did it come from?"

"My ancestors built this road," he said proudly. "The dwarves of the Obrun Mines."

"They're true then? Hoysta's stories?"

"You still can't believe it, can you? That the dwarves are capable of something the humans are not?"

"It's not that, Haret," Abisina tried to explain, though she worried that there was some truth in what he was saying. "But Hoysta's cave . . . it's nothing like what she described of the Obrun City."

"Humph" was Haret's only response before continuing up the road.

Abisina followed, excited but nervous. The Mines marked the beginning of her mother's directions. Arriving there would make Watersmeet so close! Would Haret understand what Sina's directions meant, or would he think them as flimsy as they sounded to Abisina?

The road began to climb more steeply. Haret set a pace that left Abisina far behind, her limp more pronounced after a night of walking. She caught up with him when he stopped in the middle of the road. Dawn had arrived, and in the cold light Abisina could see slopes of loose rock falling away on either edge of the road. A few scraggly trees clung to the slopes, but mostly the bits of green came from clumps of grass, weeds, and wildflowers. Cut into the side of the mountain directly ahead of them was an immense archway. The road disappeared into the darkness beyond.

They had reached the entrance to the Obrun Mines!

Abisina stared. All but a few of the top stones of the archway had fallen out. On the center stone Abisina could just make out what remained of intricate carvings and words, now eaten away by weather, lichen, and time.

Haret's voice startled her. "I've done my part and gotten you to the Mines, human. Now tell me what you know of the passageway."

"You want to search for it now?" Abisina said, stalling. "But we've been walking all night."

"I don't need rest," he said, that familiar superiority back in his tone, the hunger back around his eyes.

Abisina shifted her weight. It was time to speak.

"My mother said the pass to Watersmeet could be found at the entrance to the Obrun Mines, between Mount Sumus and Mount Arduus." She tried to sound confident, as if pronouncing the key to a confounding riddle.

"Sumus and Arduus?"

"That's what she said. Aren't they the names of those mountains?" Abisina asked, her show of confidence rapidly evaporating. She peered up at the slopes bathed in the light of the rising sun, their summits swathed in mist.

"Dwarves don't name mountains," Haret grunted. "What matters is what's under them. What else?" he demanded.

"What else?" Abisina echoed nervously.

"What else did your mother say?"

"W-Well, there's more once we get through, but that was all she said about the pass."

"But that tells us nothing, human! I knew *where* the Mines were! I need to know *how* to get through them!"

"Between Mount Sumus and Mount Arduus. Doesn't that mean something to you, as a *dwarf*?" Abisina said stubbornly, but inside her heart sank. She had hoped the names of the mountains held some clue Haret might recognize—though Hoysta, and now Haret, told her that dwarves don't name mountains.

"Tell me everything," Haret said through clenched teeth.

"Maybe we should rest first. Wait for the—" Abisina was cut off by a bellow of "Human!"

She gave up. She had no choice.... "She said that I would find Watersmeet at the meeting of three rivers."

"Three rivers," Haret repeated. "What else?"

"That's all."

"You must have forgotten something," he insisted.

"I haven't forgotten. That's all."

"Then your mother must have forgotten!"

"She didn't!" Abisina shouted back as she fought tears. These were some of the last words her mother ever spoke to her! She knew every syllable.

Haret shook his head fiercely. The two patches of beard on the sides of his face twitched.

Then he exploded. "I trusted you! Do you have any idea what this cost me—what this cost my grandmother—coming here? You were supposed to be the answer!" His voice broke as he threw his bag on the ground and strode back down the road, away from Abisina.

She did not follow him. *Let him go*, she thought.

But after a while, she picked up his bag and stowed it with hers inside the entrance to the Mines. She sat in the darkness where she couldn't be seen by any roaming centaurs, but where she could keep watch for Haret's return. The bees buzzed around the wildflowers growing between the cracks in the paving stones, and she longed to be out in the warmth of the sun. There had been no centaur tracks or abandoned fires since the Cairn—no minotaur tracks either—but even with her bow, she wouldn't risk it.

Especially after we just told anything in hearing distance where we are.

Abisina had been up all night, but she stayed awake, staring down the road, hoping to see Haret climbing back up to her. He wouldn't *really* give up on the passage, would he? Surely he would come back, and together they could figure out what to do.

The sun hung low on the western horizon when Abisina left the archway. There was still no sign of Haret. But she let hunger absorb her attention. She hadn't eaten since the night before. In the twilight, she searched for supper on the slopes of one of the mountains (she didn't know which was Sumus and which was Arduus). The footing was tricky among the shifting rock slides, but she managed to find a few edible plants in the tufts of grass and weeds. It wasn't a feast, but it would be nice to have some fresh greens after days of eating nothing but smoked deer meat. Abisina took water from the carrier and rinsed her share of leaves, waiting for Haret to grunt and reprimand her for washing off the best part. But the mountainside remained silent.

She arranged the greens in two piles—washed for her, unwashed for Haret—pulled out the deer meat and a few nuts, and sat back to wait. Her head was light with hunger, but she refused to eat alone. It would be an admission that Haret was not coming back.

She sat against the arch and tried to keep her mind blank. But thoughts surfaced like moths drawn to a dangerous light.

Can we find Watersmeet? Does it even exist? And what if I have to find it alone?

And then, he was there.

"Gone and ruined supper again, I see," Haret noted as he threw down a load of firewood and some long strips of reddish-yellow bark.

Abisina said nothing but couldn't hide her smile.

"I found more slippery elm," he said, ignoring the relief on her face. "It makes a tolerable gruel. But it will take a while to prepare. So eat." Haret had already helped himself to the greens and spoke the last with a dandelion leaf poking out of his mouth.

Abisina dug into her supper.

When they finished, Haret set about building a fire. They hadn't had one since they left the cave by the Cairn. "What about centaurs?" she asked.

"Not around here."

With supper eaten and the fire prepared, Abisina's hopes rose. Now they could figure out what to do. But Haret's next words froze her.

"It's time to tell me everything. Why you left your village. How your mother came by the necklace—if this part of your story is true—and how she knows Watersmeet. No lies, human."

"I've told you no lies!" Abisina insisted.

Haret snorted. "Tell me everything," he repeated. "I've brought you this far; you owe me that at least."

Abisina bit her tongue to keep from flinging back, "I owe you nothing!" She did owe him; she could not have gotten here on her own. She hesitated, not knowing where to begin, but at Haret's "I knew it! Plotting lies!" she launched into her story.

She began with Vranille, Sina saving her life but her being outcast—"So human!" Haret muttered—and the arrival of Charach. As she described that lurid scene in the burial ground, Haret sat up straighter. Somehow, Abisina told Haret about the fire, about the cries of the villagers, about the bodies. Her voice didn't even shake. But when she got to the sudden wind and snow, Haret jerked so violently that Abisina broke off.

"No, no. Keep going."

"That's when I found the necklace. The wind blew away all the ash"—Abisina winced—"and there it was, on the altar."

Haret frowned. "But where did your mother *get* the necklace?"

"From my father. I told you that."

"But *who* was your father?"

"We've been through this. My mother told me he was from Watersmeet," she said wearily.

"You don't look like the typical human, you know, with your coloring and those eyes, and—well, you've shown yourself to have some bit of ingenuity and courage, which aren't exactly human qualities. You couldn't be, er, part dwarf?"

"No!" Abisina spat.

"Oh—and that would be so terrible!" Haret snapped back.

Abisina flushed. "It's not that. It's just—"

But Haret didn't let her continue. "I don't understand the instructions!" he said in frustration. "According to your mother, the passage is at the entrance to the Mines. But my family has been searching there for ages. There must be fifty different tunnels dug in there." He pointed to the darkness of the Mines behind them. "No—eighty! And most are filled with the skeletons of one of my—"

Haret shook himself and continued. "My ancestors have dug and dug in search of the passage, but they've come up with nothing. Every tunnel ends against that rock, that infernal rock that breaks tools like twigs! When you appeared with Obrium, I thought—but how could you know what a dwarf could not? We are bred of the Earth, bred of stone! If anyone were to find this passage, a dwarf would. All I've learned from you are the names of these mountains—useless."

Haret got up from the fire and walked into the mine entrance, disappearing in the darkness. Abisina also left the fire, walking a few steps down the road; then she turned and stared up at the peaks, dark against the starry sky. The moon had risen, the thin crescent visible between the two mountains, its light glinting off the snow on the summits.

Abisina stared at the spot where the slopes of the two mountains met. *"If anyone were to find this passage, a dwarf would."* But I am supposed to find it now.

Abisina headed back to the fire. She hadn't thought about

what it would cost Haret to go to the Mines; she had thought only of how he could get her to Watersmeet. She settled on the hard ground, her head on her sack, waiting for sleep to come. Her mother had always said that wisdom came in the morning, but as Abisina drifted off, these seemed like more empty words.

She woke with Haret standing over her. As her eyes fluttered open, he sprang back. The pendant on her chest felt heavy with Haret's stare. His eyes looked hollow, haunted. "I leave at twilight," he said bleakly. "I've dug all night in the one promising place in the archway—and once again hit the hard, black rock that has bedeviled my family for generations. I will sleep for the day and then head home, never to visit this cursed place again. I swore to my grandmother that I would look after you. I will take you back to her, safely. If you don't want to return, I consider my obligation fulfilled."

"So *you're* giving up," Abisina said. "One night of digging. That's it."

"It's not one night!" Haret shouted. "It's been hundreds of nights! Don't you see, human? My family has been driven beyond the edge of madness hunting for Obrium. I swore I wouldn't become like that. Not after my parents . . . Then I saw your necklace, heard 'Watersmeet,' and I became like all of them— thinking of nothing but that mythic metal. But your passage, like all the other hints and clues and hopes we've chased, is only a chimera." He clenched his fists. "I leave tonight."

But Abisina was staring past Haret. "My passage," she

murmured. "My *passage*. Wait, Haret! That's it!" She leapt up and grabbed his arm, dragging him under the archway and onto the road, pink in the early dawn.

"Leave me!" Haret cried, pulling away.

"But that's it, Haret! Passage! You've been saying 'passage' all this time, but my mother said 'pass'!"

"Pass, passage, what does it matter?"

"It does matter! You've been thinking about this like a dwarf!"

"I *am* a dwarf!"

"Yes, but my father was not. He didn't go *under* the mountains; he went *over* them!" Abisina pointed to the meeting of the slopes of Sumus and Arduus, the rocky peaks stark against the clear sky.

"Over the mountains?"

"Yes!" Abisina nearly danced with joy. "Don't you see? Thinking about mines and tunnels and dwarfish things, you assumed that the only way to get to the other side of the Obruns was to go under them. But that isn't the only way! There's a *pass* between these mountains, a notch of some kind that we can climb to and then down the other side—to Watersmeet!"

"You don't know what you're saying. Look at the height of them, the rock faces! There's no way over those mountains."

"Humans have climbed mountains before," Abisina heard herself say, though she could hardly keep up with the speed of her own thoughts. "'Vran led the people down the Mountains Eternal.'" She repeated the line chanted so many times by the Elders; the words chilled her, but she rushed on. "Why can't we do it again?"

Haret straightened his shoulders. "I am a dwarf. I'll not follow Vran."

Abisina's face clouded for a moment. But then she remembered her mother's words. "It's not Vran we're following. It's something else. My mother told me the night before—she told me that what Vran did was miraculous, but he was a man, and miracles come from beyond mere men. Hoysta tried to say this, too," she added quietly, thinking of the old dwarf's gentle words at their parting. "She said that no good had come from our hate—the dwarves and the humans. But some good might come from our friendship. And that's what's happening now, Haret. You have to trust me."

She had caught his attention. The bitterness left his face as he considered her words. "Is it possible? All these years we've searched—" Haret rubbed his beard. "I don't know, human. I know nothing of going—up."

"You said yourself, the pass cannot be in the Mines or your ancestors would have found it. But my father told my mother it *is* here—between Sumus and Arduus."

"We don't even know if that's what those mountains are called!" Haret looked at the steep slopes warily.

"They must be," she said. *The instructions seem so clear now.*

Unconvinced, Haret stared again at the peaks, his face shadowed by the same fear that had haunted Hoysta when she stood at the mouth of her cave.

"We have to try. We've come this far," Abisina said firmly.

By midmorning, they'd refilled their water sacks, gathered a few more handfuls of greens, and tied up a small bundle of firewood. Before leaving the Mines, Haret stood alone in the archway, staring toward the abandoned shafts, holding a clod of dirt in his cupped hands.

Then he joined Abisina in the sun and they began to climb. They picked their way up the treacherous rock slides, working toward the saddle between Mounts Sumus and Arduus. After hours of the uncertain footing, steep incline, heat radiating from the rocks, and Haret's increasing nervousness, Abisina doubted what had seemed so certain before. She could see no sign that anyone had ever come this way or of a pass between the two mountains. They crested a rise, and a precipitous cliff blocked their way like a wall. The cliff's face, striated with white, black, and gray ribbons of rock, glittered in the light. *How will we get up that?* she wondered, with a glance back at Haret's anxious face. *But we have to*, she told herself and kept climbing.

The field of boulders leading up to the cliff looked deceptively small. Abisina expected to reach the base of the cliff in an hour—two at the most—but the sun was well past noon and still they toiled over, around, and between huge boulders worn smooth by wind and storms. At every footfall, rocks rasped at Abisina's toes and wobbled under her boots. Her right foot ached terribly. Twice she fell hard, and Haret fared little better. Though more comfortable moving among rocks, he couldn't take his eyes off the cliff towering ahead.

They rested in silence in the long shadow of one of the boulders. They'd already had some water, munched some of the wilted greens, and should have been back on their feet, but neither moved. Absentmindedly mimicking a gesture she'd seen Sina make countless times, Abisina reached for her throat and pulled out the necklace, running her fingers along the strands of cool metal. "We should keep on," she said with forced conviction.

"Hmm," Haret murmured, eyes closed.

With effort, Abisina stood up and then bent down to pick up her bag and water skin. As she did, the necklace fell forward, catching the light of the sun. She was about to hide it from Haret when she saw before her—winding among the boulders—a narrow, gravelly path. It was barely discernable but for tiny bits of mica that reflected the light of Sina's necklace. She took a few steps, pausing before she rounded the next corner. The path continued. It wound and winked around the next boulder, and when she ran to where it turned—Haret yelling behind her—she saw it leading on.

The pass! She'd found it!

She raced back to Haret, who stood bewildered where she had left him.

"Haret, it's right here! It's been here all the time."

"Put it away!" he cried, pointing a shaking finger at the necklace.

"But that's what is doing it! Look!" She pointed to the sparkling stones at her feet. "Can't you see it? It comes from the necklace. Watch!" Abisina tucked the necklace into her shirt, and the path disappeared; she yanked it out, and the path shimmered to life again. "See?"

Haret looked at her suspiciously. "What are you up to, human?"

"Haret, it's right there! You don't see it?"

"I see nothing. And I told you, put the necklace away!"

"Well, I see it," Abisina asserted, her excitement undiminished. "Just follow me. I'll lead you."

Haret's frown deepened.

"What is it, dwarf?" Abisina asked, imitating Haret's gruff voice. "Don't like to be led by a human?"

Haret took a step toward her. She slid a few more steps along the path.

"Human," Haret rumbled, but he followed. Abisina leapt on ahead. Haret followed once again but cried out at Abisina's retreating figure, "Not so fast!"

It was all Abisina could do to keep from laughing.

They made steady progress after that, Haret getting more and more comfortable following an invisible path. By late afternoon, they had reached the cliff. The path snaked back and forth across its sheer face, rising higher and higher. But from the bottom, the shining line looked thin, feeble; could they really climb it without tumbling off? She held the necklace for a moment. "It's worked so far," she whispered and took a few steps onto the narrow path.

"Are you crazy?" Haret's face turned a sickly shade of gray. "You plan to climb that?" He stabbed a finger toward the top of the cliff.

Abisina backed off the path and returned to Haret. "The path is clear all the way up."

But Haret was having none of it. He crossed his arms and said flatly, "I will not go up that."

Abisina looked toward the cliff in desperation. The sun was sliding down the sky. The path already shone with an orange tinge; with the fall of night, it would be gone.

She tried again. "Haret," she coaxed, "we can do it."

Silence.

"Come on, you stubborn dwarf! Are you going to stand there like a stone until—until what? You practically killed me those first few days out, but now that you have to face something hard, you refuse?" She realized she was yelling.

With glacial slowness, Haret faced Abisina and spat through clenched teeth, "I—am—afraid—of—heights!"

"What?"

"You heard me, human. Don't make me say it again." Haret's ears reddened.

Abisina fought the urge to smile and raised a sober face to Haret. "We have to go up. What else can we do?"

"I don't know," said Haret, dropping his crossed arms helplessly.

"Would it help if you could see the path?"

"Maybe."

"Then try the necklace," Abisina offered, pulling it over her head.

"No!" Haret took a step away, even as his hand reached for it, twitching with desire.

"Go ahead. Take it," Abisina urged. "I know you'll give it back."

Haret licked his dry lips. "You trust me?"

"Yes." Abisina sounded surer than she felt.

Haret snatched the necklace and threw it over his head. As the pendant came to rest on his chest, he sighed deeply and stared down at it.

"Well, do you see it?" Abisina asked.

Haret started as if he'd forgotten she was there.

"The path, Haret. Do you see it?"

"Oh." Struggling, he squinted toward the cliff. "I see *something*. It's faint."

Abisina could see nothing but sheer cliffs now, and her stomach lurched. "Faint? It was there a moment ago."

"Well, it's faint," Haret snapped as he stared again at the necklace.

"Let me try again." Abisina held out her hand, but

Haret shrank back, curling protectively around the necklace.

"Haret!" Abisina spoke sharply, and he blinked a few times. "Let me try the necklace."

Haret's eyes flamed, and then, as if a candle had been snuffed out, they dulled. His shoulders slumped as he fumbled at his throat and took off the necklace with trembling hands.

Abisina slipped it back on, and it settled over her heart. The pathway sprang to life, redder now, but clearly defined. "It's bright, Haret. I can see it as easily as I can see you."

"It's *your* necklace," he said morosely. "The power resides in you."

"Power?" Abisina repeated vaguely, studying their path.

"The necklace belongs to you, human. It sought you out. I've known since you told me about the snow and wind at the altar. That was the necklace, too."

"At the altar?" He had her attention now.

"The wind blew the ash away—so you could find the necklace. The snow prevented pursuit. This path is the same. You're *meant* to go to Watersmeet. But the necklace's power— it works only for you."

"But it was my mother's—and my father's before that. It really isn't mine."

Haret shrugged. "It is now. Come on, human. Let's get going. I'll walk with my hands on your shoulders."

Abisina couldn't imagine how Haret made it up the cliff essentially blind. The path in front of her ran into long, narrow switchbacks chiseled into the cliff face, and each step terrified her more. At times, the ledge was so narrow they had to sidle along it; any misstep on the loose gravel threatened to send them both over the edge. Haret's hands were like iron on her shoulders. She learned early the mistake of looking down—her head spinning at the sight of the jagged rocks below—and the terror of looking up—feeling as if the wall above her were tumbling down. She kept her eyes locked a few feet ahead on the path and thought only about putting one foot in front of the other.

The sun was sinking fast now, the night chill already biting at her hands and ears. Abisina knew they would not make the top of the cliff by sundown, but they had come too far to turn back. As the path faded from orange to red to gray, her thoughts raced: *What will we do when the sun sets? There has to be a wider spot here somewhere, a place where we can sit safely until the moon rises.* But when the sun dipped below the edge of the horizon and the path snuffed out, they were at a place as narrow as any they had yet encountered.

Abisina stopped.

"What?" Haret croaked behind her.

"Sun's down," she said. "I can't see the path. We can't go on."

"We have to stay here? All night?"

"Just till moonrise," Abisina said as lightly as possible. "And we'll have to stand. There's no room for us to sit down."

Haret knew as well as she did that the moon would not rise until after midnight. A low moan escaped his lips.

Time crept by as Abisina and Haret waited for the moon. The warm rocks at their back provided a little warmth but, even in early summer, nights at this elevation were cold and Abisina's muscles soon cramped. She tried to talk to Haret; he could barely utter a word. Exhaustion overtook her, but trickles of falling rock brought images of rock slides and avalanches, and once she nearly screamed as a puff of air hit her face and she sensed a large body winging by her. *It's only an owl*, she thought. Still it took several moments before the rush of fear left her.

Worst of all, Abisina started to nod off. Without realizing she had shut her eyes, she was lost in a swirl of color—blues and purples and reds, drawing her into their midst. In the center of the maelstrom, a blond man, somehow familiar, smiled at her, his lips forming her name. Abisina started to take a step, unable to resist, though she knew that this man was dangerous.

"Human!"

Abisina jolted awake, her head slamming against the cliff behind her. Haret's arm was across her chest. "What—I—what—?"

"You almost stepped off the cliff!" Haret panted. "I think I'm going to be sick."

Abisina's head pounded. The pain drove sleep and the dream from her mind. "I think I saw—" But she wouldn't say Charach's name.

Haret groaned in response.

Please, she pleaded to the sky above her, to the hidden moon, to anything that might be listening. *Please help us!*

And, as if hearing her call, a bit of moon did peek over the horizon, a soft beam of light reaching toward Abisina and finding her necklace. Before her feet, the path reappeared, shimmering across the face of the cliff to the next switchback.

"I can see it, Haret!" she cried. "We can keep going."

Haret's hands fell heavily on Abisina's shoulders, telling her how much this climb was costing him. They groped across four more switchbacks before the path curved over the top of the cliff.

"We're almost there!" she said. Haret's steps dragged, as if he had stopped lifting his feet. She struggled on, legs protesting, until they crested the cliff and the path disappeared. Abisina fell forward, Haret falling on top of her like a dead weight. She crawled away from the lip of the cliff and collapsed. Haret rolled off, panting in the dark.

Abisina woke with the warmth of the sun on her face. She opened her eyes and squinted into the blue sky. Sitting up, she saw the edge of the cliff just beyond her outstretched legs. Below her, she could make out the field of boulders and the lower slopes of Sumus and Arduus, first rocky, then giving way to forest. To her left, the Obrun Mountains stretched like the backbone of a huge animal off into the brightness of the rising sun. To her right, several more peaks reached toward the Mountains Eternal. A mist rose from the foot of one of the westernmost Obruns. As the light of the sun hit the water droplets, they bent the light into two rainbows arching like bridges between the high peaks.

"Haret!" she called softly. He lay on his belly nearby, sleeping. "Haret, it's morning." He groaned and pushed himself up onto his elbows. He glanced at Abisina, then back at the edge of the cliff, and groaned again, dropping his head between his hands. "I'll not soon forget last night."

"What do you think that is?" Abisina asked, pointing toward the rainbows. Haret looked up, then buried his head back into his hands.

"Waterfall," he said, his voice muffled. "I've heard stories of it. The waters of the Great River run through the Obruns. But don't make me look again. Makes me dizzy."

Abisina gazed toward the rising mist, enjoying the sun kissing her face, the journey up the cliff and her vision of Charach pushed to the back of her memory. Her stomach grumbled. "Breakfast," she muttered and reached for her bag. Haret stirred, getting to his hands and knees.

"Oh, the Earth!" he cried, and the note of wonder made Abisina turn quickly.

Only fifty or sixty paces behind where they had slept, set in the notch between the upper slopes of Sumus and Arduus, a cluster of rock pinnacles pointed like bony fingers into the sky, pink in the light of the rising sun. "Those spires! What are they?" Abisina echoed Haret's reverent tone.

"I—I don't know. But they're *something*. Do you see the path?"

Abisina turned her body toward the strange outcropping, letting the necklace catch the light. "Look!" she cried. The light from the necklace reflected on the largest of the spires, making a perfect, luminescent archway at its base, as if the rock were glowing from the inside.

"What do you see?" Haret asked urgently.

"There's an arch! Can you see it?"

Haret got to his feet. "No, but let's go. The necklace hasn't led us wrong yet."

With Abisina in the lead, they walked toward the arch, the light intensifying. When they were within five paces of it, Abisina had to close her eyes against the brightness.

Groping blindly, she expected rough rock on her fingertips, but instead, her fingers were seized by—something that felt like a cold, hard hand. "Haret!" she called as a powerful wind arose, ripping the words from her lips. Abisina was being pulled apart—the wind forcing her backward while the crushing grip pulled her forward. Haret's arms closed around her waist as the gale blasted them toward the cliff's edge. With her last energy, she clutched the cold hand with both of her own, pulling Haret, step by laborious step. The force of the wind lessened, the brightness on her eyelids dimmed— and in one more step, the wind disappeared altogether. Silence pressed on her eardrums. The hand crumbled to sand in her grip. Trembling with fatigue, Abisina opened her eyes.

They stood in a round room carved out of rock, lit by a soft, reddish light, though Abisina could not see its source.

The ceiling hung with stalactites. Ten or twelve passageways opened onto the room, but there was no sign of the enormous archway in any of the walls. It seemed as if the mysterious hand had pulled Abisina and Haret through solid rock.

CHAPTER XI

"WHAT NOW?" ABISINA WHISPERED.

"Try the necklace," Haret said, his voice low also. His hair was blown back from his face, his beard in tangles, as he looked from tunnel to tunnel.

Abisina held the pendant up to the soft light but no corresponding glow appeared. "Nothing."

Haret picked up a handful of dirt and sniffed. "It smells—empty. And no tracks. I don't think anyone's been here for a while." He stepped down the nearest tunnel, then picked up a fleck of dirt and put it on his tongue. "Not this way," he murmured, moving on. "Or this," he said after another taste. At the fourth tunnel, Haret nodded as the dirt hit his tongue. "This way," he said firmly.

"How do you know?" Abisina asked, trying to remember where they had started.

"I'm a—"

"—dwarf," she finished. "I know. But what's down there?"

"Food, for one thing. And water. And—it's the right one. Come on."

Abisina cast a wary glance around the room again, but with no other plan, she agreed.

In a few steps, the glow from the first room faded, but around a bend in the tunnel, more light beckoned. They turned the corner and another pool of light appeared. They had gone only thirty or forty paces when the light's quality changed— from dull red to the yellow hues of daylight. Another archway stood before them opening onto grass dotted with trees, brilliant blue sky overhead.

Their steps slowed as they both peered out, cool air on their faces. Gone was the arid landscape of the mountain peak. Dew spangled the grass. The leaves of the trees shone in the sunlight, pieces of fruit peeking out, and the delicate odor of ripeness filled the air. Running water tinkled nearby.

"What do you think?" Haret asked.

"Food and water," Abisina said, nodding toward the fruit trees.

"There's a wall, too." Haret pointed through the trees where a high stone wall was visible. "Looks safe."

Still, Haret drew his hatchet and Abisina readied an arrow before they stepped out of the tunnel. The odor of fruit grew as they neared the trees. Abisina plucked a soft yellow fruit, planning only to inspect it, but the perfume that washed over her made her take a bite, her mouth flooding with sweetness.

The flesh melted on her tongue, juice ran down her chin, erasing any doubt she had about entering the garden.

"Orf, the Earf!" Haret sighed around a large mouthful of yellow fruit.

Abisina gobbled two more before she wandered on. And then she regretted eating so much—if you can regret eating the finest piece of food you have ever tasted—because the next tree was laden with smaller, red fruit, spicier in flavor, but still sweet and juicy. And the next offered thin green ones, dry and crunchy. Then she was finished, her stomach not straining and sore, just extremely satisfied.

Now wanting a drink, she followed the sound of water to a stream that bubbled out of the orchard wall into a deep basin. Although it had no visible drain, the basin stayed filled to the brim without overflowing. Haret emerged from the trees, juice soaking his beard. She wiped her own chin self-consciously.

Cupping their hands, they leaned over the basin and lifted mouthful after mouthful of the icy water to their lips until Abisina plunged her whole head in and came up spluttering, her ears aching with the cold. Haret took one look at her and burst out laughing, the deep boom echoing off the walls. She grinned—and the next time he bent to get a handful of water, she dunked his head, too. Now it was her turn to laugh at the surprise on Haret's dripping face.

"Quite a place, eh?" he said, after joining Abisina on the grass. "The fruit! I've never tasted its equal."

"No, I imagine you haven't," she said dryly, thinking of Hoysta's gritty soup.

"Oh—and you have? I've seen enough of humans to know what you're used to eating. Coarse bread and mealy potatoes, breakfast, dinner, and supper!"

Abisina smiled. There was no edge to their banter now.

They sat watching the sunlight on the leaves until Haret spoke: "I think I'll investigate those tunnels. After crawling like an insect up the side of that mountain, I need the strength of walls around me."

"Mmm," Abisina murmured, vaguely aware of Haret getting to his feet and wandering away. She lay back on the grass and peace settled over her—a peace she had known only on nights in the hut with her mother, sitting before the fire, learning her letters, while a storm raged. On those nights, when no one from the village would come out to disturb them, she could almost believe that Vranille was an illusion, that she was not outcast, that somehow she would wake up in the morning to a world where she was accepted.

She may have dozed. Her stomach prompted her to rise when the sun shone directly overhead, and she wandered again through the orchard, sampling different fruits, humming.

She lost track of her path but didn't care. Nothing would happen to her here, she was sure. She came to a break in the trees, and the peace that saturated the orchard became almost palpable in the clearing before her. A single rowan tree grew in the middle; she recognized its long, thin leaves and the clusters of white blossoms. Her mother had always hung a rowan branch over their doorway, warding off evil. Did the peace she felt around her emanate from this tree? Near the trunk, a spring bubbled up, providing the soothing sound of water. Beneath the tree, white stones outlined what Abisina immediately knew was a grave. Could this somehow explain the wonder of this orchard?

She sank down on the grass, letting the whisper of the leaves and the song of the water fill her. The murmurs surrounded her and—without fear—she felt that something or someone had entered the clearing. She closed her eyes.

A voice spoke inside Abisina's head. *This is my garden, my grave. I brought you here.*

The voice felt female and old. Very old. And as it spoke, the necklace radiated a warmth on Abisina's chest.

You wear my necklace. Have you felt me?

Abisina thought of the lighted archway on the wall of stone, the ribbon of light up the cliff and through the boulder field, the light glittering against the black stone of the altar. *Yes. You've been with me since Vranille. Who are you?*

I am Vigar. I brought the folk to Watersmeet, made it their home. And now, I am bringing you to Watersmeet. And to Rueshlan.

Abisina fought to keep her eyes shut. *Who is he? Is he my . . .*

The voice said nothing, but she knew the answer.

When the voice came again, Abisina felt a new urgency. *You must warn him as I warned him myself. Tell him my ancient enemy has returned. Tell him you have seen Charach. It is the beginning.*

The air rippled around Abisina, the rowan leaves rustling. Abisina hated to hear that name uttered here. *You know—Charach?*

He is everyone's enemy.

Again, the rowan's branches stirred.

How do I get to Watersmeet?

Northwest. To the River Deliverance, then follow the river due north. You will find Watersmeet where the Fennish, the Middle, and the Lesser Rivers meet. And Abisina?

Yes?

We are all with you—those who wore the necklace. When the time comes, you will know what to do.

What time? What will I have to do? Wait!

Abisina's eyes flew open as she felt Vigar's presence leave the clearing.

What could it mean? Vigar had said that she founded Watersmeet, but she was buried here, in the Obruns. And Hoysta and Haret spoke as if the founding of Watersmeet happened long ago, but Vigar said she had warned Rueshlan—*my father*—as if she had spoken to him. *Was he here once—in this very garden? Did Vigar speak to him as she just spoke to me?* Abisina looked around her, studying the place anew. Had her father sat beneath this rowan? Listened to this spring?

But Vigar said to *warn* him. Abisina went cold. Her mother had said the same as the village burned around them.

And Mama wore the necklace. Did my father, Rueshlan—the name felt strange—*wear it? Are they with me, too?*

Haret was skeptical when Abisina told him what happened. "You spoke to a *ghost*? And she gave you directions to Watersmeet?" But he couldn't deny the magic pervading the orchard.

Abisina had not meant to say anything about Charach. She had decided that the world of the Vranians and Charach no longer concerned her. But Vigar's warning slipped out as she told Haret the story.

"Charach is seen as an enemy here also? On the northern side?" Haret's eyebrows pulled together. "There's no way across the Obruns that we know of except the way we just came. Surely Charach doesn't know about the pass."

Abisina said nothing. Every time the name was mentioned, the peace around her was disturbed. To her relief, Haret dropped the subject.

They slept in two nooks chiseled in the tunnels Haret had explored that morning. The nooks had mattresses already stuffed with something soft, springy, and smelling of fresh herbs. Warm blankets lay at the ends.

"I guess your ghost was expecting us," said Haret.

Abisina woke, feeling as if she had slept for days. Her muscles were so relaxed, the bed was so soft, and her body fit it so well. Even the ache of her missing toe had lessened. She was sure Haret must have gotten up without her, unable to rouse her from such a wonderful slumber. And the thought didn't bother her; she was too contented. Light fell across her bed from a window carved in the wall. Lifting onto one elbow, Abisina peeked outside. The yellow sun of morning bathed the orchard, and fruit-perfumed air blew in. Her belly responded with a rumble to say that it was time for breakfast. She swung her legs off the mattress.

Across the passageway, Haret stirred in his bed, opened a sleepy eye, and said, "'S'it morning?"

"Yes."

"How long've we slept?"

"I don't know," she admitted. "I thought you were up."

Haret didn't seem concerned about this either. "Should we find some breakfast?"

But as Abisina stood, she felt a tremor in the garden's tranquility—the same feeling she had when Vigar spoke to her of Charach. "Bring your axe," she said to Haret as she put her bow and quiver over her shoulder.

Haret raised an eyebrow at her but tucked his weapon into his belt.

They gathered fruit and took it to a weathered bench built around the base of a tree. Abisina began to relax. The orchard was calm.

Between bites, Haret said, "Did your ghost tell you how many days it is to Watersmeet?"

"She didn't mention," Abisina responded with similar sarcasm.

Suddenly a terrifying bellow reverberated around the orchard.

They were both on their feet in an instant. "Centaurs?" Abisina hissed.

Haret shook his head. "I've never heard that sound before."

It came again, and the ground shook. "Is it *in* here?" Abisina asked.

The bellow sounded a third time and was followed by a crash as if the rock wall had been blown apart.

"It is now," Haret said grimly, loosening his axe.

Abisina nocked an arrow and gave Haret a quick nod.

They headed toward the noise, which had changed from deafening bellows to guttural snorts and grunts, punctuated by sharp cracks. Abisina gripped her arrow tighter. *What is it?*

The answer came all too soon. They followed the cacophony, not to the destroyed wall as they expected but to the very center of the garden, where only yesterday Abisina had basked in peace. That memory was far from the sight that now met her eyes: rocks from Vigar's grave lay strewn across the clearing, which had been trampled to a muddy mess. Many of the rowan's branches had been ripped from its trunk. In the middle of this destruction stood a minotaur with tiny, hate-filled eyes, poised to impale them on its vicious horns.

For an instant, no one moved. And then the monster lowered its head and charged.

Abisina let her first arrow fly seconds after Haret threw his hatchet, and she had another on her string before either had a chance to hit their targets. With a clumsy swipe, the minotaur batted aside Haret's hatchet, but he lifted his head to do it and Abisina's arrow, aimed at the minotaur's eye, caught him instead in the shoulder. Abisina loosed her second arrow, but this one went wide. The minotaur wrenched the first arrow from its shoulder and stared at it in surprise before Haret, dashing to retrieve his axe, caught its attention. With a roar the minotaur lunged for the dwarf, turning its back on Abisina.

She took another shot and managed to hit the minotaur on the upper arm. It stopped and roared again, but still bent its fury on Haret. Abisina grasped a branch and swung into a tree. From this vantage, she watched Haret face the monster, hatchet again in his grasp, and she readied another arrow. Haret dashed in and struck the beast's shin with his blade. The minotaur reared back in pain. Here was Abisina's chance! Her arrow lanced the minotaur's ear beneath its horn, and it spun around to find this new tormentor.

Abisina was ready. This arrow found a vulnerable spot— its left eye. The minotaur clamped a hand over its face, blood seeping between its fingers, as it staggered around the clearing. Haret closed in, hitting it in the thigh, on the knee, and in its belly. Abisina got off three more shots, two sinking deep in the minotaur's back and side.

The minotaur had had enough. One hand pressed to its face, the other to its stomach, the beast turned and lumbered away from the burial place. Haret and Abisina pursued until it reached the breach in the wall, stumbled through and slipped down the mountainside, leaving clots of blood on the sun-drenched stones.

Halfway down the slope, a slight figure with a staff met the minotaur and followed it out of sight.

Abisina sank down on the rubble of the ruined wall.

"How did you learn to shoot like that?" Haret choked out between labored breaths.

"Everyone in Vranille learned in case of a centaur attack," Abisina answered, panting.

"I thought he had me there, then your arrow ripped his ear in two!" Haret dropped next to her, his bloody axe still clutched in his hand. "Minotaurs!"

"This is what I sensed," Abisina said. "It is the beginning."

"What is?" Haret asked.

"It's what Vigar said when she told me to go to Watersmeet and warn my father. She said her ancient enemy had returned. Maybe this minotaur is part of that. It shouldn't have been here. Can't you feel how it's broken the peace of the garden?"

Haret nodded. "I'm not sure about this ghost of yours, but it sounds like the sooner we get to Watersmeet the better."

They stayed one more day in Vigar's garden at Abisina's insistence. It felt wrong to leave it torn apart. While Haret repaired the break in the wall, she cleaned the grave. She put the stones back in a circle, cleared the dirt away from the spring, and cut back the broken branches on the rowan. It didn't look perfect when she was through, but some of the peacefulness returned. Maybe the minotaur *wasn't* a harbinger of a larger evil, Abisina told herself. Haret waited for her by the archway until she had said her good-bye to Vigar's grave.

Their sacks bulged with fruit, and the water skins dripped. Abisina picked up her gear and put it on; despite the load, the sack hung comfortably at her side. Haret led her to the central room and then through a maze of passages and down a steep slope to a crack in the wall that looked out onto another world: the thin air and chill of the high mountains.

Abisina and Haret squeezed into the sunshine, slipping down the gravelly slope before they could get their footing. Behind them, a jumble of rocks with a few knobby points jutted into the sky, but when they glanced back they could find no trace of Vigar's garden—no wall, no archways, no hint of the sweet fruit on the wind. They couldn't even find the crack they had just come through.

They stared back for a moment longer before setting their gaze forward and making their way down the mountain.

PART III

CHAPTER XII

THEY HEADED NORTHWEST, AS VIGAR HAD INSTRUCTED. Without talking about it, they had taken to traveling by day, eager to see the features of this new land. On the second day, they came to the torrent of a large river cutting its way south through gorges and stony beds. Abisina had never seen a river this large, and she stood transfixed by it, absorbing its power, its roar, its call. "The River Deliverance," she said, sure that this was Vigar's river. As if in agreement, the necklace at her throat glowed warm against her skin.

"It has to be," Haret replied. "And it runs due north as your ghost said it would. Let's go."

But Abisina lingered by the river, head tilted toward the sky, eyes closed, ears filled with the water's thunder.

Then she felt a shadow pass over, and Haret was hissing at her to stay silent and pulling her urgently toward the trees twenty paces behind them. When they reached cover, Haret stopped and looked skyward, his face tight.

Abisina followed his eyes as she put an arrow to her bow.

An enormous creature—terrible and beautiful—flew away to the west, sunlight glinting off its shiny wings. Its great head was balanced by a long, tapering tail whipping through the air behind it. Even from this distance, they could hear the rush of wings pumping up and down and the wind whistling through the spikes that marched from its head to the tip of its tail.

Dragon. The word came to Abisina with no prompting from Haret, a creature Sina had brought to life in countless stories by the fire. "Did it see us?" she whispered.

"I don't know. Either it didn't—which would be very strange; they have sharp vision—or it's not hungry. Either way, we are very lucky."

Is it another sign? Abisina wondered. *Like the minotaur?*

"Are they—common?" she asked as she stared after the dragon, which had become indistinguishable against the rocky slopes.

Haret shrugged. "Not in the south. But I would have said the same about minotaurs, and now we've met four!"

"Will it come back?"

"We'd better stick to the trees for now."

The dragon did not return, but Abisina glanced skyward whenever the tangle of brush, trees, and vines drove them to the riverbank. And she kept an arrow nocked, though she knew it would do little against the hide of a dragon. Then Haret discovered some wolf tracks: "the strangest wolf tracks this dwarf has ever seen—no front feet and back feet bigger than a large man's. They shouldn't be out much in the day, but keep that arrow ready, human," he concluded, drawing his own axe.

Despite her fears, anticipation grew with each step. As they rounded bend after bend in the river, she expected to see Watersmeet before her. Neither of them knew what it would look like. Haret insisted that Watersmeet was underground, populated with survivors from the Obrun City. But Abisina disagreed.

"It's going to be beautiful," she insisted.

"The Obrun City was more beautiful than anything you've ever imagined!" Haret contended hotly.

"I know, I know. But Watersmeet will be—different, somehow." She frowned. What did she expect of Watersmeet— a city of stone? A tower? A fortress on a hill? None of these pictures was grand enough. "It will be beyond what we can imagine" was all she could offer.

Her father, too, was beyond her imagination. Sina had described him as having raven hair, dark eyes, copper skin like her own, and . . . beautiful. How could all this be true? She conjured up the vision she had always held of Vran—tall and broad, golden hair, piercing blue eyes, a look of judgment on his face. She tried to shade his features, darken his hair and eyes. Would her father have that look of judgment when this daughter from the south appeared before him?

It was almost evening on the third day since they left Vigar's garden. Abisina climbed among the boulders on the edge of the river, well behind Haret. Tall pines grew thickly there, leaving only a small margin of rock between the forest and the torrent. Her pace had slowed and she was lost in the wild rhythm of the water, half expecting Vigar's voice to speak through the roar.

Ahead, the river made a turn toward the west, and Haret stopped. *Maybe he's found a place to spend the night*, Abisina thought. But this seemed unlikely. The daylight of early summer lasted late in the evening, and Haret never stopped until the light was completely gone. *He's probably waiting to scold me for going slowly*, she decided. But Haret did not stare back at her with arms folded as he usually did. Abisina's curiosity peaked, and she scrambled on as fast as she could, ignoring the lingering ache in her right foot.

She caught up with Haret, who stood perfectly still, hands at his side, gaping at something.

"What is it?" she asked, breathing hard.

"What do you think *that* is?" Haret said, pointing.

Abisina followed his finger. Before them, roots spanning the width of the river, stood—what could she call it except a tree? But its girth and height made the pines around it look like saplings—pines that until that moment she would have judged to be taller than any tree in the forests near Vranille.

Twenty men couldn't hold hands in a ring around this tree, Abisina guessed. It was some kind of fir with a straight, tall trunk, branchless for a third of its height, then opening to a sudden skirt of limbs, which tapered to a point at the top. The light from the setting sun gilded the top of the tree like a jewel in a crown and turned the river to gold.

"Watersmeet," she murmured as Haret nodded. "Do we—do we just walk up to it then?" Now that they were here, she was terrified.

"I guess we should," Haret said without stirring from his spot.

"Well, then, let's go."

"Yes. Let's."

Neither of them moved.

"Maybe we should spend the night here?" Haret suggested.

"It might be better to arrive in the morning," Abisina said.

They both began taking off their sacks when she stopped herself. "Haret! What are we doing? We're almost there! We have to go on."

He sighed. "You're right. But what if—"

"I know. I'm scared, too."

They put their bags back over their shoulders and kept going, side by side.

The details of Watersmeet became clearer. That first tree was the beginning of a grove of giants that widened and stretched north, several rivers winding among the trunks.

Their great, gnarled roots arched across the current like bridges. The closer they came, the taller the trees seemed, until Abisina could see the tops only by leaning back so far that she almost toppled over.

In the last moments of twilight, they arrived at the spot where one of the roots spanning the river plunged into the opposite bank, creating a natural bridge leading right into the island of trees.

Haret bent down and studied the root. "The top is worn. This is where they cross."

"Do we go over?"

"Maybe I should scout around more first," he said doubtfully.

Abisina was studying the mass of dark trees when a spark of light flashed from between the trunks, glittering on the water, as if someone had lit a lantern.

"Look!" She pointed as another spark shone out over the water.

When a third spark appeared, Haret said, "Let's go then. But be careful."

Abisina stepped onto the bridge and walked steadily until they began to descend the bridge's arch. Then her steps slowed. Ahead more lights shone, and in the lights, something that stopped her heart: something—someone was down there. Many someones. One of them might be her father! All her dreams were about to be realized. She was about to arrive in Watersmeet. She froze.

Haret stopped when she did, focused on the scene before them. The light of torches circled a clearing among the roots. As Abisina and Haret watched, figure after figure stepped forward to light a torch from a central fire, and then carried this light deeper into the trees, where it blinked out as its bearer moved among the enormous trunks.

"It's Midsummer!" Haret exclaimed.

"What?"

"Of course! The bonfire—the lighting of the torches. It's the Midsummer ritual. Don't you celebrate it? The longest day of the year?"

"Vran's birthfest? We celebrate that on the longest day of the year."

"It has nothing to do with Vran! It's a celebration of light—the sun rises the earliest and sets the latest. I've seen the fauns observe the ritual. They light the fire and carry it around their dancing grounds. Some even jump through it, and they burn a bit of holly, too. And look—there's a faun!" They had crept down the bridge as Haret spoke, and the scene had become clearer. Haret pointed toward the bonfire where Abisina could make out a figure with horns on its head silhouetted against the flame.

"Fauns?" She hadn't expected fauns in Watersmeet.

"Let's go," Haret said, all the worry erased from his voice.

Abisina hung back, but when Haret walked confidently down the slope of the bridge, she followed. He didn't stop until he stood just outside the circle of light.

"And there are dwarves, too. And—and humans," he whispered. "Look, Abisina!"

But she had already seen the human figures and taken a step back up the bridge. Entering the circle of light would mean humans staring at her again. Would they see right away that she was an outcast?

"What is it?" Haret asked, but before Abisina could answer, they were spotted.

"Hail the Midsummer!" A voice called from the fire, a human coming toward them with a flaming torch. Abisina tugged at the cord tying her hair back and let it fall in front of her face.

"In the dark, friends? This is the night of light!" The human was a woman, her tone friendly, but Abisina wouldn't lift her eyes from the roots at her feet.

Light poured over Abisina's boots as the woman held the torch high. Abisina stiffened, but the woman's voice when she next spoke was curious, not cruel.

"Do I know you?"

"We're—we're not from around here," Haret stammered.

"Are you from the northern wards, then? I thought I would recognize most from up that way."

"That's right," Haret said hurriedly. "We're from the northern wards."

Abisina stole a glance at the woman.

Her skin was as white as bone, and her hair fell down her back in waves of ebony streaked with gray. *But the way she speaks, the way she holds herself—she's clearly not outcast!*

"I'm Frayda," the woman continued, and then, catching sight of their tattered leggings and stained tunics, she asked, "Have you been—"

"Hunting!" Haret jumped in, and Abisina touched her bow as if in agreement.

"Well, you're back just in time. We're ready to move on to the Gathering." Frayda went back to the fire, picked up two smoldering torches, and blew on them. Most of the others had already taken their fiery brands and were leaving the clearing to head deeper into the trees. Abisina looked around her. Brightly painted doors peeked out from between the gaps, caves, and nooks created by the roots, opening right into the tree trunks.

"Here." Frayda held out the now flaming torches. "You can have these." As Abisina reached for the torch, her hair slid back, and Frayda, catching Abisina's eye, smiled. With growing hope, Abisina followed Frayda into a maze of pathways paved with roots.

The trails wound in and around the huge trunks, smaller trails flowing into larger ones, and then into larger ones still, creating roads and boulevards that dipped and dived, arching over the rivers and their tributaries. Torchbearers traveled along the pathways, the light streaming like tails of fire off into the distance.

Abisina studied the human faces she passed, and each one filled her with more hope. One woman had loamy brown skin and hair only slightly lighter than Frayda's; a young boy's brown hair flopped over his Vranian blue eyes; a little girl had hair the color of sunset braided down her back. The dwarves and fauns traveling the trails were as varied as the humans.

But then Abisina stopped again. In front of her, four or five paces away, where their root trail joined a wider one, three centaurs waited.

A pair of dwarves had just stepped in front of the centaurs and though Abisina did not catch the words that passed between them, the lead centaur threw back his head, his laugh booming off the surrounding trunks.

Haret grabbed her around the waist before she fell, holding her tightly. "Steady, human!"

"Centaurs!" she gasped.

"I know. But human—they're welcome here. There are some more—" Haret pointed to his left, but Abisina refused to look.

Frayda slowed. "Is everything all right? Is she ill?"

"Weak with hunger," Haret said. "We were hunting pretty far out and had to push hard to get here by Midsummer. She's worn out."

A shadow of confusion crossed Frayda's face, but she moved to the side of the pathway. Haret lowered Abisina to the ground. "I'll step into this ward," Frayda said, indicating a clearing with ten or twelve doorways opening on to it, "and find something for her to eat."

"I'm sorry," Abisina whispered as Frayda left and Haret

raised his water skin to her lips. "I saw those centaurs, and I—" but Haret shushed her and made her drink.

By the time Frayda returned, Abisina had taken several sips of Vigar's water—still cold and invigorating, and bringing Abisina a little of the garden's peace.

"We're lucky," Frayda said as she handed over half a loaf of bread and a piece of cheese. "All the wards are emptying, everyone gone to the celebration, but I managed to find something for her."

Abisina took a bite of the bread, trying to look famished, but she could barely choke it down.

"Er—thank you," Haret began, "but don't let us make you late. You go on ahead—to the Gathering. We'll follow as soon as she's up to it."

Frayda looked at Abisina as if for confirmation.

Abisina took another big bite of bread and nodded.

When Frayda had gone, Abisina gave up the pretense of hunger. "Centaurs, Haret! Here!"

"It's not what we expected, but these centaurs—they're different than Icksyon's herd. They're part of things here. They look—I don't know—civil."

Abisina shook her head. "They're *centaurs.*"

The light of the torches faded around them as the last stragglers hurried along the root roads toward the meeting place. Abisina got to her feet. "We'd better go. Before there is no one left to follow."

They jogged the rest of the way, always choosing the

larger trail when they came to a junction. They crossed at least three bridges, one disconcertingly high, and ran into several fauns and a dwarf hurrying in the same direction. One young faun mumbled, "Fell asleep! Father will have my horns!" as he rushed by them. Thankfully, the only centaurs they saw were far ahead.

At last, they came to the top of the highest bridge they had crossed yet. At the end, bars of light from thousands of torches glowed between heavy trunks. "That must be it," Haret said. Abisina nodded, not trusting her voice.

The bridge brought them between two gigantic trees to the top of a great amphitheater. Fifteen trees stood in a perfect ring around the theater, and between each, root trails emptied the last of the assembling crowd. The sides of the theater sloped gently down from their feet. A whirlpool of roots created tier upon tier of steps filled with the folk of Watersmeet, each holding a burning torch. The light rose far up the trunks to the canopy of branches. The theater throbbed as humans, dwarves, fauns, and centaurs produced a note deep in their chests that rose with the light toward the sky.

Abisina and Haret joined two graying dwarves and a family of dark-skinned, brown-haired humans—a man with a baby, a woman, and two girls about Abisina's age. The closest centaur was many paces away along the edge of the theater.

The hum of the crowd filled Abisina, lifted, and held her. She stretched her torch arm as high as she could and added her voice to the swelling sound. And then, in response to some cue that she didn't see, the humming rose and fell, rose and fell, rose and fell until it was gone, leaving the theater silent but for the hiss of torches. All eyes focused on a point somewhere below and she stood on tiptoe, trying to see what held the crowd's attention.

"Watersmeet!" came a strong, female voice, traveling around the sides of the theater.

"Hi-yah!" the crowd answered as one.

"Watersmeet!" the voice came again.

"Hi-yah!" said the crowd.

And again: "Watersmeet!"

"Hi-yah!"

"As is our custom, we gather together to welcome Midsummer," the voice went on. "We've carried the light through our homes and through all of Watersmeet, driving out any darkness, chill, or illness left from winter. Tonight, we revel!"

Joyous shouts swelled as the folk shook their torches aloft. Two young dwarves a step below Abisina linked arms and spun around and around until one of the gray-haired dwarves to her left bent over and spoke to them. They stopped spinning and grinned sheepishly at their elders; Abisina couldn't help but smile.

"But first!" the high voice rang out. "We have news!"

A murmur swept the crowd. The dwarf next to Abisina said to her companion, "Can he be back so soon?" and one of the younger dwarves turned to add, "That's what I heard, but your ears were like rock when *I* spoke, Mama!"

"Folk of Watersmeet!" The crowd quieted, expectation thick in the air. "I give you the Keeper of Watersmeet, Rueshlan!"

For the second time, Abisina's knees gave way. She reached out to Haret, but before she caught hold of his shoulder, the crowd around her shuffled to clear a space at the lip of the amphitheater.

"Step back," the human father with the baby reminded his daughters. Haret, his hand suddenly on Abisina's arm, pulled her a few steps along the rim of the theater.

A figure stood in the shadows on the bridge behind them. As an aisle formed, the figure stepped into the light.

Abisina heard a cry and realized it had come from her.

The tallest man she had ever seen was walking past her. He stood a full head taller than Misalan, the biggest man in Vranille. His skin was burnished copper, and his hair, raven-colored, fell beyond his knees. As he stepped past, he paused, and Abisina saw his profile—a strong, straight nose, full lips—and caught the glint of torchlight on his black eyes.

She knew immediately who he was.

Abisina wanted to leap forward and slink away at the same time. She was sure he would hear the pounding of her heart or feel her hungry stare—and what would she do then? But after a pause, he descended the tiers of roots, flanked by a centaur on either side.

"That's him," she breathed to Haret. "That's my father."

A few tiers from the top, a faun greeted Rueshlan in an embrace. Then the two centaurs at his side stepped behind him and blocked Abisina's view.

A hush settled over the theater. "Watersmeet!" a new voice called in rich tones that made Abisina shiver.

My father's voice.

"Hi-yah, Rueshlan!" the crowd responded, and the greeting was repeated twice more.

"Hail the Midsummer!" he called, and cheers echoed around the bowl. "I will not hold you long from your feasts and dancing and merrymaking!" Another cheer swelled from the crowd. "I am so glad to be back among you in time for our most joyous celebration." Abisina could hear the smile in his voice. "And I come with good news from the fairies' Motherland!" Rueshlan continued as the shouts subsided. "We have long hoped to bring the fairies to our Midsummer revels as recognition of the ancient friendship between Watersmeet and the Motherland."

Excitement buzzed around the amphitheater. The dwarfmother near Abisina said, "It can't be!" while her child said, "I told you that, too, Mother!"

"This year"—Rueshlan spoke over the hum—"we will indeed welcome the fairies. At our final Midsummer Gathering in three days' time, Lohring, Daughter of the Fairy Mother, and her attendants will lead our celebration!" The crowd's response was jubilant. The light intensified as torches were raised again.

"Look around you, Watersmeet!" Rueshlan could hardly be heard above the cheers. "Look at the light you bring! Hail the Midsummer!" And the shouts redoubled.

Before the roar faded, the crowd was on the move, streaming up from the bottom of the amphitheater toward the bridges. The folk on the bottom tiers left first, working their way through hastily cleared aisles, calling greetings, clasping hands, embracing. Each tier followed in succession. Abisina was in the tier that would leave last, and if Rueshlan followed the same path out, he would again walk within feet of her.

Haret must have had the same thought. As the merry fauns, dwarves, humans, and centaurs paraded by them, he whispered, "You have to speak to him!"

Abisina's stomach clenched. "I can't!"

"It's why you're here, human! We can't keep pretending we're folk from the 'northern wards' just returned from a hunting party. It's time to let yourself be known."

Abisina cringed as a centaur passed close to her, her nostrils filling with the smell of grass and horse sweat.

"Come on, human. He'll be passing by any moment. Get ahold of yourself!"

"But Haret—he's a leader here! He's too busy right now. He doesn't even know I exist! And what if he hates me?" Was she ready to face the father of her dreams?

"He's coming!" Haret cried, but Abisina stared at the ground. She could hear the cries of "Rueshlan!" as he approached, and she thought that she could discern a low, rumbling laugh. The tip of his boot stepped into her field of vision, but she didn't move.

Haret took matters into his own hands. He stepped around Abisina and stood in Rueshlan's path, calling out, "Rueshlan! I bring you Abisina of Vranille!"

The boot stopped. "What did you say?" The deep voice rumbled over her head. Every pore of her skin tingled.

"Abisina of Vranille!" Haret said, louder this time, and the crowd around them quieted.

"Sina? Did you say Sina of Vranille?"

"I—I bring you her daughter!" Haret said, shaking slightly. "I am Haret, son of Harland and Marrah from the southern side of the Obruns."

The crowd stirred at these words, and Abisina strained to hear the rumble of Rueshlan's voice.

"Where—where is she?" he asked.

"Here." Haret took Abisina by the hand and pulled her from the crowd so that she stood facing the boot tips. Slowly, as if moving through a thick liquid, she raised her head, hair tumbling back from her face until at last she stared into his searching gaze.

"Who are you?" he whispered.

"Abisina." Her voice cracked. "Sina was my mother."

"*Was?*"

Abisina nodded, unable to turn away.

"Look," she said. "This was hers." She fumbled at her neck. She could see the metal's glow reflected in Rueshlan's eyes.

"Vigar's necklace!" His face drained of color.

Abisina had to gather every shred of courage to utter her next words: "She—she told me it belonged to my father."

CHAPTER XIII

ABISINA SAT NEAR THE HEARTH IN A LARGE ROOM BUZZING with activity. Rueshlan had brought her to this dwelling in one of the enormous trees to escape the crowds leaving the amphitheater. But many of the folk of Watersmeet had followed them. A steady stream now came to take her hand and welcome her, some wiping their eyes and touching their hearts. She was thankful that no centaurs were there. But all this activity was a backdrop to the only thing that felt real: her father, sitting next to her, clasping her shaking hand in his own strong one. Abisina hardly heard the greetings and welcomes around her or noticed one dwarf leave and another faun arrive.

Abisina pulled her attention away from Rueshlan as he spoke with a dark, heavyset man with white hair. She wanted to find Haret. It was hard to see him in the crush of bodies, but she spotted him deep in conversation with two dwarves, one a redhead, the other bent double with age, his white beard sweeping the floor. Both had the same dark skin as Haret and the other dwarves she'd seen. She couldn't hear Haret, but his hands flew around in agitation as he spoke. The redheaded dwarf was shaking his head, looking serious.

Abisina wanted Haret to share this moment with her, the joy that lifted her beyond the top of Watersmeet's highest tree. She was trying to catch his eye when Frayda, the woman who had first greeted them, approached. "Kyron is waiting for you outside, Rueshlan. He longs to meet your daughter." She smiled warmly at Abisina.

"I wondered where he had gone." Rueshlan turned to Abisina. "You must meet Kyron and the centaurs. They—"

"No!" Abisina leapt to her feet. "No centaurs!"

Conversations stopped across the room.

She lowered her voice. "Please. No centaurs."

"But—why?" Rueshlan said, concern—and something else—on his face.

Abisina didn't want to speak here, in front of everyone. She knew she had insulted them, but she didn't back off—she *couldn't*.

"Sir, if I may." Haret jostled through the crowd. "The human—er, Abisina"—he reached Rueshlan's side and motioned for him to lean closer—"she's had a terrible run-in with centaurs. Her people have been at war with them for generations. And then Icksyon—do you know him?" At the shake of Rueshlan's head, Haret continued quietly, "Icksyon terrorizes parts of the south, and Abisina was captured by his followers and taken to him. He—he bit off her toe before she managed to escape—"

"Bit off—?" Rueshlan choked.

"The littlest one. It's healed well. . . ."

Rueshlan's eyes flashed. "Thank you, Haret. I didn't understand." He took Abisina's hand again.

Now they know, she thought.

But she felt betrayed somehow. On hearing Haret's explanation, her father seemed angry, but also surprised, disbelieving. And what had she seen on his face when she insisted that she meet no centaurs? Disappointment? She braced herself for questions about Icksyon. She didn't want to go through it all again, not here.

But Rueshlan didn't ask her any questions. Instead, he said to Frayda, "Please, tell Kyron that I will"—his glance flitted to his daughter—"that I will find him as soon as I'm able."

Frayda opened her mouth to say something, thought better of it, and headed toward the door.

As Rueshlan was turning back to Abisina, a cry came from the doorway: "Hail the Midsummer! The feast is here!"

A copper-skinned man carrying a heaping tray on his shoulder worked his way into the room; behind him came two dwarves carrying a large table, five fauns with more trays, and two men rolling in a cask of beer. The crowd pressed tighter to let them pass. The red-haired dwarf, who had been talking to Haret, cried out, "At last, some food!" and a wave of laughter broke over the room. The food had not even been set on the table before the crowd descended. Someone placed a wooden plate in Abisina's hand piled with thick slabs of brown bread, the light meat of fowl, a creamy lump of cheese, and a disk of golden dough covered with nuts and dripping honey. It had been hours since her few bites of bread from Frayda, and she was famished.

As she took her first bite, Rueshlan introduced her to the two dwarves who had been talking to Haret.

"Abisina, you must meet Gilden, one of the oldest in Watersmeet. And this is his great great-grandson, Alden. It's Alden's house we've taken over." She now noticed that Rueshlan, though seated, had to duck to keep from hitting the ceiling. The chair he sat in was twice the size of any other in the room. Of course, this was a dwarf's house!

"Thank you," Abisina said to Alden around her bite of bread as Gilden wrung her hand with surprising strength.

"At your service, Rueshlan's daughter!" Alden said. "And you missed a 'great.'" He winked at Rueshlan. Then, turning soberly to Abisina, he added, "Don't you worry about Haret. We'll do all that we can for him."

"Haret?" she asked in surprise, but before he could answer, a female faun stepped forward, arms open wide.

"And this is Glynholly." Rueshlan chuckled as the faun gathered Abisina into an embrace.

"Rueshlan's daughter!" Glynholly cried as she held her at

arms' length, her light eyes dancing. "It's such an honor!" She pulled Abisina into another crushing embrace.

"Glynholly is another of my advisors and a dear friend. She spoke at the Gathering tonight," Rueshlan explained as Frayda rejoined the group. She gave Rueshlan a short nod before offering her hand to Abisina.

"Welcome to Watersmeet—again—Abisina."

"I—I'm sorry we didn't tell you who we were," Abisina said awkwardly, still recovering from Glynholly's hugs. "We were afraid we might not be welcome—"

"Unwelcome in Watersmeet?" Rueshlan broke in. "This is your home, Abisina!"

Abisina looked at him, and the crowd around them seemed to disappear. "My home?"

"Of course! But you'll want to think about it, I'm sure," he added hastily. "You've only just gotten here."

"No," Abisina blurted out. "I don't need to think about it at all!" Her wide smile perfectly matched her father's.

She was still smiling when Haret approached her late that night. A welcome breeze blew in from the open door as the crowd thinned out. Rueshlan had gone to talk to Kyron and the centaurs, but even this dimmed her happiness only for an instant. Haret sat down in Rueshlan's vacated seat, legs dangling. His eyes darted around the room, and his hands wandered from his beard to the dagger at his waist, back to his beard.

"Haret, can you believe we're here?" Abisina said. "I've found my father—and you've found the dwarves of Watersmeet!"

His fingers drummed the arms of the chair. "They're from the Obrun City, as my parents and grandfather and great-grandmother believed. All those years. . . ."

Abisina sighed and leaned back in her chair. "Can you imagine how happy Hoysta will be? We've both found our families, Haret. We've found just what we were hoping for."

"Have you told him?" Haret asked abruptly. "About Vigar's warning? The minotaurs?"

"Not yet," Abisina said. After meeting her father, the minotaurs seemed like a small concern. "I'll tell him tomorrow—"

But Haret wasn't listening anymore. His fingers continued to drum on the chair; his gaze roved the room. Abisina was glad to avoid his question. She didn't want the threat of Charach ruining her first night with her father. But Haret's agitation worried her. He seemed so anxious to get back to the dwarves—as if he sat with her only as a courtesy. Was the companionship they found on the trail over?

Abisina leapt out of bed the next morning ready to see her father. Her clothes lay rumpled on the floor, where she'd flung them after Alden led her to this bedroom just before dawn. She threw on her tunic with fumbling fingers and rushed out to find Rueshlan waiting for her in the adjoining sitting room.

"There you are!" He took her hands in his. "When I woke this morning, I thought you might have been a dream! Midsummer madness!"

Abisina basked in the pleasure on his face.

They ate breakfast together in the same room as before, though this time they sat at a small table by a window looking out on the clearing—or ward, as they called it here—with the dappled light of the sun filtering through the enormous pines. Folk with baskets over their arms passed in front of them, calling out Midsummer greetings. The ashes from last night's bonfire still smoldered, and two fauns were already stacking wood near the stone slab for the next celebration.

The holiday mood matched Abisina's. "Those trees!" she exclaimed, leaving her bread and honey to peer toward the canopy of branches far above.

"The Sylvyads. I sometimes forget how remarkable they are." Rueshlan looked toward the distant branches, too. "They're thousands of years old. They grow where the three rivers meet to form the River Deliverance. Their thirst is deep, and only the rivers together can quench it."

"Have people lived here all those years?" Abisina still stared upward.

"For generations, since Vigar came from the mountains and settled her people."

"Vigar," Abisina repeated, her hand on the necklace. "I— I met her," she began tentatively. "Well, not the real Vigar," she continued quickly. "But Haret and I, we found her orchard in the mountains. And she spoke to me. . . . She was there."

Rueshlan leaned forward. "What did she say?"

"That she had led me there. With this." She pulled the necklace out of her tunic, and the light from the window caught the metal, reflecting on the walls.

Rueshlan watched the light for a moment before saying, "It's a symbol of many rivers coming together." He pointed to the ribbons of metal twisting into a single strand.

"Vigar told me about you, told me your name. She said that you were all with me—all the wearers of the necklace."

Rueshlan continued to look at the pendant. "They say that her spirit still protects Watersmeet."

Abisina knew that she should warn him now—tell him about her mother and Charach. But something inside her rebelled. *No! I've left that behind!* The light streamed in; cheerful voices called to one another in the ward. It felt wrong to bring *his* name into all this beauty. She could wait. Just a few days.

"She was also Watersmeet's greatest teacher. The Sylvyads provided shelter for her small band of humans and for the others who soon joined them—dwarves and fauns and centaurs." If Rueshlan noticed Abisina flinch at the last mention, he did not let on.

"Why—how did they all come to live together?"

"It was Vigar's idea. The forests and glens around Watersmeet were dangerous then. In the Sylvyads, she welcomed anyone who needed protection. And it has remained our home. Would you like me to show you Watersmeet?"

Rueshlan stood and offered Abisina his arm. She took it, struck by the sight of her copper skin against his. *This is my father*, she said to herself, flooded again with happiness.

They had stepped out into the ward, Rueshlan finally able to stand to his full height, when Abisina stopped. "Haret!" How could she have forgotten him?

"I'm sure he and Alden stayed up past dawn, so Haret could meet all of his cousins," Rueshlan said.

"Ah, he's where he wants to be, then. As he told me countless times, he's had more than enough of humans on our journey."

But something bothered her as they left Alden's ward. Haret had not been himself last night—drumming fingers, agitated surveying of the room. "Will we see him tonight?" she asked, her worry showing in her voice.

"All of Alden's family have been invited to my ward. They'll bring him with them," Rueshlan assured her.

Abisina could hardly take in all the sights, or make sense of her feelings, in the next few hours. Wandering on root trails among the Sylvyads, she stared at the shifting sea of green as distant as the sky, turning in tides of wind she couldn't feel from the sheltered ground. And standing next to a trunk was like standing next to a wall, the trunk's curve almost indiscernible in the tree's massive girth. Their steps were cushioned by fallen needles three times longer than the pine needles in Vranille's woods. Like fir needles, these were flat, but as wide as her little finger. She could almost call them leaves, but they had the waxiness of evergreens.

She was in for another surprise when she laid her hand on one of the trunks. The reddish bark was rough with coarse hairs, and through the wood came a sensation Abisina could only describe as *aliveness*. She looked up at Rueshlan. "They're—breathing!"

"You feel it?" He sounded pleased. "Not everyone can. They're most alive for the fauns, but some others, too, sense them as you do."

"Can you?"

"Yes." He smiled. "There's nothing like them."

As they strolled on, they crossed countless root bridges that spanned the churning water of the rivers, sometimes at dizzying heights. She loved the song of the water that followed them wherever they went. She felt in her veins the current of the rivers mingling under Watersmeet.

With particular pride, Rueshlan showed Abisina the three wards that comprised Watersmeet's library—neat rows of white doors marked with black letters. "The letters indicate which texts are in the ward," Rueshlan pointed out. "From the beginning, Vigar trained scribes to collect the stories, songs, and legends that the folk brought with them: the fauns' classification of trees, the dwarves' odes to the Earth, the centaurs' hero legends. We even have some of the stories the fairies collected from birds. No song is too trivial, no legend too obscure."

"You mean you have stories here, written down? The folk of Watersmeet can read, too?"

"Of course, Abisina!" Rueshlan laughed, but then his eyes clouded. "The Vranians. I'm sorry, Abisina. I'd forgotten about their rules. . . ."

"I can read," Abisina said. Then, softly: "My mother taught me." Abisina knew her father wanted her to continue, to tell him what happened, but she couldn't bring herself to speak.

The silence was broken when a woman laden with large tomes emerged from one of the white doors. "Rueshlan!" she said in surprise.

With a last look at Abisina, Rueshlan greeted the woman. "Hail the Midsummer, Agna. I want you to meet my daughter, Abisina. Abisina, Agna cares for the library—but today she should be celebrating. It's Midsummer!"

"The bards are checking one of the odes they will recite tomorrow," Agna replied. "I won't be long!" She opened a door, and Abisina heard a deep bass voice ringing out until the door closed behind the woman and her books.

"Can you show me more?" Abisina asked her father. There would be time later to talk about Sina.

Throughout Watersmeet, folk were bustling from ward to ward. Rueshlan explained to Abisina that the first day of Midsummer was Visiting Day; all the inhabitants brought food, flowers, and small gifts to friends and family. And they all knew who Abisina was: word of her arrival had been carried throughout the community. Fauns with chains of vines in their hair cried, "Hail, Rueshlan, on your return! And happy news of your daughter!" Dwarves of all ages—from toddling children following their mothers to ancient grandmothers like Hoysta, stumping along with canes—stopped to wave or smile or wring her hand. Abisina saw only two centaurs the whole morning and they hastened away at her approach—as if they'd received a message as well.

Most fascinating to her were the humans: every man, woman, and child was a new mix of hair, skin, and eye color. Of the hundreds of humans who greeted her and Rueshlan, only one—a girl four or five winters younger than Abisina—would have been accepted in Vranille. This girl and her older brother stopped to talk to Rueshlan, and Abisina fought the instinct to retreat behind her hair.

"Findlay! Meelah! I've got someone I want you to meet!" Rueshlan put his hand on her tense shoulder. "This is my daughter, Abisina, just arrived from beyond the mountains."

Meelah grabbed Abisina's hand in both of hers and squeezed. "Welcome to Watersmeet! It's so wonderful that you've come!"

Though she had begun to get used to folks taking her hand or even hugging her, Abisina blanched at the girl's touch—she looked so Vranian! So like her tormentor Lilas!

Seeing Abisina's discomfort, the boy reproached his sister:

"Meelah! Give her some time to get used to us." He offered Abisina an apologetic smile. "My sister can be very bold." Findlay shared his sister's fair skin and blond hair, but his eyes were a comforting brown. Holding out his hand to Abisina, Findlay had the self-assurance of a boy on the brink of manhood, as well as some of the awkwardness.

Abisina shook Findlay's hand, and his touch stayed with her even after they let go.

"I'm sorry for being *bold*," Meelah added, dimples showing. "But it *is* wonderful that you're here."

"You must come to our ward tonight," Rueshlan urged them. "Abisina's arrival will make our celebration even greater!"

"Thank you, Rueshlan. It would be an honor to join you," Findlay said, the respect in his voice reminding Abisina that her father had an important position here.

As they moved off down the trail, Meelah called, "Goodbye, Abisina!" and Abisina lifted a tentative hand in response.

They continued to stroll through Watersmeet, and Abisina told Rueshlan a little about her journey there. Rueshlan never pushed her to talk, and she said nothing of her life in Vranille. Abisina spoke freely about Hoysta and Haret, but when she got to the escape from Icksyon, she gave no details and Rueshlan didn't ask. It felt better to tell him about the necklace leading them up the cliff, emphasizing perhaps more than necessary her bravery and Haret's fear.

"That necklace will always lead you here," Rueshlan said.

"Your mother was wise to give it to you." She did not correct his error. Instead, she asked a question that had been on her mind since meeting Meelah and Findlay. "You're called the Keeper of Watersmeet—what does that mean?"

Without answering, Rueshlan pointed to a loop of root in the trail that jutted out over a small tributary of one of the rivers, creating a natural lookout. "Hungry?" he asked. "We can sit here." So she sat in a crook of roots, while he sat on the ground—and still towered over her. He brought out cheese, nuts, and apples from the leather bag across his shoulder.

They had started eating, the gurgle of the river in the background, when Rueshlan answered Abisina's question: "As Keeper of Watersmeet, I am charged with preserving Vigar's vision for this community. Vigar wanted us to remember that all are welcome here, that we are stronger together than divided. She gave me the necklace to symbolize that."

"*She* gave you the necklace? But you said she lived generations ago."

Rueshlan was watching her closely. "Yes, Abisina. I am very old."

"But—" She stopped, not sure what to say next. She didn't want to press him when there were so many things *she* didn't want to talk about. Her father looked younger than Sina with his dark hair and firm cheeks. Only his eyes, now that she looked carefully, showed any sign of age. And it wasn't laugh lines or wrinkles—it was the depth of wisdom.

"I—I'm not sure I understand," she said.

"There is going to be a lot to get used to here, Abisina," Rueshlan responded gently.

"This necklace!" she said, shifting their focus. "If this necklace belongs to the Keeper of Watersmeet, you should have it back." She lifted it off, trying to appear happy to return it.

"No, no, Abisina! I don't need it anymore. I want you to keep it."

Abisina gratefully put the chain back around her neck.

To her relief, Rueshlan turned the conversation to the folk they'd met, the feasting and dancing they would enjoy that night, and the Gathering for stories, poems, ballads, and songs the following day. "I don't think you celebrate Midsummer in Vranille," he said. "We owe everything to our Sylvyads, so we celebrate the height of the growing time with abandon. On the final evening, the fauns will dance through each ward with torches to bring the light—now that is something to see! And this year the fairies will be here, too. It's as if they knew you were coming and wanted to help us celebrate!"

Abisina finished her apple and looked out over the water. "I can't believe I'm here, that I can call this home."

"Speaking of home—" Rueshlan stood up. "It's high time you saw yours." He held a hand out to Abisina. "Come on, Rueshlan's daughter, let's go home!"

CHAPTER XIV

RUESHLAN AND ABISINA ARRIVED AT HIS WARD IN THE coolness of late afternoon. Rueshlan's house was on the east side, where the wide and slow-moving River Fennish ran below the island of Sylvyad roots. There were several other doorways on the ward, much wider and taller than those in Alden's, and as they stood there, one of them opened. A huge, roan centaur stepped out and stopped when he caught sight of them.

"There's nothing to worry about, Abisina," Rueshlan said, as she stepped behind him, her face pale.

But Abisina cried, "Please tell him to leave!"

"It's all right," Rueshlan soothed. He faced the centaur and said in an apologetic tone, "Kyron, could you—leave us?"

"You're not helping her, Rueshlan," the roan rumbled. Though he was as big as the centaurs of Giant's Cairn, the roan had to look up to meet Rueshlan's eyes.

"Please understand," Rueshlan said. "She needs more time."

From behind her father, Abisina watched the door close on the retreating centaur, the click of hooves fading away.

Rueshlan knelt next to her. "Please believe me, Abisina. He would never hurt you. None of them would!"

She stared at the closed door. "*He* lives there?"

"Yes. That is *Kyron*. I told you about him. He's the leader of the centaurs here." She knew he meant to be comforting, but all she could think of was Icksyon. She felt a twinge where her little toe should have been.

Abisina looked from doorway to doorway around the ward—all were large. "Do centaurs live in more of these houses, then?"

"Yes, there are more. I've asked them to stay away for now. I know they make you uncomfortable."

"Why do you live with them?" she asked.

He looked sad, even pained. "I know it's hard for you to believe, but most centaurs are nothing like those you met in the south, nothing like Icksyon. But like any race, there are some who destroy the good in themselves."

"I'm sorry," she said quietly. "I—I just don't believe that."

"Abisina, promise me this: keep your heart open to them. Please."

Reluctantly, she nodded, though she couldn't imagine doing what he asked.

They entered Rueshlan's house, and Abisina tried to ignore the clues that centaurs visited him here. Like Alden's house, Rueshlan's opened onto a large room with a fireplace built into the curving outside wall, but the scale here was much greater: higher ceilings, larger doorways. *He's Keeper*, she tried to reassure herself. *He needs to welcome everyone.*

"Our houses are quite different from what you're used to. We live in the outer layers of the Sylvyads, one room leading to the next like links in a chain. If you need to rest, your room is four down in that direction." He pointed to the left. "You should have everything you need."

Abisina wanted to slip away to her room, to be alone with her thoughts, but the pain in her father's face persisted. "I think I'll stay here with you for a while," she said.

His jaw relaxed. "I was hoping you'd say that."

As twilight began to fall on Watersmeet, a host of visitors with enough food to feed twice as many arrived in Rueshlan's ward. Some faces were familiar: Alden and Glynholly, Meelah and Findlay, and Frayda, who was asked countless times to tell of first meeting Haret and Abisina. "I knew they were not from Watersmeet—deerskin boots!"

Abisina remembered Haret saying that centaurs could talk to deer, that it was barbaric to slay animals you could communicate with. She also realized that the new clothes she found in her room were made entirely of woven cloth, the boots made of small animal pelts.

"I welcomed them," Frayda went on, "as anyone would. Of course, I never dreamed who I was talking to!"

The one face missing was Haret's. Abisina looked for him every time the door opened, until Rueshlan, sensing her growing worry, brought Alden to her.

"Rueshlan's daughter," Alden said, bowing low. "You are wondering what has become of your companion."

"I was sure Haret would be here tonight," Abisina said. "Ruesh—my father said he was with you."

"He was." Alden nodded. "And he struggled mightily. . . . In the end, there was nothing left to do but take him to the Mines."

"I don't understand—the Mines?" At Alden's continued nodding, Abisina cried, "But they're days away! Why would he go now, during Midsummer?" She *knew* there had been something wrong!

Rueshlan and Alden exchanged glances.

Abisina tried to take the edge out of her voice. They were holding something back, afraid she would be too upset. "I need to know," she said, "I wouldn't have made it here without Haret."

After a look from Rueshlan, Alden said, "It's the Obrium-lust. He needed to see for himself. The Mines are closed off from us, the same as on the southern side, but he wouldn't believe it." Alden rubbed his forehead as if it hurt. "All dwarves feel the Obriumlust, but some worse than others. Last night Haret demanded again and again to see my collection of Obrium trinkets. We had some hope that he would withstand it. At times he was quite lucid, even checking on you. But as the night wore on, it took firmer hold. He accused us of hiding the precious metal from him, hoarding it for ourselves."

"But he fought it," she protested. "He gave this back to me." She clutched the necklace. "It was hard, but he knew I needed this."

"It can seize at any time, I'm afraid. It must have come from seeing so much Obrium at once—items our ancestors wore when they fled. Many of us have some bit of the metal. I wear this," Alden added, showing Abisina a plain Obrium band on his finger, "and my brother, Waite, has a kilt clasp. Haret noticed these immediately, and that's when I saw it growing on him—he was ready to go off and search right then. We tried to talk him out of it. Thought we had, but then it came back stronger than ever. That's when a few of my cousins agreed to go with him. Two centaurs offered to take them. They left before dawn."

"Centaurs?" Abisina stepped back. "You let centaurs take him? They'll kill him!"

"They're helping him, Abisina," Rueshlan tried to explain, but she would not listen.

"You cannot trust them!" she cried.

"Not trust them?" Alden said. "Why, Rueshlan—"

"—would never have sent Haret and his cousins with them if I wasn't absolutely convinced that he would be safe," Rueshlan finished.

He led Abisina to a chair in the next sitting room, out of the crowd. "But why did you let him go?" she asked.

"It's the only way, child," Rueshlan said sadly. "If they hadn't taken him, he would have snuck away on his own. They always do. This way, the dwarves will be with him in the Mines. He may respond to his kin. As you said, he's fought it off before. There's reason to hope."

Haret did not return the next day. As Abisina attended the Midsummer celebrations and thrilled at her father's every word, her happiness was chilled by thoughts of Haret riding with centaurs, or perhaps by now, digging his own grave.

That afternoon, hundreds of punts put forth from the bank of the River Deliverance to watch an archery contest. Abisina sat in the front of one with Meelah and Findlay. Rueshlan stood at the back, propelling the punt with a long pole, while Frayda sat near him, conversing in low tones. Here below the Sylvyads, the river ran gently, the torrents higher up smoothed out by the thirst of the trees. On the western bank, the archers prepared their bowstrings, tested the wind, and calculated the angle between them and the target—a series of rings hung from branches on the far bank.

Abisina had never been in a boat before. She loved the sensation of floating and the sound of moving water. She was less comfortable sitting so close to Meelah, who chatted about those in the boats around them and that evening's bard performance. Abisina had to fight her instinct to speak in monosyllables, to hide in the face of Meelah's Vranian beauty. Despite his brown eyes, Findlay flustered her, too. Abisina was acutely aware of his presence and blushed if he happened to brush against her.

It was a relief when the archery contest started. Abisina was riveted, evaluating the archers' form and predicting the accuracy of each shot based on angle, wind speed and direction, and the draw of the bow.

"Too sharp an angle with the wind northwest," Abisina murmured under her breath as she watched one of Alden's arrows fly wide of the last ring.

"I think I'll have to see you shoot sometime." Findlay laughed next to her. "That's the third archer whose shortcomings you've diagnosed correctly before the arrow came near the target!"

"I—I love to shoot," Abisina admitted, embarrassed that Findlay had heard her.

"Watch Glynholly." Findlay pointed to the faun who was about to take her turn. "It's the only time you'll see her so serious."

"Glynholly has won the last two years," Rueshlan called from the back. "At this rate, they'll make her retire like Frayda!"

Abisina glanced toward her father. The pride on his face

as he looked at Frayda unsettled her. And Frayda's shining eyes disturbed her even more. Was it the glow of a compliment from Watersmeet's leader, or was it—something more?

"Frayda has never been beaten." Findlay leaned toward Abisina and spoke confidentially. Abisina's pulse surged, though she didn't know if it was the look that passed between her father and Frayda or Findlay's closeness that made her so jittery.

"No one would challenge her anymore," Meelah added. "She still runs all the drills, though. Our mama's one of her drill captains."

"Drills?" Abisina asked.

"All of Watersmeet drills on one team or another," Findlay explained. "Alden handles the axe-play, Frayda the archery, and a man named Neiall, the fencing."

Cheers erupted across the water as Glynholly's arrow passed through the final ring without moving it a hair's breadth. Abisina cheered, too.

"Look at Alden," Findlay said, touching Abisina's hand lightly—and taking her breath away—as he pointed out the dwarf. "There is quite a rivalry between those two. Alden looks ready to explode!"

Abisina followed Findlay's finger, but before she could pick out the dwarf among the archers, there was an alarmed shout from farther down the bank. A palomino centaur broke from the trees followed by two others, all galloping hard.

"Überwolves!" The cry rang across the water. "Half a league from here!"

The boat lurched beneath her as Rueshlan sent it hurtling toward the shore. All along the bank, the archers of Watersmeet put arrows to strings, while those who had other weapons drew them and gathered around the centaurs.

The punt struck the shore with a jarring thud and Rueshlan leapt out, followed by Frayda, who was handed a bow and quiver before she had even climbed the bank. Findlay was on his feet, too, Abisina close behind him. But Rueshlan called out, "Stay in the boat, Meelah! And you, too, Abisina! Findlay, stay with them!"

Abisina was about to argue when an eerie howl filled the air.

"Over there!" someone cried as two hulking figures came through the trees. They stood a least a head taller than the centaurs who reeled to meet them. Their yellow eyes gleamed, their black lips drawn back to reveal long fangs. Like their wolf brethren, silver fur covered their bodies, but they stood on hind legs and carried crude spears in their clawed forefeet. The hair around their necks and down their backs stood on end, and Abisina could smell a wild, musky odor. She remembered the strange wolf tracks Haret had seen as they neared Watersmeet.

Arrows rained down on the überwolves the moment they left the cover of the trees, but none penetrated their thick coats. It was the palomino centaur who got off the best shot, close as she was, sinking an arrow deep into the belly of the first überwolf.

Frayda leapt onto a boulder, took aim, and shot in one liquid motion. The second überwolf fell dead, and the palomino got another shot off to finish the first.

Thinking the danger over, Abisina was surprised to see the three centaurs dive back into the trees in pursuit of something beyond her sight. Kyron and a group of others ran farther down the riverbank before plunging into the woods.

"Where are they going?" Abisina asked.

"There must be more!" Findlay said.

Meelah had scrambled out of the punt. "I want to see them!" she cried and set off running.

"Meelah!" Findlay yelled, but the little girl didn't stop.

Findlay and Abisina raced after her.

When Abisina reached the edge of the trees, she found Rueshlan standing over the bodies of the fallen überwolves, directing the pursuit. "Alden, take your group north along the river. Glynholly, you head south. We'll follow Torden." He pointed where the palomino centaur and her partners had disappeared into the forest. Then he caught sight of Abisina, Findlay, and Meelah. "Abisina! You and Findlay must take Meelah back to Watersmeet."

"But, Father—"

"No, Abisina." His tone brooked no argument. "I want all of you safe. Wait for me at home."

They could only watch as Glynholly, Alden, and Rueshlan led their teams away, leaving behind the unarmed folk who had scrambled ashore when Torden sounded the alarm.

Several agonizing hours passed as they waited in tense silence. Once Meelah clasped her hands together and cried out, "Oh, Vigar, protect them!"—and then she was quiet again while Abisina and Findlay took turns pacing before Rueshlan's hearth. Twice Abisina stood up and announced, "I'm going."

"We train for this," Findlay argued. "Überwolves are the most common threat, but sometimes it's minotaurs—"

"Minotaurs?"

"Vigar got rid of most of them long ago, but now and then they threaten us. There's even a dragon that flies over occasionally. They're looking for folk straying from the protection of the Sylvyads. It's been a long time since someone's been taken. Our training takes care of that."

The minotaurs and the dragon aren't signs of an advancing evil, Abisina thought with some relief. *Vigar's warning in the garden has nothing to do with them.*

But as evening approached, Abisina could not contain her anxiety. "I can't wait any longer, Findlay," she said. "I have to go out there!"

"We promised Rueshlan we would stay here." Findlay sounded firm, but his eyes cut toward the door, and she knew he wanted to be out there, too.

She had just retrieved the bow that Haret made her, with the intention of going after her father, when Rueshlan walked in.

"Father!" Abisina threw herself at him.

"It's all right, Abisina," Rueshlan spoke with little energy. Hugging him, Abisina smelled fresh air on his tunic, but wrinkled her nose when she caught a whiff of centaur.

"Thank goodness you're back," Findlay said. "She was about to walk out after you!"

"Abisina!"

"I didn't come all this way to lose you again, Father!" Abisina insisted. "What happened?"

Rueshlan sank into a chair. "It was a large pack—far larger than anything we've seen in years. But they must not have been ready for a fight, because they headed toward the Mountains Eternal as soon as our teams came together. A cadre of centaurs is still on the trail, but the wolves were moving fast. I doubt they'll catch them." Rueshlan rubbed a hand over his eyes.

"Are—are the bards still singing tonight?" Meelah asked, bringing a smile to Rueshlan's face.

"Of course! It takes more than a pack of überwolves to interrupt Midsummer! And Abisina has never heard our bards."

"They're wonderful!" Meelah said rapturously.

Abisina could see the strain behind her father's smile. He'd said the pack was larger than anything seen in years. Could *this* be a sign? She had to tell him about Vigar's warning.

But the danger had passed. And Rueshlan looked so tired. She could wait to tell him—until after the Midsummer celebration.

The folk of Watersmeet filled tier upon tier of the amphi-theater again that night until it overflowed with the light of their torches. News of the überwolves must have traveled through the community—the mood was more subdued than the night Abisina had arrived—but as the folk poured in, they seemed ready to throw themselves into the celebration at hand. Frayda came and whispered something to Rueshlan that made his eyebrows pull together, but when he caught Abisina look-ing at him, he squeezed her hand in reassurance. "There's nothing to worry about, Abisina. Just enjoy the music."

She studied the stage at the bottom of the theater where the performers gathered: two dwarves, four fauns, five humans, and two centaurs. The bards stood among a cluster of instruments: harps of various sizes; lutes ranging from smaller than Abisina's forearm to one that she could hardly imagine Rueshlan handling; drums made of animal skins stretched over stumps, hollowed logs, and what looked like an enormous mushroom cap. Two fauns played a light and merry tune on a harp and a flute until everyone had filed in. Meelah hugged Abisina in excitement, and Findlay smiled at her over his sister's head.

Before the fauns' song ended, Abisina caught Alden's eye, but at her hopeful look, he shook his head. Haret had not returned.

The performance began when one of the centaur bards came forward and called out the familiar greeting: "Watersmeet!"

"Hi-yah!" the crowd boomed.

Abisina thought everyone would sit down, but all remained standing and she soon understood why. The echo of the crowd's "Hi-yah!" had not yet died away before the dwarves struck a chord on two lutes and a faun sang a jolly, reverberating note. Abisina's feet stirred beneath her. Four beats later and she was humming; four beats after that, she was dancing with the rest of the amphitheater. The first song was followed by another rollicking tune performed by two women on lutes and two of the fauns singing in close harmony. By the third song, Abisina's face ran with sweat as she twirled with abandon, elbow locked with Glynholly's. From Glynholly, she reeled to Meelah and then to Findlay, whose brown eyes held hers steady against the whirling scene around them.

The song ended, and Findlay and Abisina came to a stop, laughing. She had expected something like the recitation of the story of Vran—the ritualized call and response, the steady martial beat of the verses, the story that never varied. But like the enormous Sylvyads, the wide variation of Watersmeet's inhabitants, and the wonder of Rueshlan, the music defied her imagination.

Then the mood shifted. Two of the men sang a heart-rending story of a faun's unrequited love, followed by a dwarf narrating the tale of his ancestors' search for the Obrun City.

Abisina went cold as she thought of Haret on this same journey. Near her, unchecked tears streamed down Alden's face.

She was still thinking of Haret when the two centaurs began to sing. She bit her tongue, but sensing Rueshlan's eyes on her and remembering her promise, she did not look away. Their voices rang out: one a vibrant soprano, one a deep bass. They sang a song of the land—towering mountains surrounding deep valleys, rivers tumbling toward thundering cataracts, vast forests giving way to equally vast oceans. Their voices beat the air like hooves on stone, like Drolf's hooves carrying her to Icksyon. The fear she felt as she approached Giant's Cairn gripped her again. She slipped her hands under her hair and covered her ears—anything to block the sound.

As the song ended and the amphitheater shook with applause, she pushed her hair away from her face and glanced toward her father. Like the rest of the crowd, his cheeks were flushed, his eyes glistening. As he turned to her, Abisina forced herself to smile back at him. He nodded and looked again toward the stage, leaving Abisina both relieved and disappointed that he had not noticed her fear.

Several more hours of music, dance, and recitations passed. Abisina knew that dawn was near, but no yawn tickled the back of her throat, no heaviness pulled at her legs. Then one of the women on the stage stepped forward, and a hush fell over the crowd. She was tiny—shorter than the dwarves—with a waist Abisina could span with her hands.

She had a white, pinched face lost in a sea of red hair. Abisina realized that of all the bards, only this woman had not yet sung or played.

"Oh, Abisina!" Meelah said, barely holding her voice to a whisper. "You get to hear Sahnda! She hardly ever sings—and then it's only of Vigar!"

At that moment, Sahnda opened her mouth. The first note—high and sweet, but so lonely—hung in the air, and in it Abisina heard all the pain of her days in Vranille. The note rang on until Abisina thought she would cry out—then it faded to nothing.

There was a long pause before Sahnda sang again, and when she did, she sang of Vigar. As Abisina tried to focus on the words, the mood of the music moved into her head, peeling back layer upon layer of memory: her hand in Rueshlan's at Alden's hearth; the peace of the orchard; the stench of Icksyon; the comforting time underground with Hoysta; the flight from Vranille. Abisina waited for Sahnda to lift the last layer and expose the wound of her mother's death, but instead the music became discordant and Sahnda spoke a name that stopped Abisina's breath.

Had she heard it? In coming so close to the pain of Sina's death, did she imagine Sahnda had named its cause? But there it was again—Charach—the name that she had been avoiding since she got to Watersmeet. *It should never be spoken here*, she thought. Next to her, Rueshlan shuddered.

A third time Sahnda sang it, and this time Abisina

understood: Charach had killed Vigar. Her own loss, Watersmeet's loss, all stemmed from the same evil.

Then the song spiraled upward, growing lighter and more beautiful with each note. The pain remained, coloring the echoes that shimmered around the amphitheater, but there was resolution, too. Sahnda sang of Watersmeet, her voice as high as the Sylvyads, as gentle as the flow of the River Fennish, as airy as the bridges that connected the wards throughout the community. Charach was defeated! Watersmeet remained!

But Abisina knew that Charach lived.

She hated the fear that the name evoked in her, in the folk of Watersmeet. She hated the idea of telling her father of Vigar's warning and reawakening the dread she had seen on his face.

The song ended, and the crowd stood in awe, unmoving, until Sahnda took a step back. It was a stumble really; she looked even smaller, her pale skin now a shade of gray. A faun and dwarf rushed to support her, and the crowd woke from its trance. Waves of applause flooded the stage as Sahnda was led off and the performance was over.

Abisina and Rueshlan didn't need torches to get home—dawn lit their way, but for Abisina, the light was touched by the darkness of Charach.

Tomorrow I'll tell him.

Abisina woke well past noon to the news that Alden was waiting for her. She rushed from her room, tying the waist-cord of her new, pale green tunic, a gift from her father.

"Haret's returned," he said.

"He has! Can I see him?"

"That's why I'm here. He's with my brother Waite. But I have to warn you, Rueshlan's daughter, he is not himself."

Abisina hurried behind Alden through the shady pathways that were still a maze to her. They arrived at a ward on the western side where the River Lesser provided a backdrop of falling water as it joined the Middle and Fennish Rivers. The doorways in this ward were smaller, some obviously built for dwarves, others for humans and fauns as well. Outside a bright yellow door with a green *W* on it, stood a knot of dwarves, their faces serious. As Abisina approached, they stepped aside.

"You'll want to prepare yourself," Alden told her, and the rest of the dwarves mumbled their agreement.

At her tight-lipped assent, Alden opened the door and led Abisina through a chain of rooms to a bedroom with a small balcony overlooking the river. Haret sat in a chair on the balcony, wrapped in a wool blanket, though the day was warm. He looked tired, withered. Alden went to Haret and spoke softly to him, then left the room. Abisina stood alone in the doorway, waiting for Haret to look at her, to speak, to somehow acknowledge her presence.

He didn't move for a long time, and when he did look in Abisina's direction, a tremor passed through him.

She willed herself not to cry out when she saw Haret's face. He had aged ten winters, his eyes sunken, his cheeks hollow. He tried to smile but grimaced. "Hello, human."

"Haret." She was unable to say more, unsure if she should go to him.

"Your face tells me that you are shocked. I know I don't look myself." He ran a hand through his hair, and Abisina noticed strands of gray against the jet-black. Had they always been there and she just hadn't noticed?

"You need some rest," Abisina offered. "We've had such a long journey, and now . . ."

"Yes," Haret said harshly. "A long journey to find my heart's desire. I just didn't know how twisted my heart is."

"No, Haret!" Abisina went to him now and touched his hand. It was cold. "Your heart is not twisted! Think of what you did for me. How many times you saved me!"

"As you pointed out then, human, I saved the Obrium." He spat the final word. "No. I will not shy away from the truth. My grandmother said that finding what I was looking for might be worse than not finding it at all. I didn't think I could live with not knowing, but it's far worse to know—what I am."

"Don't say that! You tracked those centaurs for leagues to rescue me—a human! It wasn't just the Obrium. You knew that no one deserves what the centaurs were going to do to me. You *cared* for me. And Alden said that all dwarves have the Obriumlust."

Haret shook his head. "That first day—we didn't have to travel all day and night. I wanted to show that you were weak, that you didn't deserve all you've taken from us—and from the others who lived in the land before you. I wanted to break you, human. Was that caring for you?"

Haret's voice had never been so bitter, but Abisina would not be put off. "Then I am guilty, too, Haret. I believed the worst of you—and Hoysta. Despite all that you did for me, I couldn't see beyond what I'd been taught. But you both made me look beyond the Elders' words. Haret,"—she took his hands—"you can't let this one moment become all that you are."

Haret sighed. "No. I'm—I'm leaving tomorrow. I can't face the other dwarves." He pulled a hand away and ran it over his face. "I will return to my grandmother, far from the Mines. Where it's safe." He straightened slightly. "I said I would get you to Watersmeet, and I have. You've found your father." Then his shoulders rounded again. "But it was you who brought us here," he said, his voice just above a whisper. "I would never have thought of going *up* the mountains. And the necklace—it needed to be with you."

"And *you* gave it to me, Haret, despite the Obriumlust. Many dwarves couldn't have done that! We helped *each other* get here. Please, please don't leave. No one thinks any less of you. And—and you're not strong enough to travel. Promise me you will wait till you're stronger. You—you owe me that," she said, desperately trying to think of something that would reach him—"if only for that first night of our journey when you tried to 'break me.'"

They argued until Haret cried "Human!" with a touch of his old energy. But Abisina prevailed. He would stay in Watersmeet for another week.

A pudgy, blond dwarf led Abisina back home—after Alden

reassured her that he wouldn't let Haret leave. "The humiliation is common, Rueshlan's daughter," Alden explained. "It isn't often that we have to confront the impure sides of ourselves."

Abisina returned to Rueshlan's ward and intended to find her father immediately to tell him about Vigar's warning, but first she was greeted by Meelah. She received the girl's ecstatic hug and managed to look directly into her blue eyes as Meelah chatted about the fauns' and fairies' dance that night. When Findlay approached them, Abisina was surprised at how easy it was to meet his gaze.

"I hope my sister let you say *something*." He laughed as Meelah darted away to greet a girl her age. "She forgets that a conversation is supposed to go two ways!"

"Really, it's so nice to have people to talk to. She does whatever she can to make me feel welcome here."

"You *are* welcome here," Findlay said warmly, and Abisina wondered if he noticed her blush.

By the time Abisina resumed her search for her father, so many visitors filled the ward that it was impossible to get him alone. The crowd moved between the bonfire in the center of the ward and Rueshlan's laden table, talking, laughing, singing songs, and demanding Rueshlan's attention every time Abisina opened her mouth to speak. She would have to wait a little longer.

Late in the evening, Abisina stood at Rueshlan's elbow, listening to a dwarf sing about an ancestor who longed to dance with the fauns. The description of the dwarf practicing his leaps with false horns on his head was ridiculous, and the listeners were shaking with laughter. Abisina, laughing too, glanced toward the bonfire and caught sight of the sparks spiraling toward the Sylvyads' tops. For a second, she stood again in Vranille's burial ground, watching Charach's eerie fire spike into the sky as the people fed the flames with bodies.

She felt her father's hand on her shoulder. "Abisina?"

She looked into his concerned face, felt the weight of his hand, and the world of the ward became distinct again.

"When you're ready to tell me, Abisina, I'm ready to listen."

Now. She had to tell him now. But Rueshlan's focus shifted to something across the ward. Looking over, Abisina saw Kyron emerge from his door.

Some silent communication passed between Kyron and Rueshlan as the huge centaur came into the circle, driving all other thoughts from Abisina's mind. She backed up into her father, and he put his arm around her, saying, "There is nothing to worry about, Abisina. I promise." Kyron did not look at her and never moved more than a few paces from where he stood, but neither did he go away. Abisina stayed facing him and kept close to Rueshlan.

Just before midnight, Alden bustled in. She'd hoped he would bring Haret, but he was alone. "Still quite low," he told her. "Not up to a party."

"But he loves the fauns!"

Alden nodded sympathetically. "I hope to get him to the Gathering at dawn. It might revive him a bit."

The arrival of the fauns cut their conversation short. One stood at the entrance to the ward, two torches held high above his head, his dark, handsome face solemn.

"Get ready," murmured Findlay, who had been near Abisina much of the evening. "You've not celebrated Midsummer till you've seen the fauns dance."

After the lead faun captured everyone's attention, he strode into the ward at a regal pace, followed by eleven more fauns bearing torches in each hand. They stationed themselves at equal intervals around the ward, and the crowd stepped back to join the ring they'd created. Abisina was separated from Rueshlan by one faun, but Findlay stood on her other side. Kyron was across the ward.

For a moment, there was silence. Then, the ward filled with a high-pitched whistle that Abisina recognized from watching the fauns with Haret. Seconds later three fauns vaulted through the entrance between the Sylvyads, swinging their torches, crouching low then leaping high, their hooves pounding the ground faster than raindrops in a cloudburst. Absorbed in the movements of these three, Abisina hardly noticed another three, and then three more, spring between the Sylvyads until the ward teemed with fauns—moving, gyrating, lunging, leaping, the music dipping and diving right along with them. Torches swung in all directions, and Abisina was sure one would hit a dancer or an onlooker, but the fauns' timing did not falter.

Just as Abisina began to grow dizzy from the fauns' mad caper, they fell back into a ring two deep, lining the inside of the circle. The music stopped abruptly, and then a new song emerged, higher and wilder than the fauns' pipes, and achingly beautiful, somewhere between a human voice and the call of a nightingale. Abisina couldn't tell the source, but two figures at the ward's entrance stood illuminated by the strange glowing orbs they held. A breeze ruffled Abisina's hair, and she smelled deep, old forests.

Abisina knew very little about fairies—mostly stories of devilish beings told to scare Vranian children. The two who stepped into the fauns' circle, and the many who followed behind them, were decidedly not human. They were the same basic build and size—as tall as most men—but the grace with which they moved, the way their hips swayed, the fluidity of their arms— made even the fauns look clumsy and lumbering.

Their skin was as black as a moonless night; their hair, as long as Rueshlan's, rippled through the air in waves; their loose, silky tunics and pants reflected the burning torches and the orbs they carried; even their skin shimmered. They moved with such weightlessness, tossing their orbs to one another in intricate patterns, that Abisina was sure they would leave no footprints behind. At the height of the dance, she counted thirty fairies, losing track twice in her awe of them.

"Those balls they carry," she asked Findlay, without looking away, "what are they?"

"Moonlight," he breathed back.

"Can they—fly?" Abisina asked a moment later when another fairy leapt into the ward, head almost touching the Sylvyad branches.

"Not quite. But they are not held to the earth as we are. They have an affinity with birds. They communicate with them in their own language."

The fairies' expressions were inscrutable, their almond-shaped eyes touched with blue. Each became a small part of a larger whole. And though Abisina assumed that the music came from the fairies, she never caught their lips moving. Through the whole of the dance, she didn't know if she watched men or women, or if gender was as immaterial to the fairies as gravity.

At some unseen cue, the fauns with their pipes joined the fairies in a dance of circles inside circles inside circles, each one moving in opposite directions, so that Abisina looked into the heart of a whirlpool, felt the tug of its current. She took a step forward and next to her Findlay did, too, and others around them until the circles melded together, and the fauns and fairies clasped hands, weaving through the onlookers toward the ward's exit.

At the melding of the circles, the watchers made their own chain and began to follow the dancers to the next ward. But Abisina, totally absorbed, did not stir. So she came face-to-face with the last fairy to leave. This fairy stood taller than any of the others, had hair which shimmered with strands of silver, and wore a circlet of silver leaves around its brow. As the fairy stepped toward her, their eyes met.

Abisina's world turned upside down, her head dangling toward the center of that cool blue eye and the infinity beyond it.

The fairy spoke: "Our ancient enemy has returned. This human has seen Charach."

CHAPTER XV

"LOHRING!" RUESHLAN SPOKE STERNLY BUT QUIETLY, breaking the spell of the fairy's gaze, and bringing Abisina tumbling back to earth. He put his hands on Abisina's shoulders as the rest of the crowd filed out. "Let them go, let them go," he murmured until the last dwarf had disappeared along the trail. Findlay had started to follow, but hung back when he saw that Abisina was not with him. Sensing that something was amiss, Alden, Frayda, and Kyron stayed behind, too.

Rueshlan faced Lohring, jaw clenched. "Do you know what you're saying?"

Lohring stood up taller, eyes flashing. "Do you doubt me, Rueshlan? Do you forget that I am the Daughter of the Fairy Mother?" The tones in her voice rang high and low, reverberating through Abisina.

"I do not forget, Lohring," Rueshlan answered. "But you speak of very dark things—and at the height of Midsummer."

"We cannot wait, Rueshlan. Every moment is precious. Charach is back and on the move—and your daughter knows him!"

The others gasped at Lohring's words.

Abisina looked to Rueshlan for help, but he focused on the fairy.

"How do you know this?" he asked.

"It is in her eyes," Lohring said. "The White Worm leaves his mark."

"Abisina," Rueshlan took her hand, "is what Lohring says true? Have you seen the White Worm?"

"Y-yes," Abisina stammered. "I didn't know that you knew Ch-Charach until last night when Sahnda . . ." Her voice faded.

Rueshlan bent closer to her. "Tell me, Abisina. Tell me what you know."

She took a deep breath. "My last day in Vranille, he came. But he came as a man and the people thought he was a hero. He promised to lead us—the Vranians—to defeat our—*their* enemies—the dwarves, the fauns, the centaurs." She glanced nervously around the group. "He came during the Ritual of Penance. He—he was beautiful. At first. I thought he was Vran. But then—his eyes! That's when I saw it." Abisina's voice shook.

"What?" Rueshlan asked, leaning still closer.

"I—I felt like I was being swallowed by darkness. And at the center, I saw—" She couldn't get out the words.

"Yes?" Rueshlan urged.

"I saw the White Worm. And I knew then that he was evil—a shape-shifter," Abisina whispered.

"Did others see it?" Rueshlan asked in the same steady voice.

"I don't think so. Maybe one." She remembered the outcast Jorno, helping her lift Paleth as the rest of the crowd fell apart in a frenzy, telling her to run. "They cried out to him, Father. They wanted to touch him. They *loved* him. Then— then he turned on the outcasts. They chased us, and they killed us. They got—they killed my mother. . . . But—she— and Vigar—told me to warn you, to tell you about Charach. That this is the beginning."

There. It was out—what she had avoided for so long.

No one moved.

Rueshlan stared off, past the Sylvyads, pain clouding his face. "I'm sorry, Abisina," he said, focusing again on his daughter. The lump that had risen in Abisina's throat threatened to dissolve into tears, but she fought to stay dry-eyed.

Rueshlan straightened up. "Charach is back," he said dully. "Call the Council."

The small group scattered. Kyron reared up and galloped away, carrying the news to the farthest wards. Lohring stayed long enough for a hurried, whispered conversation with Rueshlan, before setting off to catch up with the fairies who still danced through Watersmeet. Findlay was the last to leave, tentatively touching Abisina's hand before he turned to go. The lump in her throat threatened to dissolve again.

There were several hours before dawn and Abisina spent them with Rueshlan sitting before the smoldering fire, the remains of the banquet still spread on the table. Rueshlan asked her again to tell him what she knew about Charach, why he had come to Vranille. He wept with her when she told him about the fire in the burial ground. When she described finding the necklace, he stood abruptly. "I thought she had given it to you," he said.

Abisina shook her head. "I found it after she—was gone. Haret thought the necklace *knew* me. He said the snow and wind at the altar were the necklace's power."

"He may be right. Through the necklace, Vigar—and your mother—brought you here."

Mama was with me. We went on the journey together. She held the necklace tightly. "Vigar said something like that. And soon after that, a minotaur got into Vigar's garden."

"Minotaurs in the *garden*? It's always been a refuge. . . . The signs are becoming quite plain. Charach's power is growing."

His words made Abisina feel sick. "I'm sorry, I should have warned you earlier," she said. "But I didn't want to bring *him* here."

Rueshlan laid a hand on her arm. "It's all right, Abisina. All this time, I've been defending Watersmeet, as if her folk were the only ones that needed me. I should have seen that

Charach would take any opportunity, use any foothold. It's been so long since—I had begun to think he was truly defeated."

The question that had been lurking in the back of her mind tumbled out before she could stop it. "Sahnda said Charach killed Vigar. So is he old—like you?"

"Much older. The stories of Charach go back as far as there are stories. And he has many guises. He can look quite beautiful, as he first appeared to you. That is one way he gains followers. Charach was here when Vigar came to Watersmeet, but she defeated him."

"Was Vigar *human*?" Abisina asked.

"Yes, she was—as were her original followers—but she embraced all beings. That was her power. Charach grew weaker as more and more joined Vigar. They were strong enough to drive him out. The folk of Watersmeet believed he had been killed, but Vigar knew better. Did he slip into the Fens? Cross the Mountains Eternal? Head south to the sea? Or did he go underground?" Rueshlan sighed. "Wherever he went, Vigar knew he would be back. I have had the same fear. Charach does not take defeat lightly, and he is patient. But lately, I let myself forget."

Abisina mulled over Rueshlan's story. "Why did he come to Vranille?"

"He feeds on hatred. The Vranians provide plenty, born of their fear. It's another reason to kill the outcasts—it shows the people that he will defeat what they fear."

"The Vranians don't fear the outcasts!"

"But they do. They fear what they cannot control. Since they descended the Mountains Eternal, the Vranians have viewed this as a hostile land. They have struggled to control it by deciding who lives, who dies, and how each life will be lived out. Killing a centaur or dwarf—even a helpless infant—provides them with a sense of power, but they fear deeply that this power is an illusion. And Charach feeds on this fear."

The windows of the room were no longer dark, but gray. It was time to go to the final Midsummer Gathering. Abisina had one more question. "Why did I see the Worm?"

"Perhaps Charach offered you something you didn't want. The villagers longed for a hero like Vran to lead them. But you know in a very deep way that Vran—and Charach—are your enemies. Eventually all the Vranians will realize this. Then Charach's outer beauty will fall away and his followers will behold the White Worm—but it will be too late."

Abisina stood next to Rueshlan as the fairies and fauns entered the Gathering Place for the climax of the Mid-summer celebration. Abisina wanted to feel the beauty of the ceremony—the light of the torches and the fairy orbs greeting the dawn, the music climbing to impossible heights, the lithe dancers moving with the same intensity and passion that had delighted her only a few hours earlier—but she viewed the scene as if through water. The outlines of the dancers wavered and bent at odd angles, the music came to her from a distance, and the roar of the crowd sounded hollow.

The Council met as soon as the Gathering ended. The crowd heading wearily but happily home did not notice the strain on their leaders' faces.

Abisina was relieved that Rueshlan took her with him to the Council. She was afraid to ask—it wasn't really her place—but she couldn't imagine waiting alone while they discussed how to respond to Charach.

The Council House stood at the center of Watersmeet where the First Sylvyad had grown. Rueshlan had described it to her while they first toured Watersmeet. The enormous tree had fallen, leaving its splintered base, twice as tall as the fence around Vranille and double the girth of any other Sylvyad. The shadow of the fallen giant lingered on the forest floor, a clearing that reached straight to the bank of the River Fennish. The folk of Watersmeet had hollowed out the center of the trunk and built two wide doors opening into it.

Abisina was sure the Council included centaurs, and she braced herself as she entered, walking a little closer to Rueshlan. The mood was somber, the merry greetings of the Midsummer replaced by terse nods. The whole Council—one representative for every ten wards—knew that danger had come to Watersmeet.

Before Rueshlan could tell Abisina where to sit, Lohring approached, pulling him aside, and Abisina was left standing alone in the middle of the floor. She searched the room, hoping to find a familiar face. She spotted Frayda and Glynholly and others she recognized, but all the Council members stood huddled in conversations. There were many she didn't know. And there were centaurs—more than she'd seen since Icksyon's lair—chestnuts, blacks, dappled grays, palominos, and whites—and she forced herself not to back out of the doors behind her.

Cut into the wall were at least sixty seats of varying heights as well as over a dozen rooms dug out at various points around the circle. To Abisina's surprise, two dwarves headed straight for the highest seats, which appeared too high even for a tall man. But when the dwarves climbed steps hacked into the wall, she understood: the seats were built so that all sat at the same level. The lower seats were for the humans, the middle height for the fauns, and the highest for the dwarves. The rooms carved into the walls were for the centaurs. When Kyron entered his room, he went down several steps, his great height necessitating a large drop to keep him level with the others.

She was wondering where she should sit when Glynholly trotted forward and said, "Follow me, Abisina." Benches ran along one side of the circle, some close to the floor, others higher up the wall. Sizing up Abisina, Glynholly sat her on several benches until the faun found one that brought Abisina to the same level as those in the Council. Ten or so fairies were seated on a long, lower bench to Abisina's left. As Abisina took her seat, she felt as if everyone were staring at her—the one who brought Charach to Watersmeet.

Rueshlan finished his consultation with Lohring and headed to a place to the right of Abisina. No mark or sign on Rueshlan's seat indicated that he was the Keeper of Watersmeet, but his feet reached comfortably to the floor. Abisina realized then that the other seats had been built to put the Council on Rueshlan's level.

When all but three seats were filled, Rueshlan stood and the nervous whispers around the room stopped. He looked from fauns to dwarves to centaurs to humans to fairies, his gaze resting briefly on an empty seat.

"Where is Alden?" he asked. "He is the only one I cannot account for."

"I'm here!" came a cry from the doorway, and Alden rushed in with—to Abisina's great relief—Haret. He still looked haggard, his eyes sunken, but he managed a hoarse, "Human," as Alden led him toward the benches.

"Is it true?" a faun called out. "Charach has returned?"

"It is." A chorus of alarmed cries met Rueshlan's words. He held out his hand for quiet and continued. "Lohring, Daughter of the Fairy Mother, has talked with several eagles she dispatched to the south during the night. Charach leads a Vranian army due east, destroying the country as he goes. He has shattered communities of dwarves and fauns, taking those who survive as his prisoners. To the north, groups of dwarves, fauns, and some centaurs have raised small bands to try to stop him, but these are pursued by a gang of centaurs who are taking advantage of the chaos. Judging by the number of human bodies left behind, some of the Vranians recognize Charach's evil and have started to resist."

Abisina thought of the people she knew. Who among them would have resisted? Corlin, the boy who had saved her from the mob? Magen and Robia, who had worked surreptitiously against the Elders? Were they dead now?

She felt Haret's eyes on her. When she looked at him, he mouthed the word "Grandmother." *Surely Hoysta is safe!* she told herself. *She lives north of Vranille, and Rueshlan said that Charach was headed east!*

Alden spoke next. "The news is grave indeed. But I see little that Watersmeet can do. Charach is in the piedmont below the Obruns, and we've never been involved in the affairs of the south. No disrespect to Rueshlan's daughter," he continued, nodding toward Abisina, "but from what we know of the Vranians, they are hardly worth saving. Rueshlan has told us how they treat their own people, not to mention the folk who have lived on that land since—well, since time began, I suppose. It's no accident that Charach has chosen to return in their villages. Maybe they deserve him!"

"Alden!" Frayda cried. "Think what you're saying. Have you forgotten Vigar's teaching—that Watersmeet will aid any creature who needs help? And what of Rueshlan's daughter? They are her people!"

Abisina's head shot up. Is this how they saw her? As *Vranian*? But even as she thought this, she heard her mother's voice: *If I were to act as a follower of Vran, I would have had to deny you, and that will never happen.* By denying the Vranians, was *she* now denying her mother?

A dwarf spoke, her face reddening underneath her dark skin. "I must agree with Frayda. I have no love for Vranians, but Charach is beyond the evil mere humans—or any of us—can possess."

"These southerners are not our concern!" a fat faun with copper skin and curly red hair spoke. "They don't even know we exist! They won't expect us to help."

"Barlus!" cried another faun, this one black from head to hoof. "That is no reason not to help them! Are you forgetting what Charach did to us, the trees he slaughtered to dam the rivers in the battle against Vigar? Please do not assume, my friends, that Barlus speaks for all fauns."

Heated words flew, though Rueshlan remained silent. For a while, Abisina followed the discussion avidly, but as the argument continued to weave around her, she went numb.

A large portion of the Council advocated going after Charach—and traveling into Vranian territory to save the Vranians. Although Abisina had been in Watersmeet only five days, it had become a home—a real home in a way Vranille never was. A great anger welled up in her. Would Charach take this from her, too? Alden was right—the Vranians *deserved* Charach! Her mother had said there was good in the Vranians, but what had Abisina ever seen of that? No, she couldn't bear one drop of Watersmeet's blood being spilled to save a Vranian.

But a small voice echoed from the back of her mind. *Jorno, Corlin, Paleth—they all tried to help you.*

And so many hurt me! she argued back. *Lilas, Theckis—and countless others who called me dwarf-dirty, bastard, Outcast. No!* She shut down that voice. She had no pity for the Vranians.

Lohring stood to speak, her melodic voice silencing all arguments. "Charach will never be satisfied with the southern side of the Obruns. He will use the Vranians to bring chaos to all the land, from the Mountains Eternal to the farthest reaches of the Obruns, from the sea in the south to the Fens in the north. Saving the Vranians or letting them die—that is not what matters. What matters is stopping Charach." Lohring drew all eyes to her by invisible threads.

But then the spell of the fairy's voice was broken. A tall man stood. His eyes were almost as light as the fairies', and his hair and skin were white, though his cheeks were as smooth as a young man's. Abisina recognized him from Rueshlan's feasts but did not know his name.

He spoke slowly: "My ancestors were some of the last to join Vigar in Watersmeet so many years ago, and they suffered until they did. I cannot forget her lessons. I stand with Lohring. We must go south and meet Charach wherever he is—no matter the cost." Shouts broke out, but Glynholly's voice rose above the rest.

"My family suffered, too, Neiall," she said with a pointed look at the white-haired man. "We all did. But I have seen no evidence that Charach is going to launch an attack on the north."

Lohring spoke again. "You continue to ignore the inevitable, Watersmeet. Charach is well past Vranille, the easternmost village—heading directly toward the Low Col."

A murmur swept the room. *What is the Low Col?* Abisina asked Haret with her eyes, but he only shook his head.

"The Vranians have never been known to go east," Alden said doubtfully.

"No Vranian has ever come through the Col," Glynholly added. "And though it is a lower place to cross the Obruns, it is still very difficult. I suggest we send a small scouting force to monitor the Col. If Charach does intend to move into the north, our scouts can ride to Watersmeet and we will be ready to meet him."

"The centaurs stand ready to be this small force," came Kyron's rumble.

"A small force?" Lohring's voice shook with rage. "And when he marches through, the centaurs will return to Watersmeet, leaving the fairies' Motherland as a sacrifice to Charach!" Lohring glared around the room. "I expected more support from Watersmeet!" The fairies stood as one. "We will have no choice but to make a truce with the enemy, to secure our own safety."

"No!" shouted Frayda. "Watersmeet will not abandon the fairies! What have we been training for all these years? We must stop Charach where he is and free the folk he has already captured."

At this, the entire Council was up, shouting, pointing, pummeling the air with their fists. Throughout, Rueshlan had sat with his head bowed, as if unaware of the furor around him.

Rueshlan, Abisina thought. *Father!*

He met her eyes as if she had spoken. He smiled sadly and got to his feet. Silence. "I will not turn my back on the fairies," he said quietly, but his words sank into the stillness like stones in a pool. "Frayda is right. Should we use our training to defend only ourselves? Was that why Vigar established Watersmeet? But I cannot—I *will* not—compel anyone to follow me. We may lose many of our brothers and sisters in this battle. Each of you must decide whether to stand with me. I will go—alone, if I must—through the Low Col and to Charach."

Rueshlan's words rang in Abisina's mind like a death knell. She would lose her father to Charach—just as she had lost her mother.

"Centaurs always stand as one! We ride with Rueshlan!" shouted Kyron, followed by shouts of "Centaurs!"

Next Frayda pledged, then Neiall, and soon the air was full of voices pledging to follow Rueshlan. Even Alden offered his support. Glynholly was the last, waiting until every faun had risen before slowly getting to her feet.

Rueshlan looked around the room. "Thank you," he said, with his hand to his heart.

Lohring said nothing but glared around the circle as if daring folk to change their minds.

The meeting ended. At a Gathering that evening, Rueshlan would invite all of Watersmeet to march on Charach, if they chose. And then the work would begin—it would take several weeks to ready Watersmeet's army. Small groups of Council members gathered in the middle of the floor talking excitedly, while others headed toward the bright square of the open doors. Abisina stared at those doors as the sun poured in, wondering how it could be light outside when inside she felt so dark.

"Human." Haret stood next to her, offering a hand.

"He can't go, Haret!"

"I know," he said heavily, helping her off the bench. "Let's go outside," he suggested, and they headed toward the doors.

"Abisina!" Rueshlan called to her.

"I'm walking home with Haret, Father," she answered, trying to keep her voice steady. "I'll meet you there."

He nodded and turned back toward Frayda and Lohring, who both started speaking at once.

Knots of folk stood talking outside the Council House. "Let's go to Alden's," Haret said. "There's no one there, and we can talk." Abisina followed him down one of the trails.

For several minutes they walked without talking, and then Haret paused, scratching his beard.

"What's wrong?" Abisina asked, pulled out of her jumbled thoughts.

"Don't know where I am," he muttered. "Trees! I thought

I had this route figured out."

Abisina took in the gigantic trunks and the three trails that forked in the mottled light. "I don't know either. I came a different way this morning."

Haret peered down each of the trails. "They all look exactly the same to me."

Abisina glanced down the trail that led to the Council House. "That's the way back."

"I know the way back. It's forward I don't remember! And there's been too much traffic for me to *taste* the right way. Oh, to be in a cave! I'll go get someone to lead us, human. You wait here."

Haret set off, and Abisina sat down on a gnarled root to wait, trying to sort through what she'd heard at the Council meeting. She pulled in her feet and wrapped her arms around her legs, but before she had sat for long, the thud-thud of hooves approached. *Centaurs!* She heard the rumble of voices, and the instinct to escape flooded her. She got up and started down the right-hand trail, but stopped. What if they came that way? As the voices neared, she spied a notch between a root and the trunk of one of the Sylvyads, and she pressed herself into it, praying they would walk by her.

Two centaurs came to the crossroads; one was the palomino, Torden, who had shot the überwolf. Her yellow flanks, white tail, and light skin were bright even in the dim light. The other was a dark chestnut, with spots of white on his hindquarters. The smell of horseflesh brought Abisina right back to the moment she had entered Giant's Cairn.

"Here's where we part, Morrell," Torden said. "I'll wait in my ward for Kyron. He'll pass my way when the Council's finished."

"Did Kyron say what it was about?"

"He couldn't tell me. But we're sure to follow Rueshlan—centaurs always stand together. We cannot let our brother down."

The centaurs clasped each other's forearms before turning down two different paths, Torden heading in the same direction as Haret.

Abisina began to unfold and crawl out of her hiding spot, Torden's words ringing in her ears. *Our brother.* Kyron had said something like that at the Council: *Centaurs always stand as one. We ride with Rueshlan.*

An avalanche of images made her sink back onto the root. The height and breadth of all the doors in Rueshlan's ward: *Do centaurs live in more of these houses?* she had asked, and her father had said yes. She remembered Rueshlan's reaction—and the reaction of the whole company—when she had refused to meet the centaurs that first night. His sadness when she told him she could never trust a centaur and his pleading with her to be open to them. His apology to Kyron, asking for "more time" when she had found Kyron in the ward.

It all had new meaning now. It all spoke to the truth.

Her father was a shape-shifter—a demon like Charach.

Rueshlan could shift his shape from man to—and as the word formed in her head, she almost fainted—*centaur*.

She stared again into the blackness of Charach's eyes. For five days she thought she had found her father, a family, a haven, a home. But now she didn't know what she had found. Who was Rueshlan? Who—or *what*—was her father?

Abisina felt even more alone than when she'd fled Vranille. At least on the journey north, she had hope to follow. Now, she had nothing.

The despair crushed her. She could not rise from that root. Not ever.

But she did rise. With one thought in her mind. The same thought that had sent her from Vranille. *Run.*

CHAPTER XVI

THE STILLNESS OF THE GARDEN SURROUNDED ABISINA—
the coolness of the dewy grass; fruits' sweet odors drifting
from the boughs overhead; bees' soft hum; a light wind caressing her skin. But the peace of the garden eluded her.

She sat on the bench at the base of one of the fruit trees,
the rough boards biting into her thighs. Her elbow and knee
ached from falling as she ran along the River Deliverance.
Her fingers were ripped ragged from clawing her way up the
slopes of Mt. Sumus. Her right foot throbbed where her toe
had been taken. And she was tired, so tired, after her flight
from Watersmeet.

She hadn't slept at all during the two days and nights it
took to return to the garden. And she slept little once she got
there, unable to find the alcove where she'd spent the nights
of her first visit. Mostly, she walked among the trees waiting
in vain for the release of her anger and pain.

This was where Haret found her. She was wandering through the orchard, so distracted by her thoughts that she didn't hear his approach.

"Human."

She spun to find Haret's black eyes fixed on her. His tunic was soiled, and a trickle of dried blood snaked across his shin. "Haret! How did you know I was here?"

Haret shrugged, his gaze never moving from her face.

"You want to know why I left." Abisina answered his unasked question, "It's about my—Rueshlan." Abisina looked at him pleadingly, but his eyes were cold.

"I know about your father. And though I hoped otherwise, I knew that's why you ran."

"You knew about my father and you didn't tell me?"

"I didn't tell you for the same reason that he didn't. You're Vranian."

"I am not!" she seethed.

"Well, you're acting like it, human. You've learned nothing from Hoysta, nothing from me. Nothing even from Watersmeet. You found out Rueshlan is a shape-shifter, and like every good Vranian, you fled."

"He lied to me!" Abisina cried, the disdain in Haret's voice stoking her anger. "He's a—*centaur!*"

"He had to lie! What choice did he have? He knew you'd see him as a demon."

Abisina looked away, hating her silence but unable to disagree.

"Was Hoysta a demon then?" Haret demanded. "When she saved you? Nursed you?"

"Of course not."

"You can't have it both ways, human. If you listen to the Vranians about centaurs, you have to listen to them about dwarves. Are you prepared to condemn us all?"

"Stop! It's not fair! Hoysta and you are different. I know you—as people."

"We are *not* people!" Haret was yelling now. "You can't stop thinking like a Vranian, can you? Judging the whole world with yourself at the center. Look at me! What do you see?"

"What do you mean?" Abisina stepped back.

"When you look at me, you think short, hairy, ugly. Don't deny it."

"Haret—"

"But that's only because you're holding up some human form, some form of yourself, as an ideal. To me, *humans* are ugly. Spindly. Weak. Blind."

"But don't you understand, Haret? I can accept that he's not Vranian, or human—or even that he's a shape-shifter. . . ." She waited for Haret to nod in agreement, though she knew that what she had said wasn't all true.

But Haret didn't budge. His eyes bored into hers.

"No, you couldn't understand." She turned away. "Icksyon didn't hold you. He didn't put his hands on you, bite you— You will never convince me that he isn't evil."

"I have no intention of trying," Haret said flatly. "I'm not saying evil doesn't exist. But you've met one evil centaur—"

"One?"

"Fine, Icksyon's whole band is evil. But from this experience you've decided that *all* centaurs are evil."

"You don't understand," Abisina repeated. "My whole life I've been called a demon. I tried to ignore it—to believe my mother when she said I was gifted and beautiful. But I worried. What if it were true? I could feel something inside me—something different—something bad. But I hoped that what they said was wrong." The words hurt, sand raking across the flesh of her tight throat. "Now I know. I know that what he is—it's part of me. In me. I *am* a demon." Abisina had just spoken her deepest fear, and she sank to the ground under the weight of the words.

Haret sighed, his own shoulders slumping. "We all have evil in us, Abisina." The sadness in his voice made her look at him again. His cheeks were hollow, and shadows lingered under his eyes, a reminder of his time in the Mines. He sat down next to her. "Come back with me to Watersmeet. Your father's sick with worry. Search parties have been formed. They're wondering if you were taken by überwolves. . . ."

"I can't. I can't face him. Or any of them."

"Then let me bring him here."

"No—Haret, I just need to think. To figure this out."

"Human, he is your father."

Haret's voice reached her from a distance.

"Abisina?"

She knew he was waiting for her to get to her feet, to fight back.

But she didn't. And after a while, she felt Haret rise quietly and move away through the grass.

Still she sat on, Haret's words tumbling through her mind in fragments—until one thing he said rose to the surface— fully formed and heavy with meaning.

He is your father.

The storm broke.

Her sobs were the shrieks of an infant left alone while her mother worked behind barred doors; the pain of a child bruised by cruel words; the suffering of a girl hating herself as a demon, the bastard with dark hair and skin. She wept for flame and heaps of ash. For cold metal against colder stone. For Icksyon's mad eyes staring into hers. She cried for disappointment, betrayal, anger.

And finally, she cried because she had believed. She had believed that her mother could protect her, that her father was the hero she had come to love.

They were both gone now.

When Abisina's sobs quieted at last, she was lying face down on the ground. She rolled onto her back. The sky stretched endlessly above her, framed by shifting leaves. She felt empty.

But the emptiness did not last. Memory filled her: she felt her mother's lips pressed to her hot forehead testing for fever; she recalled the comfort of Paleth's pebble tied into her tunic; she heard Hoysta's chuckling prattle in the warmth of her cave; she saw Rueshlan before her, his face filled with joy at the discovery of his daughter. And always there were the questions: Would he come to her? Did she want him to?

She had avoided the clearing with the rowan tree and grave. Vigar had said: *We are all with you—those who wore the necklace.* But the necklace hung around her throat like a weight: cold, hard, dead.

When she had clawed her way up the mountains from Watersmeet, no path appeared, no archway, not even a crack that she could slip through to return to Vigar's garden. For hours in the dark, she had groped her way along the face of the mountain, slipping her fingers into any fissure until they bled. As the sun rose, she found a dusty cave with a low tunnel at its back. And then she had wandered through inky tunnel after inky tunnel. No reddish light glowed at her approach, no odor of fruit beckoned to her. She had even tasted the dirt, but her parched tongue told her nothing, and she was left with greater thirst and less hope.

When she at last stumbled into the garden, exhaustion and despair had so dulled her senses that she didn't recognize it for what it was. The midnight sky heavy with clouds left the archway indistinguishable from the darkness she had wandered through, and only when she fell and felt grass on her cheek did she realize that she had found the orchard.

It was fury that drove Abisina to seek out Vigar after days in the orchard.

"Where are you?" she cried, as she stepped into the clearing. "You said the wearers would be with me—but they're all gone now. My mother. My father. And now you! Watersmeet is readying for war. Isn't that what you wanted, Vigar? You need nothing more from me and so you're gone!"

After her shouts died away, the silence was thick, impenetrable. She yanked the necklace over her head, threw it onto Vigar's grave, and ran.

She ran until she came to the wall, and then she fell, curling into a ball, as if she could squeeze into the empty space at her center.

Before her panting had quieted, Abisina knew that Vigar had come back—and was with her in the garden.

But the voice that spoke was real, not the ethereal voice of someone long dead.

"Abisina?"

For one glorious second, she was dazzled again—the sun glinting off his black hair, his bronze face, and broad frame. The word almost came to her lips: Father.

But the instinct drowned in the wash of anger that pushed her to her feet, ripped the words out of her throat, and blinded her to the pain in his eyes: "Get away from me! Get away!"

He stopped. "Abisina—"

"No!" She put her hands in front of her, warding him off. "Don't say anything."

"Please, Abisina. *Daughter.*"

"Don't call me that! Do you know what being your daughter"—she said the word as if it were a curse—"has meant to me? Bastard they called me! Dwarf-dirty! Demon!" She relished the anguish her words brought to his face. "Because of you, I was outcast. Spit on. They wouldn't even touch me. And they were right! I am a demon." She fixed Rueshlan with her green eyes. "I am a demon," she repeated. "I've got *you* in me."

She had expected—no, *wanted*—him to reel back, crushed. But now, with her greatest insult ringing in the air, he met her gaze steadily.

"No, Abisina. You are not a demon. Neither am I. I have many flaws, but I am not evil—as a man or a centaur. I am not Icksyon."

"Icksyon! Kyron! Rueshlan! It's all the same. You're all monsters! Perversions! And you're worse! You are a *shape-shifter*. Like Charach. And now that's part of me." She collapsed against the orchard wall. "And you *lied* to me," she choked out.

"Abisina, you are *Vranian*—"

"I don't want to be!" she yelled, back on her feet.

"But you were raised Vranian. I couldn't risk losing you. As I lost your mother. I thought you'd despise me—"

"I despise you for lying to me!"

"Abisina, please try to understand!"

But she rushed on. "I don't want your excuses. You left my

mother! You knew what Vranille was and you left!" It felt so good to yell and rant. She could no more stop the words than she could stop the shaking in her hands or the tightness in her chest.

When Rueshlan next spoke, his voice seemed to be pulled from deep within. "I know. I've thought the same thing every minute since you arrived in Watersmeet. If I had known about you, if I had stayed, if I hadn't been too proud to go back for your mother . . ."

"You never loved her, and you've never loved me. You've moved on. To Frayda."

Rueshlan took a step toward her. "This has nothing to do with Frayda. I loved your mother deeply—but I could never stay in Vranille. They would never have accepted me. And I had Watersmeet to think of. Sina felt she had to stay; she had work to do there."

"You should have come back. You should have tried harder."

"You're right," Rueshlan said. "But I was hurt. She had rejected me. Or that's how I felt. And she didn't even know that I was a shape-shifter."

"So you lied to her, too!" Abisina sounded triumphant, but it hurt to say it.

"I planned to tell her the truth." Rueshlan's words were labored. "I should have. . . . Abisina, your mother was different, but she was still Vranian. Would she have been able to accept who I am? Can you? When you came to Watersmeet, you were terrified of centaurs. With good reason. But I thought if you had some time to get used to me, if you could know *who* I am before you knew *what* I am . . . Abisina, I can't lose you again."

At his pleading words, Abisina's anger was replaced by a sadness that threatened to engulf her. She couldn't lose him either, but how could she love him—as a shape-shifter and a centaur?

Then Rueshlan's hand was there to hold her up, to pull her into his warm and solid embrace.

She fought for a moment. "No!" she whispered. "I hate you!" But his arms were strong, his tunic smelled of the Sylvyads, and his words were balm for her wounds.

"I love you, Abisina," he said, his voice rumbling through his chest. "You can hate me all you want, but I will always love you. I will always be your father."

Before they left the orchard, Abisina ran back to Vigar's grave and retrieved the necklace, warm and shining in the sun. As she slipped the chain back over her head, she heard Vigar's voice on the breeze: *When the time comes, you will know what to do.*

Abisina set out for Watersmeet with a lighter heart, wanting to think only of her father striding beside her and to hold on to this short time together. Rueshlan needed to return as soon as possible to oversee the preparations for the coming battle, but they stole time in the summer sun over long meals and built their evening fire before the sun had set. During the night, they slept under a carpet of stars.

Abisina tried not to think about their arrival in Watersmeet. Everyone would know why she had run. At the Council meeting, Alden had said that the Vranians were "hardly worth saving"; would they all see her now as Vranian? Would Alden and Glynholly and—Findlay?

As they drew closer, her anxiety increased, until Rueshlan stopped in the middle of the path. "What is it, Abisina? You've been picking up the pace for the last league. You're practically running."

"I—I think I'm ready."

"Ready?"

"Ready to—to see you as—to see your other shape." Her palms were sweaty and her voice quavered, but her jaw was set.

"You don't have to do this, Abisina," Rueshlan said after a pause.

"Yes, I do." She managed a tight smile. "Before we return."

Rueshlan took a step back but never looked away. She knew something was happening, sensed movement, but she kept staring intently into his eyes, saying over and over in her head, *This is my father. He would never hurt me.*

His face relaxed, though his eyes were nervous. "Well?"

Abisina braced herself for a wave of fear and revulsion

that never came. Rueshlan's transformation changed nothing about his torso, but his hips now disappeared into the muscular legs of a horse, as black as the hair on his head. Abisina looked at him—taking in his body, his flanks, his hooves, his tail. The light shone on his skin and rippling muscles. He took a few prancing steps backward on his impossibly slender ankles. His tail swished from side to side.

"Well?" Rueshlan said again, and Abisina saw that he was waiting anxiously for her response. "Are you all right?" he asked.

"Yes," she said quickly and realized she was. She smiled up at him as the relief spread across his face.

They walked together for a league—a centaur and a human beside him.

Abisina broke the long silence. "Do you feel *different* when you're one way or the other? I mean," she said, not sure if she might offend him, "I feel my toe sometimes, though it's not there. I was wondering, do you feel like a centaur even when you're not?"

"I never thought about it in those terms," Rueshlan said. "It's not that I 'feel like a centaur,' but there are certain situations when I am more myself as a centaur, while in other situations I am more myself as a man. In fact, that was how I discovered that I had the power to shape-shift. I was a little older than you are now—"

Abisina faced her father. "You *discovered* that you were a shape-shifter?"

"Yes, I was born just human, or so I thought. But when I reached sixteen or seventeen winters, as I grew into manhood—"

"Stop!" Abisina felt as if the air were being forced from her chest. "Don't say any more. I'm not ready for this."

"Not ready for what?"

"To think that this could happen to me." She watched understanding dawn on his face.

"Just because you're my daughter—"

"Your parents, were they shape-shifters?"

"I didn't know my parents," Rueshlan said softly.

Abisina started walking in agitation. *What if I*—she didn't want to finish the thought. She was just getting used to her father! But against her will, she searched herself, testing her legs, her hips, her feet—*Are there any signs?*

"Abisina," Rueshlan said behind her. "If you *are* a shape-shifter, you'll know—you'll know when it happens."

She slowed down, self-conscious. "How?"

"It was so long ago, I can hardly remember. I had been wandering in a forest for days—maybe weeks. I longed for sun, open air, and wind. And then I came to the end. The trees didn't even thin; they simply stopped and this green, undulating meadow began, shining in the sun. It was like another world. And I leapt into it—from the darkness of the forest into the light and air of the meadow. I was running and leaping and—I didn't even know it had happened. I just *was* a centaur, galloping toward the horizon.

"That's how it was for a while," Rueshlan continued, and Abisina could sense he was dusting off old memories. "I couldn't control it. I would just *be* a man, or just *be* a centaur. Sometimes I went to sleep as one and woke as the other, as if I needed the other shape in my dreams."

"Did it scare you?"

"I wanted to control it, I remember that. I never knew what was going to happen next. But I wasn't scared, because it always felt right—the shape fit the moment. And I learned I *could* control it. If I was a centaur and for some reason I wanted to be a man, I would imagine myself doing something man-like. The easiest was sitting. Centaurs don't sit, so if I imagined sitting, I'd be a man." Rueshlan chuckled. "I had forgotten all about that. I'm not even conscious of wanting to change now."

They walked on, and Abisina's fears receded. But as she curled up in her cloak by the fire that night, she couldn't help but think, *Please, don't let me be a shape-shifter!*

When they arrived at Watersmeet the next evening, Abisina could barely keep her feet moving across the root bridge. *I hope no one is around*, she thought. *Let them all be at the Council House or supper or something!*

But as she followed Rueshlan, now a centaur, into his

ward, a crowd met them: somber dwarves, fauns, and humans talking in hushed tones. In the center stood Kyron, flanked on either side by more centaurs, and it was on him that Abisina focused.

Someone called, "Rueshlan! Abisina!" Was it Frayda? Abisina didn't turn to the voice. She knew what she had to do.

Without giving her fear time to catch up, she walked past Rueshlan. The distance seemed to grow longer with each step. The crowd stepped back, clearing a path, but she saw only Kyron—his thick roan legs, his taut torso, his red beard on his chest.

When she finally reached him, she couldn't speak, but she met his blue eyes. She was surprised to find that he looked—nervous.

"Rueshlan's daughter! I—I—"

Abisina fought the urge to shrink back. "Kyron," she managed and summoning all her strength, she held out her hand. She felt the stares around her as Kyron grasped her forearm in the centaur greeting. The strength of his grip sent a tremor through her, but she refused to look away; instead she returned his firm grasp.

"Welcome, Abisina." There was relief in his voice.

"I—I owe you an apology," she stammered into the deafening silence.

"There is no need to apologize." Kyron smiled.

Rueshlan put one hand on Kyron's shoulder and another

on Abisina's. He looked from one to the other, beaming. The crowd let out its breath.

"They must eat!" A scratchy voice broke the stillness, followed by a voice that Abisina immediately recognized.

"They've just gotten here," Haret growled. "Give Rueshlan a moment to consult with his advisors!"

Glynholly, who Abisina now realized was standing next to her, stepped aside to let into the circle a dwarf with long red hair and a wooden spoon clutched in her hand. Haret was right behind her.

Abisina was glad for the distraction. Her cheeks still felt hot, but her heart was beginning to slow down. *I did it*, she told herself. *Not very gracefully, perhaps, but I faced Kyron. Now for the rest*. She looked at the folk around her: Glynholly, Alden, Frayda, Neiall, and others she recognized from parties, celebrations, and Gatherings. Did they see her as the girl who ran from her own father? Someone with the blood of Vranille in her veins? She saw frank smiles and open faces. There would be some—the centaurs particularly—for whom it would take more time. She could face that, too. For now, there were no reprimands, no reproaches. Just acceptance.

"Abisina?" She looked up to find her father smiling at her. "We've been invited to have supper with Breide here. She has some fine wild rabbit stew waiting for us—"

"And anyone else who needs it!" the redheaded dwarf cried, looking triumphantly at Haret.

Breide's tone and accent were so like Hoysta's, Abisina couldn't help but grin.

They set off through the Sylvyads, Breide in the lead. Many more joined their group to cry out greetings to Rueshlan and Abisina. Before they reached Breide's ward and her steaming stewpot, Haret fell into step next to Abisina. "I don't know why he's humoring her," he grumbled. "Alden told her to leave Rueshlan alone, but she insisted."

"You like her!" Abisina pronounced, looking at her friend.

"What?" Haret exploded, his eyebrows lowering like a thundercloud. "Don't be ridiculous, human! She's Alden's daughter!" But now his cheeks were red.

"You do!"

"If you say one more word," Haret warned, but Abisina didn't need to—one sidelong look was enough to send Haret off into another bluster of "Ridiculous humans!" and "The idea!"

Breide had just handed Abisina a bowl of delicious-smelling stew when Meelah came hurtling out of nowhere, throwing her arms around Abisina and almost knocking her over.

"We were so scared!" she cried. "We thought you'd been taken by the überwolves!"

Abisina tried to hug Meelah back, balancing her brimming bowl. Findlay came up behind his sister. "She was scared," he agreed, and then added, "So was I."

Abisina smiled at him before burying her face in Meelah's embrace.

For a moment, sitting there cross-legged on the ground between Findlay and Meelah, eating wild rabbit stew, listening to the hum of conversation from those crowding Breide's ward, Abisina felt again that she was *home*.

But then Glynholly's voice reached her. The faun was speaking to Rueshlan, and her words brought Abisina back to reality.

"—another hundred swords, and now we're waiting for word from the fairies—their eagles will have news about the movements of Charach's army."

Watersmeet was going to war.

CHAPTER XVII

DURING THE NEXT TWO WEEKS, RUESHLAN AND THE COUNCIL talked strategy; the centaurs combed the forest to recruit wild donkeys and stags to carry gear; the forges glowed far into the night as dwarf blacksmiths made and repaired swords and axes; teams gathered to string bows and fletch arrows; fairies arrived and left with news gathered by their eagles; and everyone honed their peacetime fighting skills to the sharpness needed for war.

Abisina joined in the preparation, assigned to work with Frayda's archers after Haret told about her saving him from the minotaur in Vigar's garden—much to her embarrassment and her father's delight. Abisina was amazed at the feeling of camaraderie she found working with a host of archers: the teamwork, the strategy that depended on all doing their part. She made several friends—another revelation—particularly with a dark-skinned, curly-haired girl named Elodie who stood near her in the ranks. Elodie's ready laugh and immediate acceptance put Abisina at her ease and their friendship grew quickly.

She also discovered just how good her skills were. Frayda quickly recognized Abisina's superior marksmanship and ability to weigh all the elements that might affect an arrow's flight. Frayda asked her to work with some of the younger archers, and Abisina loved sharing the gift that had given her such comfort during those lonely days in Vranille. One afternoon, after the archery drills were over for the day, Glynholly took her to the row of rings used in the archery contest. Abisina managed to shoot through all but one. When the faun brought Abisina back for dinner, she told Rueshlan how his daughter had done. "I'll warn Frayda!" the faun said in mock dismay. "This young woman will soon be challenging both of us for title of best archer in Watersmeet!" Then Glynholly turned serious. "She'll be a great help in the coming battle."

But that night, Abisina decided that she could not join the battle. She had tossed in bed for what felt like hours, before finally getting up. Voices came from one of the sitting rooms, and she crept toward them, peeking through the half-closed door. A single candle sat on the mantel, lighting Rueshlan as he stood facing the cold fireplace. Frayda sat on a chair nearby staring at his back.

"Remember Vigar!" Rueshlan's voice was laced with agitation.

"Of course," Frayda replied. "But you don't have to do it her way."

"What if I'm asked to make the same choice?" He turned to Frayda. The worry on his face made Abisina bite her lip.

"There are no 'same choices,' Rueshlan. You are not Vigar."

"But I am *Keeper*." He started pacing. "Vigar's life bought us years of peace. She was willing to die for that—and I was, too—before Abisina came. I would have traded my life easily if it meant Watersmeet would endure for even another generation. I cannot do that now. But Charach must be stopped. For Abisina, as much as for Watersmeet. . . . There is no other way."

Abisina had heard enough. She slipped away to lie awake until dawn. She knew she could not watch her father die.

She told Haret of her decision the next day. Rueshlan was out inspecting the stag herd with Kyron, and Findlay was expected any minute; he had said he wanted to show her his new sword. Abisina and Haret sat at a window above the River Fennish as the evening breeze stirred the surface of the water. The sun had slipped behind the trees, but the air was still warm and humid.

"Human! You're not listening," Haret said.

"I am!" Abisina insisted. Then, "Wait, what did you say?"

"I said that we are at most a week away from being ready to go."

"A week?" Abisina had been slumped in a chair, but now she sat up. "You'll march to meet the fairies in a week?"

"The weaponry is all but ready, as are the provisions. We're waiting for Torden to bring in more supply animals. That should take two or three days. I'd say *less* than a week."

"But Haret!" Abisina cried. "How can I say good-bye now?"

"Good-bye?" Haret stared at her.

"I can't go back there, Haret! I can't watch my father—or anyone from Watersmeet—destroyed by Charach."

"But human, Charach must be stopped."

Her father's words. "Then let's stop him from coming through the Col!" At Haret's dark look, she defended herself: "It's not such a bad idea. He can stay on the other side of the mountains with the Vranians! They deserve each other!"

Haret's eyebrows came together dangerously. "And Hoysta? What about her? Or the fauns we watched dance in the clearing? Do they deserve Charach?"

"I didn't mean—"

"I have hated the Vranians as you have, human." Haret's voice was flinty. "They have hunted the dwarves like beasts, destroyed Stonedun—what you call Vrandun—and started a war with centaurs that has affected all of us in the south. But I've learned something, and it was you who taught it to me. When I returned from the Mines, I hated myself. But you wouldn't listen. You reminded me that I had saved you from Icksyon. 'No one deserves what the centaurs were going to do to me,' you said. And I say the same to you now. No one deserves Charach."

"But the Vranians—"

"Human! Haven't you been listening? Your father has told you about Vigar. Don't you understand what Watersmeet stands for? You more than anyone know the dangers of casting out folk! I thought you understood—when you came back from Vigar's garden with your father—I hope I wasn't wrong."

Before she could stop him, Haret was gone. At Abisina's age, her mother had already left home to help free her people from the tyranny of Vran. Even after she had lost so much— Filian who had opened her eyes, Rueshlan whom she loved, her hope for her daughter's future—Sina worked to help ease others' pain. Not just with her healing, but working with all the people who did what little they could against the Elders. Wasn't Abisina being asked to continue her mother's work?

But she had watched her mother pulled from the wall of Vranille! She couldn't live through that again with her father.

The day before the army departed, Abisina still hadn't told her father that she would stay in Watersmeet. She had finished target practice and sat picking at her lunch of cheese, bread, and greens when Rueshlan burst through the door.

"What is it?" she asked, startled at the flush on his face.

"Do you want to ride?" he asked abruptly.

"Ride?"

"It may sound strange, but sometimes, when my mind is swimming in details and plans and questions—galloping across the open space, feeling the wind . . ." His words faltered as he took in Abisina's stunned expression.

But she caught herself. "Y-Yes. I want to."

"Truly? You do?" His face lit up and Abisina smiled, though her heart was in her throat.

Without waiting another minute, Rueshlan transformed. It was especially strange to see him as a centaur in their house, but Abisina approached him, staring up at his back high above the ground.

"Put your left foot here," Rueshlan said, reaching out a hand for her to step into. "That's it!" he called as she stepped from his hand onto his back. For a split second she was on Drolf again, Surl ready to wind vines around her. But before the fear had a chance to burrow in, her father's laugh rose from deep within him and the fear drained away.

"Are you ready?"

"Ready."

"Then hang on!" he called, and they were ducking through the doorway, leaping out of the ward and onto the root trails, flying through Watersmeet. Faces turned, folk called out as they cantered by, but she didn't wave or answer, too focused on keeping her balance. As they clattered over the bridge and onto the banks of the River Deliverance, she began to relax. She listened to the thunder of Rueshlan's hooves and

watched the blur of trees rushing past. She felt the exhilara-
tion of speed. At some point she grinned, and then laughed,
and Rueshlan's own laughter rang out again, his bass joining
her higher tones. It was their laughter that drove all other
arguments from her mind. She would go to the Col. She
could not leave her father again.

The next morning dawned clear and hot. Abisina stared at the
faces around her. Less than a month earlier these same fauns,
now grim and dressed for battle, had flown through the wards
with flaming torches to usher in the Midsummer. These
dwarves, belts bristling with weapons, had sung hilarious
songs around the fire. Frayda, bow slung over her shoulder,
ebony hair braided down her back, had welcomed Haret and
Abisina to Watersmeet without question and led them to the
Gathering. Charach had transformed these merry folk into
warriors.

But they were a mighty force. Five hundred dwarves and
five hundred humans, two hundred centaurs; each in charge
of two stags and one or two wild donkeys laden with food,
weapons, and supplies. There were also six hundred fauns, but
they were impossible to count, blending into the trees around
them with leaf-woven tunics and branch headdresses. And
when this host arrived at the Motherland, there would be
another three hundred fairies.

They set off to the tune of chain mail clinking, arrows rat-
tling in quivers, harnesses squeaking. The dwarves marched in

several single-file lines, each stepping into the footprints of the dwarf ahead. Haret explained to Abisina that this method was used to confound enemies' estimates of how many dwarves were ranged against them. The fauns appeared at times to report to Rueshlan that a donkey had twisted its leg or that a fallen tree was blocking the route. The centaurs and their charges followed pathways through the woods that were invisible to Abisina. While Rueshlan trotted up and down the ranks, she walked with Findlay or Elodie or Haret on a route carefully mapped out for speed and efficiency. Even with this planning, it would take at least three weeks for a force of this size to reach the Motherland.

On the third afternoon of the march, as Rueshlan walked with Abisina and Haret, Glynholly appeared with a scowl on her face.

"What could possibly make you angry this early in the march?" Rueshlan asked.

"Meelah," Glynholly answered. "Kyron spotted her marching with the dwarves, wearing one of their hauberks. I'm amazed she kept up as long as she did!"

Before Rueshlan could answer, Kyron galloped up, holding the squirming Meelah, who wore a chain mail shirt that came to her ankles. The sight of the girl held by the centaur made Abisina tremble, but she didn't cry out.

"Meelah!" Rueshlan exclaimed as Kyron set her down. "What are you doing here? You were supposed to stay home with Breide!"

"I did stay with Breide!" Meelah protested. "I followed her right in the line like she told me to!"

Rueshlan looked puzzled until another voice reached them.

"Put me down! I am perfectly capable of walking myself!" A gray centaur rode up with an irate Breide in his grip, her fiery braids swinging as she tried to take a swipe at her captor.

She, too, was deposited at Rueshlan's feet, the gray centaur only too happy to put distance between himself and the feisty dwarf.

"Breide!" Rueshlan bellowed. "Did you bring this child on the march? You were to watch her *at home*. And what about Gilden? Don't tell me you dragged that venerable old dwarf—"

"Of course I didn't!" Breide defended herself. "I left him under my sister's care; she's as capable as I am—almost. I had to come! And then when Meelah discovered I was going, she insisted on tagging along—"

"Rueshlan, I can help!" Meelah chimed in. "I'm only a little younger than Abisina—well, three or four winters—"

"At least five," Rueshlan corrected her.

"—and I won't go near the battle. I'll stay back with Breide and cook and tend the wounded. Oh, Rueshlan! Mama and Findlay are here, and I had to do *something* to save Watersmeet!"

Rueshlan's eyes softened, but his voice remained stern. "You leave me no choice. I can't spare someone to go back with you, and it's not safe to send you back on your own."

"Not that they'd even go," Haret muttered under his breath.

"Breide," Rueshlan continued, "Meelah will be in your care. You must keep her *away* from the battle—with the water carriers and the healers. I need her mother with the archers and I need Findlay's sword. I can't imagine what you were thinking, letting a child come to war!"

Breide shifted her weight uncomfortably; for once she had nothing to say.

Though she was often near Rueshlan, Abisina tried to avoid hearing the updates that scouts brought to him—the latest reports from the fairies or the estimates of Vranian swordsmen and archers—but she could never stop thinking about the advancing Vranians. There were still some in Rueshlan's army who argued that they should fight to hold the Col rather than seek Charach, and though she knew her father would never agree, Abisina guiltily hoped they might sway him. She even tried to say as much to Findlay. They were in the second week of their march, walking along the margin of a dense forest, coolness seeping from the trees into the warmth of the afternoon. The sun hung at their backs, herding their shadows in front of them.

"I don't think Glynholly is convinced that we should meet the Vranian army," Abisina began tentatively. "She thinks we can hold the Low Col—well, indefinitely."

"I've heard her say that," Findlay replied. "Some of the

dwarves agree. If we can hold Charach off long enough, they think they can build earthworks to defend the Col with a small band. But Rueshlan—and the fairies—are absolutely against it."

"Are you?" Abisina asked.

"Of course," he said with conviction. "For one thing, if we only hold the Col, we risk the fairies making a treaty with Charach. And even if they didn't and we *could* hold the Col, that's not what we're about, is it? Those folk on the other side—they need us. If we stop at the Col, we'd be sacrificing them to Charach."

Abisina took out her water skin, sipped the mossy-tasting water they had collected at the last stream, and put it back over her shoulder without answering. But the light of the sun on Findlay's blond hair triggered the anger she had not been able to erase. "They were ready to sacrifice *me*," she said.

The bitterness in her voice made Findlay stop. "What?"

"The people of Vranille," she said, looking at him, "people who all had hair and skin like yours—they were ready to sacrifice me to Charach."

"Abisina, I'm s—"

"What do you know about them, Findlay? What do any of you know about the Vranians?"

"I know it was bad—" Findlay tried to say, but again, Abisina cut him off.

"Bad? They killed babies, Findlay! Innocent babies. They killed my mother after she had cared for every last one of them—saving their lives from fevers and snake bites, easing the pain of the dying. She had to blackmail one of the Elders to keep me *alive*. My crime? I didn't look like Vran. I didn't look like *you*."

He dropped his eyes at the barbs in her words. Abisina steeled herself and went on. "It's easy for all of you to say, 'Save the Vranians!' But they're not worth the loss of one of your lives, Findlay. Not one."

Abisina pushed past him, catching the hurt in his face as she did. It was so clear to him: the right thing to do. But he was wrong! He had to be!

She still saw Findlay's face before her as she rushed on, but then it changed. The brown of the eyes lightened to blue, the shock of blond hair flopped forward to cover his right eye, and it was Corlin she saw. Corlin, who had distracted the boys who were after her with their sticks and rocks. Corlin who had saved her.

Abisina's steps slowed. Would she ever feel the way her mother felt—that there was enough good in Vranille to make it worth saving?

She reached the top of a rise, a little valley spreading out below her. There, like a beacon in the advancing darkness, she saw a yellow braid snaking down a girl's back. It was Meelah, but all Abisina could see was Lilas.

About three weeks after the army left Watersmeet, the weather turned cooler in the evening and morning—a glimpse of the coming autumn. Abisina and Elodie sat around the breakfast fire with bowls of hot soup. They had spent more time together since she and Findlay had argued. She appreciated Elodie's lighthearted chatter as much as the girl's intuition about when to leave Abisina alone with her thoughts. This morning her thoughts completely absorbed her; in two days they would reach the Motherland, and a day after that, the Low Col.

"Abisina?"

She looked up to see her father—who was always a centaur now, except at night around the fire. "I've said your name at least three times. Where were you?"

She shrugged, giving him a tight smile.

"When you finish, I'd like you to come with me," he continued. "I'm going to do some scouting."

"Do you mind, Elodie?" Abisina asked.

"I'll walk with Meelah," Elodie replied. "She said she wanted me to help her make a bow, but I think she just wants to get away from Breide!"

Rueshlan chuckled, and Abisina got to her feet, leaving her breakfast untouched. "I'm not really hungry."

He nodded. "I didn't eat mine either."

They headed south, Abisina riding, as they climbed a ridge that the army had to skirt and then descended to a hidden valley. Farther south, the jagged peaks of the Obruns stood against the sky, lower than their brethren to the west, but still formidably high. To the east, a low ridge of hills marked the horizon.

Since midday, Abisina had seen tension growing in

Rueshlan's face. Now, he sounded weary. "Let's sleep here tonight," he said as Abisina slid to the ground.

"Why?" she asked. It was well before sundown.

Rueshlan, transforming into a man, pointed to the low hills in front of them. "Behind those hills, our army will set up camp. There is a plain bordered by streams—a perfect place. In another day we will be at the Motherland, and my attention will be wholly on Charach and the coming battle. For one night, I want to be Rueshlan, your father."

Abisina nodded, afraid to trust her voice.

They said little all evening. As darkness fell, they sat near the fire, its low hiss mingling with cricket song and the babble of the nearby stream; Abisina heard only the silence between them. When they stretched out on the grass, feet toward the fire, ready to sleep, Rueshlan's sigh reached Abisina through the darkness.

She sat up and Rueshlan did the same. "I think you'd better tell me," she said. "Tell me what happened to Vigar. What might happen to you."

Rueshlan drew a long breath and said, "What we know about Vigar—much of it—we don't understand. I can't tell you what it might mean for me. I don't know if it will help to hear—"

"Vigar died because of Charach. So did my mother. You now go to face him. I need to know it all."

After a pause, he began the story. "When Vigar arrived at Watersmeet—"

"From where?"

"She and her people came down the Mountains Eternal."

"Like Vran . . ." Abisina murmured.

"Yes, I noticed that, too. Both Vran and Vigar are responsible for bringing humans back into this land; there had been none, in the south or north, for generations. But Vran and Vigar couldn't be more different. The Mountains Eternal invite myth-making. In my experience—"

"You've been there?"

"Yes, but that story will have to wait"—in the low light, Abisina could hear the laughter in Rueshlan's voice—"at least, if you want me to tell you about Vigar."

"I'm sorry. No more interruptions."

Abisina settled back, her arms around her knees, and Rueshlan continued.

"When Vigar arrived at Watersmeet, it was a frightening place. The folk in the forest surrounding it told stories of malevolent spirits that lived among the Sylvyads. But Vigar saw only shelter. There were terrible beasts around then; Charach was the worst of them. Where he came from is a mystery, but he brought with him creatures who loved evil as much as he did: minotaurs, trolls, hags, überwolves, and other strange beings who embraced darkness. Some folk native to this land joined him, too. The Great Earthquake that destroyed the Obrun City brought ruin for everyone. The fauns and the centaurs who had lived together peacefully now competed for scarce food. And then the dwarves showed up, survivors of the Obrun City—more competition. Some joined Charach because they were drawn to his evil, others because he was strong and they were afraid."

"But in Vranille, he told the people he would 'defeat the beasts,'" Abisina said.

"He knew how to manipulate the Vranians. Just as he manipulated those around Watersmeet before Vigar. They had been divided for too long."

Abisina pulled a goat-hair blanket around her shoulders, suddenly cold.

Rueshlan went on. "I can imagine a young faun or an old centaur, driven in to Watersmeet, desperate to escape the gnashing teeth of an überwolf or the horns of a minotaur. But instead of death among the trees, Vigar was there. As the stories got out, folk began to say that Vigar was a powerful new sorceress or the priestess of a new god, and that she would defeat Charach. She always insisted she was simply a woman, but who's to say?" Rueshlan shrugged. "Maybe it doesn't matter."

He was no longer talking to Abisina, but to himself. "For the coming battle—do I carry some strength that will rise when I need it, or is there something out there that will come to our aid? I know what is said about me—that I am some kind of demigod because I have lived long, because I am both man and centaur. But is any of this power real or does it just flow from their belief?"

After a moment, Rueshlan looked at his daughter.

"What was I saying?"

"You were talking about the stories of Vigar," Abisina replied, glad to have him back again.

"Yes, that's right. Vigar's followers grew, and Charach worried. This new community had to be destroyed. But it was impossible to attack Watersmeet. He tried to lay siege, but there are so many places to climb or paddle ashore for supplies. At last, he found a weakness: the Sylvyads' great thirst. Dam the rivers and destroy Vigar's stronghold.

"His armies were given a new task: felling tree after tree. It took months and thousands of trees, but eventually he dammed all three rivers flowing into Watersmeet. With Charach's followers busy hauling logs and pulling down forests, it was easy enough to slip to the shore for food, but now they needed water, too. And their beloved Sylvyads began to show the strain. Leaves fell in showers, and in a high wind the groans were deafening. Finally, the oldest and largest tree, at the very center of the community, died. And when it died, Vigar knew something had to be done. Do you remember Sahnda's song?"

"I remember rushing water," Abisina said slowly, "and something about figures—is that right? Figures in the water?"

"Yes, and along the shore—naiads and hamadryads—the spirits that live in the rivers and the trees."

"We saw them—Haret and I!" Abisina cried. "South of the Obruns, we watched fauns dance, and the trees seemed to dance with them!"

"The fauns can call them up sometimes. But in those

days, the tree and water spirits didn't just look alive. They *were* alive—provoked, I suppose, by Charach, his arrogance that he could control the river and do it with the corpses of trees. One morning, Vigar took a stand in the muddy riverbed. She offered to spare Charach a great vengeance if he would leave the land immediately. He laughed. What great vengeance could this tiny woman bring? But he was also enraged at her boldness, and he gathered his army to capture Vigar. The stories say that his followers were afraid to stand below the swollen dams. Transforming into the White Worm, Charach compelled them.

"The second his claw touched Vigar's neck, the waters rose up with a great roar, alive with the figures of naiads, mouths open in screams, hands raised in fists. The wall of water towered high above the dam. And then it burst forth, deluging the army and Charach and Vigar, racing toward Watersmeet in a roiling, raging flood filled with trees and their spirits, naiads, minotaurs, überwolves, and—bodies. In Watersmeet, there was no time to react, nowhere to flee. Most simply sat transfixed as the flood raced toward them. A young faun, Glynholly's ancestor, who had crawled onto a root far upstream, survived to tell the story of Vigar's sacrifice. One of the naiads carried Vigar high above the crest of the waves. As the water was about to reach the faun's perch, Vigar cried out to the naiad who held her, 'Leave me! Destroy Charach!' The wave struck, and Watersmeet sustained great damage. The impact took out many of the already weak

Sylvyads, and many creatures did not survive. But it also swept away Charach and his army."

"The River Deliverance," Abisina said, understanding the name for the first time. "But what about Vigar? What happened to her?"

"This is where I come into the story. I was far downstream, having just come into this land."

"From where?"

"I was a wanderer then, Abisina. . . . I have seen many lands, been part of many histories, never staying anywhere for long—until I met Vigar."

"But—why?" Abisina sought her father's eyes in the low light of the fire.

"There are many Charachs in the world," Rueshlan said heavily. "They may not all resemble him, but they are out there. I'm sure some Charach drove the humans out of this land so long ago. And Vigar and her people were fleeing their own when they came down the Mountains Eternal. I did what I could to help destroy these monsters. At the time Vigar confronted Charach, I felt called to this land. I found Vigar. She had been carried far down the river, through the Obruns where her broken body washed against a boulder. I thought she was dead, but she still carried a whisper of life. As I lifted her carefully from the splinters of trees, she said: 'You heard my call! Now listen: Charach will return. Finish my work. Watersmeet.' Every word cost her what little energy she had left. 'Take my necklace,' she told me. 'They will know

I sent you.' The necklace seemed to catch fire, almost blinding me. When I opened my eyes again, her spirit had left her body.

"The necklace led me through the mountains where I built the garden and her grave. And then it led me to Watersmeet. I found the folk distraught, needing a leader—and when they saw the necklace around my throat, they accepted that it—or Vigar—had chosen me. As you've discovered, the necklace has a . . . a power. I don't know its origin. Vigar may have, though she told nobody. She brought it with her from over the Mountains Eternal. Perhaps its power enabled her and her people to survive a journey very few have ever made.

"The necklace represents rivers coming together—and it's made of Obrium. Did her people belong to this land, to Watersmeet itself, long ago? Was she leading them home?" Rueshlan stopped speaking, his questions hanging in the air.

Abisina held the pendant and studied the flawless metal. She had seen its power on her own journey. What else could it do?

Rueshlan got up and stirred the fire, throwing on more logs, while Abisina sat thinking of all that he had told her: his life as a wanderer, the treachery of Charach, the naiads and hamadryads rising up. But she always came back to Vigar's sacrifice. In the end, the necklace could not save her.

"How did Charach survive?" Abisina asked when

Rueshlan returned to sit near her.

"Beings like Charach are hard to destroy. Only Vigar came close—it's been more than three hundred years since she died."

"But her sacrifice was for nothing!" Abisina said. "This time, instead of trolls, he's got Vranians. And instead of Vigar, there's you. Now you're going to die to save us!"

"Abisina, I have to fight him—we all do. We have no choice."

"But why does it have to be you?"

"I am Keeper of Watersmeet. I swore an oath to defend it."

"He is not threatening Watersmeet! We don't even know if he'll come through the Col." It was Glynholly's argument, the one Findlay had rejected so completely, but she couldn't help herself. "Why do you have to go looking for him?"

"He will come for Watersmeet," Rueshlan said firmly. "He will not rest until he has reversed his defeat. If we let the fairies fight, they will be destroyed. Perhaps not at first. But eventually, he will destroy them. And then we will not be strong enough to defeat him. We have to meet him together."

"But what if he kills you?" Abisina whispered.

"I won't let—" Rueshlan began but stopped himself. "Vigar made a choice that I will not make. She was not a mother when she sacrificed herself. Knowing what might be asked of me, I chose not to be a father. But now I *am* a father. I must fight Charach, but I will fight to survive." Rueshlan's black eyes glinted in the firelight. "I cannot promise you how it will end. But I promise that I will fight."

Abisina woke in the chill before dawn and found Rueshlan crouched by the coals of the fire. As she joined him, he offered her a few pieces of dried meat, but she shook her head. "I don't think I could swallow it."

He put the meat back into his bag.

It took only a moment to stamp out the fire and pack the gear. They galloped through the dusky wood and into the hills that he had pointed to the night before, coming down the far slope to the edge of a stream as the sun rose.

Rueshlan slowed. "We should meet a sentry here some-where. The camp will be just—"

"Halt!"

He stopped short, and Abisina's heart pounded against her ribs.

A figure stepped from between two trees across the stream—a faun with an arrow pointed right at Rueshlan's chest. "Halt and answer to Rueshlan!"

This brought a loud laugh from her father. "I must always answer to Rueshlan!"

The faun peered toward his prey, his mouth a stern line. He wore a quiver full of arrows slung across his back, a sword and axe tucked into his belt, and a small dagger strapped around his upper arm. But in less time than it took Abisina to assess his weaponry, he dropped his arrow.

"Rueshlan! I couldn't see you in the shadows!" He laughed nervously, and Abisina realized that he had been as frightened as she was. He was a rather young faun, his horns just small nubs peeking through his reddish hair.

"So you drew the early morning shift, Ulian?" Rueshlan asked, and the faun blushed.

"It's my first time, and Glynholly thought I'd do less harm in the daylight."

Her father trotted forward and as the faun noticed Abisina, his blush deepened. "Hello, Rueshlan's daughter," he managed.

"You acquitted yourself beautifully in your first duty," Rueshlan said, and pride swelled the young faun's chest. "I'll be sure to mention it to Glynholly."

"Thank you, Rueshlan!"

They left Ulian to his sentry duty and trotted on to where the stream left the trees. Before them lay the valley floor dotted with campfires. Plump wild donkeys and noble stags grazed nearby as the host of Watersmeet gathered for breakfast.

"I don't know if I'm ready, Abisina," Rueshlan said, slowing to a walk. "When we ride back in there, I'm Keeper of Watersmeet again."

"And my *father*. As you said in Vigar's garden: you'll always be my father."

"You're right," he said, his voice husky. "I don't have to choose."

But as they rode into the camp, Abisina could not help asking herself, *Am I ready?*

Just after noon, the army arrived at the western border of the Motherland—an unbroken line of dark trees. Abisina was relieved that they would not actually enter the forest. The trees grew close together and were hung with moss. As they skirted the edge, she felt as if the trees were watching her, ready to bar her way if she were to enter. She was sure they were *alive*—like the Sylvyads—but she didn't want to touch them. Even walking in their shadows cast a pall over Watersmeet's forces.

Lohring and several of her advisors appeared in camp that evening, materializing out of the darkness as Breide ladled out a dinner nobody wanted. The fairy army would be there in the morning to begin the climb to the Col.

As night settled, the camp had none of the usual hum of conversation, the songs of fauns, or even the sound of swords being sharpened. Everyone sat quietly, tension etched on each face around the fire. Elodie looked uncharacteristically serious. Meelah rested her head against Findlay's shoulder, brow furrowed. Findlay stared fixedly at a point on the ground. Abisina both wanted to catch his eye and avoid it; they still had said little to each other. Haret sat near Breide, brooding, and even Breide's irrepressible chatter was stilled. Alden, Frayda, Glynholly, Kyron, Torden—all settled into moody silence. Rueshlan sat alone. He had consulted with Lohring and the generals throughout dinner, but the fairy had returned to her own camp, somewhere deep in the trees, and there were no details or strategies left to review.

He looked so lonely. Abisina went to her father and put her hand in his. She knew that his thoughts matched hers: this time tomorrow, they would be on the Vranian side of the Obruns. The fairy scouts estimated it would be several days before they would meet the Vranian army, but crossing those mountains marked the end of something. There had been a lot of pain in the months—almost a year!—since Abisina had fled Vranille, but there had been joy, too. More joy than she had ever known. Tomorrow she would return to the tyranny of Vran. What would it cost her this time?

The heaviness of the camp's mood was reflected in the morning's weather. A low bank of clouds had rolled in, bringing a misty rain that woke the army from their uneasy sleep. As Elodie and Abisina stumbled out of their bedrolls, they saw Lohring standing in front of the curtain of trees, hands on her hips, head thrown back. On either side of her were four more fairies, all carrying shining swords and longbows. Glancing toward the trees, Abisina saw no one, but she felt sure that the full fairy army was concealed behind the trunks and branches.

They appeared moments later. She didn't see them step out of the shadows; they were just there. And then row upon row appeared behind the first. Abisina had to remind herself that the fairies were allies. Could there really be only three hundred?

Rueshlan was already striding forward to greet Lohring and her generals. Abisina took a few steps, not wanting to be separated from her father now that the time had come, but she stopped. He had promised she would ride with him through the Col; he would be back for her.

As Abisina crouched down to roll up her blanket, Findlay approached, holding out a piece of bread. "Breakfast?" he asked awkwardly.

Elodie mumbled something about needing breakfast herself and left them alone.

Abisina took the crust, knowing she would never be able to force it down.

"Abisina, I'm—"

"No, Findlay, *I'm* sorry."

"But you were right. It's easy for us to think we know what's best. Especially me. I've hardly been anywhere but Watersmeet. I've seen nothing of battle but a few skirmishes with überwolves. I want it to be so simple and clear, but it's not."

Abisina turned the bread over in her hand. "Maybe it *is* simple. My father—he sees what's right, and he acts. My mother did the same. But I don't see as clearly, and there is so much at stake. I think that is what's making me so me angry. I was—*am*—jealous of your certainty—of everyone's. But I won't take it out on you in the future," she added ruefully.

"Well, you can, if you need to," Findlay offered. "But maybe you could give me some warning next time?"

"I will," Abisina said, and she found herself smiling—a real smile she would not have thought possible when she had awakened in the rain.

It took all day to climb to the entrance of the Col. At midmorning, Abisina thought they must be close as they crested the peak under which they'd camped the night before. But ahead of them, across a barren plain, rose two more peaks with a low, even ridge between, like a swaybacked old horse: the Low Col. It had been described so many times, she knew it at once.

Compared to the jagged peaks stretching to the east and west, this level ridge did indeed look low and passable. But the terrain was steep and rugged, well above the tree line.

By late afternoon, Abisina and Rueshlan stood at the Col, Abisina on Rueshlan's back, ready to descend the southern slopes. Behind them snaked the long line of the army, footsore and subdued. Only the fairies, marching in their own formation to one side, looked unruffled by the demanding climb. All day, they had moved back and forth along the line of soldiers, Rueshlan conferring with captains and offering an encouraging word.

Now, he stood at the front of the column, ready to pass into enemy territory. A tremor passed through him.

"What is it, Father? Do you see something?"

"No." He sighed. "But down there, somewhere in that vast wilderness, Charach is waiting. I can feel his hate reaching toward me."

His tone was so despairing, Abisina panicked. "It's not too late to turn back! Glynholly's plan, holding the Col! We can still do that, can't we?"

"Daughter"—he reached back and took her hand—"it was always too late for Glynholly's plan. But I am glad you're with me."

And with that, Rueshlan took a step forward and they crossed the Low Col.

CHAPTER XVIII

ABISINA HARDLY CLOSED HER EYES THEIR FIRST NIGHT ON the Vranian side of the Obruns. She was not alone. The army simply paused in its march down the exposed slope, rolled up in their blankets, and waited for light. But Abisina couldn't have slept no matter how comfortable her bed. Every time she started to doze, she was sure that she heard the clank of armor or pounding feet.

She gave up all pretense of sleep when the dark sky began to lighten in the east. A few paces away, a tiny fire flickered. Lohring had just joined Rueshlan and Frayda to give them the most recent report. Straining to hear, Abisina caught Lohring's musical voice: "—the wooded terrain. At this rate, they will not reach the Col for six, maybe seven days."

"Then we have a little breathing space," Rueshlan concluded. "I've already asked Kyron and Alden to assay the land within two days' march of here. If there is any ground that will suit us, they will find it."

"That would leave four or five days then," Frayda mused. "I think the dwarves would have time for some earthwork—trenches, at the least."

"And the fairies will find the best tree-stands for our archers. We could even station ourselves along the path that the Vranians—"

"No, Lohring!" Rueshlan's commanding tone surprised Abisina. "We've talked about this before. Complete defeat of the Vranians is not our goal. Just Charach."

"I hope you do not underestimate the enemy, Rueshlan." The fairy was ready for an argument.

"Morning is here," he said, refusing to take up the fight. "The armies need to move."

With a quick nod, Lohring left the fire, and though Abisina watched, she lost her immediately in the tricky light before dawn. She knew the fairies were close by, but she hadn't seen where they had made their camp. She only knew it was not among the folk of Watersmeet.

Frayda left to oversee loading the arrows back onto the stags, and when she was gone, Abisina threw off her blanket and stood up, thankful to have some time alone with her father.

"Did you sleep?" she asked, warming her cold hands at the fire.

Rueshlan smiled. "No more than anyone. But as you heard,

we've made good time, and Charach's advance has slowed. We will be able to pick the place where the armies meet."

"Lohring sounded worried about the Vranians."

"Her numbers are small, and the fairies' Motherland lies just beyond the Col. She thinks I'm willing to be merciful because Watersmeet is not directly threatened."

"But she doesn't think mercy is wise, does she?"

"She is doubtful." Rueshlan studied Abisina for a moment. "But I have to do this my way. I will spare nothing to stop Charach, but I am not ready to sacrifice all the Vranians."

The army advanced to the base of the Obruns and into the forest. Kyron and Alden returned from their scouting with good news: between the wood through which Watersmeet's forces currently moved and the older, denser pine forest where Charach was delayed, there were several leagues of grassland. Where the wood and grassland met, Kyron and Alden had discovered a small rise of land on which they could place their archers. To the west, a finger of the forest reached into the grassy plain, providing cover and height for the fairy archers. The hills on the left and the trees on the right would protect the flanks of Watersmeet's army. If the dwarves dug trenches in front of the archers' and fairies' positions, the Vranians would be forced to attack Watersmeet at the front, allowing Watersmeet to take the preferable defensive role.

Less than two days after cresting the Low Col, the

Watersmeet army had marched to the chosen ground. And by the next morning, the dwarves had begun to dig trenches.

Haret thrived on this work: barking orders; wielding his shovel with such power that his hands blistered and bled; refusing to quit until Breide insisted he eat a bowl of soup. "It's as good as my grandmother's," Haret whispered to Abisina, "but don't tell Breide." As Abisina walked away, he shouted after her: "And should we find her again—don't tell my grandmother either!"

The discovery of a ruin less than a league from the battle-ground, back toward the safety of the mountains, further excited the dwarves. The ruin seemed to be a remnant of the Obrun City, thrust somehow aboveground by the Great Earthquake. It was hard to say what the building had been, as most of it was reduced to rubble, but there were a few stand-ing walls that provided some shelter from arrow flight. Haret and the other dwarves left the trench-digging in shifts to stand with earth in their hands and marvel at the small bits of stonework still intact.

Abisina tried to keep her mind off Charach's approach by studying the battlefield and the land around it. She talked archery strategy with Elodie constantly until the topic was exhausted. By the end of the second day at the battle site, Abisina had nothing left to do, nothing left to discuss, and her nerves were beginning to fray. Every few hours, a fairy arrived with an update on Charach's move-ments, but the reports changed little, and Abisina stopped listening to them. The dwarves still worked on the trenches, but Haret told her that she'd be no help in digging. "It's dwarf work," he said loftily. Breide had taken over the ruin and set up the healers and food preparation, but there was no one to heal yet and Breide allowed only a select few to work on meals. Meelah was always underfoot, but Breide knew better than to send her away. Abisina couldn't help but wish that *something* would happen. Anything had to be better than the waiting.

On the third day, she and Elodie were walking the eastern rise, discussing for the thousandth time how the Vranian army might approach and which shots would be most effective. Abisina had just said, "I think we've talked about every possibility, Elodie—" when a loud shout came from the brushy area on the far side of the rise. They looked at each other, and at a second shout, they set off running.

They were racing down the slope when Torden came charging in their direction.

"Did you hear that?" she called.

"Someone was shouting!" Abisina answered.

"It sounded like Ulian!" Elodie added as Ulian himself broke from the brush followed by two other fauns, who stopped at the sight of Torden and the girls. Both fauns looked unkempt: the male had a long, untrimmed beard, and the female's hair was tangled and matted.

"They're not from Watersmeet, are they?" Abisina asked.

As the centaur and the girls approached, the two new fauns bolted. But Ulian grabbed the male's arm before he got away, crying, "There's nothing to worry about. They're with me!" The male faun stopped struggling. The female ran off several paces before halting, unwilling to abandon her mate. "Really, they won't hurt you," Ulian urged, and Torden, Abisina, and Elodie threw down their weapons to show they meant no harm.

The female took a few steps toward them, tugging on her dark hair. "The tales are true, Darvus?" Her eyes darted from face to face. "They are here together—fauns, centaurs, and humans?"

"And dwarves and fairies!" Ulian added so vigorously that the female retreated again.

"Then you're not with the White Worm and his army?" Darvus whispered, peering around furtively as if Charach hid nearby. "It's *him* we're running from. We thought you were one of his captives. Erna and I were trying to rescue you," he told Ulian.

Ulian had to fight a smile. "No, we're not with them," he reassured the new fauns. "In fact, we've come over the Obrun Mountains to stop the White Worm."

"Erna! It's the stuff of legends!" Darvus cried. "An army from the other side of the mountains!"

Darvus and Erna were the first of a stream of fauns, dwarves—and a few centaurs—refugees from Charach, each with a new story of his terror.

Charach and the Vranians had been moving steadily northeast toward the Low Col, destroying the country as they went, and driving before them the folk who had once called the forest their home. One dwarf explained that the White Worm's skin oozed a poison that wiped out anything living on the land. "We'll never be harvesting roots there again, my friend," he said to Haret, shaking his head sadly. "And the creatures with him! Minotaurs driven by hags, huge wolves that can walk on their hind feet, trolls—great, scaly things that ten men keep in chains so they don't gorge on the creatures who are supposed to be their allies!"

A centaur brought tales of Icksyon and his band. They had taken up with Charach's army, fanning out to capture deserters who tried to slip into the trees. "I know what the Vranians have done to us, destroying our sacred places"—the centaur shook his head—"but I don't see how my brothers and sisters can join the Worm."

If any of the folk from Watersmeet still believed that Rueshlan's forces should simply defend the Col, the refugees changed their minds. Watersmeet was now united in the belief that Charach must be destroyed, and some even questioned Rueshlan's offer of clemency to the Vranians. If they could stand with Charach, how could they be forgiven? The fairies encouraged this line of thinking, but Rueshlan stood firm against it.

Once the stream of refugees started, Abisina spent as much time as she could at the dwarf ruin with those who needed rest and healing. Here, she kept her hands busy and her mind off the coming confrontation. Abisina spent hours making comfrey poultices, wrapping wounds, and offering yarrow tonics to those whose nightmares kept them from getting the rest they needed. The work didn't just keep her worries at bay; it felt good to twist a bandage or brew a tonic as her mother had taught her. As she fell asleep on their fourth night at the battlefield, her hands smelled like Sina's.

Abisina was at the ruin showing Meelah how to tie an arm sling when one of Alden's cousins bustled up to her and insisted she come with him immediately. She agreed—indeed, the dwarf refused any other answer—but no matter how many times she asked him why she was needed, he only said that Haret sent him and it was supposed to be a surprise.

She followed him back toward the main camp where a familiar voice rose from a cluster of folk: ". . . saw them coming and hid in a thicket till they passed. Had my axe, of course, but didn't think it was wise to take on all six. Four, I could've done!"

"Hoysta!" Abisina cried and ran forward, slipping through the crowd.

And there she was—standing next to a beaming Haret in the center of the circle, an enormous axe tucked in her belt.

"Dearie!" she cried with a now toothless grin. It was clear

that the last few months had been rough on her: she had bruises on her face—some old, some newer—and a gash on her leg. Her animal-skin tunic was rubbed bare in places, her boots were tied on with a bit of rawhide, and she stooped more. When Abisina threw her arms around the old dwarf, Hoysta felt thinner, but she held Abisina as tightly as ever. "Now don't cry, dearie," Hoysta said, patting her back. But it was too late.

"Let me look at you," Hoysta said, holding her at arm's length. "Grown so tall! You'd hardly fit in our entryway now. Not that any of us will be able to return to that dwelling."

"Destroyed?" Haret asked.

Hoysta grimaced. "Charach and his Vranians came through early in the raids, killing any creature who crossed their path. Had gone to offer my axe to folk northwest of us, but by the time I got there, they had already left. When I got home, the Worm had ripped out that tree—the one right at the entrance—and its roots pulled up the entry tunnel. Wanted to dig in and save anything left, but it was soaked in *his* poison." Hoysta ran a scarred hand under her nose and sniffed in disgust. "Nothing left for me there, so I took up with the other dwarves moving east, looking for any chance to take a stand against the Worm." She reached out to Haret. "Had to trust that somehow we would find each other, if we survived—and here we are! You made it to Watersmeet, dearie, and *you* found your father!" Hoysta looked from Haret to Abisina, smiling broadly.

"Is this the Hoysta I heard so much about?" Rueshlan's voice rolled over the group, and the folk stepped aside to let him pass. He was in his human form, and Hoysta's eyes widened as they traveled up Rueshlan's body to his face. "Oh, dearie," she said to Abisina, "you're going to be *very* tall!"

Laughing, Rueshlan got down on his knees and took Hoysta's grimy hands in his. "Thank you," he said, his voice shaking, "for saving my daughter and sending her to me."

A flush crept up Hoysta's cheeks. She had just drawn in a great breath to launch into her response when Kyron galloped up, his flanks in a lather. "Rueshlan! We've captured some Vranians!"

Rueshlan jumped to his feet. "Soldiers?"

"Deserters," Kyron said. "But they put up a good fight. We couldn't convince them we wouldn't hurt them. Granfeur took an arrow in the shoulder. It was the centaurs that really set them off. They calmed a bit when Neiall showed up, but one of them kept screaming 'Outcast!' at him."

The blood drained from Abisina's face. Her father's hand was there to steady her, but she stood strong. "Go, Father," she urged. "Find out what they know."

As Rueshlan followed Kyron, Abisina called out, "Wait! Bring Findlay with you!" Her father glanced back questioningly. "He looks Vranian," she added.

Abisina and Haret led Hoysta to the ruin for breakfast and so Abisina could tend to the hot, red cut on the dwarf's leg.

Hoysta said she longed for a true cave after "weeks crawling on the surface," but appreciated at least having stone walls around her. She told them about her journey east in detail. Abisina struggled to concentrate on the old dwarf's words, thinking of the Vranians now somewhere in the camp. Were any from Vranille? Kyron said that they were deserters, but what if they were spies? Would they take Rueshlan's offer of clemency?

"Human!" Haret shouted.

"What?"

"I said, 'Why don't you go to them, since that's all you can think about anyway.'"

"No. No," she said hastily. "Father will tell me who they are when he returns."

"Then go back to the main camp and wait for him."

"Go, dearie," Hoysta added as Abisina hesitated. "Haret will look after me."

But going back to the camp proved worse. With Hoysta and Haret she had some distraction. Now, she simply waited, and waited alone. Findlay had gone with Rueshlan, Elodie was at the ruin, and Abisina was too agitated to talk to anyone else. Finally, she headed to the archers' rise where she could pace back and forth on the hilltop.

And it was there that Rueshlan and Findlay approached her, climbing the slope as if they carried a heavy weight.

She searched their tired and grim faces. "What did they say? Are any from Vranille?"

"A few," said Rueshlan. "In fact, we wouldn't have gotten anywhere without one young man from there. . . . His name is Corlin."

"Oh!" Abisina's hand went to her mouth.

"There are about thirty of them. They wouldn't talk. I told them again and again that we had no intention of hurting them. I asked the centaurs to pull back into the trees, and Kyron went and got a few more humans—those who looked most Vranian." Rueshlan sighed. "I felt like one of their Elders, choosing people for skin and hair color! I had to move back myself—even though I was in my human form. When it was just Findlay, they started to talk. But let Findlay tell you. . . . He actually spoke to them."

"I spoke to Corlin," Findlay said. "None of the rest would say much. And Corlin was nervous, too. He didn't give me details. Mostly, he wanted to know what was going to happen to them. I explained that we wanted to help them, that we had come to defeat Charach, but I'm not sure he believed me. Abisina . . . I think you should talk to him."

"Me?"

"He knows you," Rueshlan urged, "and they may know something about what Charach is planning. It would give us an advantage. And more important, if we can convince them that we want to help them, we'll have a better chance with the others."

"But they hate me! They wouldn't talk to me in Vranille. Why would they talk to me now?"

"This is all so frightening for them. You're someone they at least recognize—"

"Yes, recognize as a demon!"

"Please, Abisina," said Rueshlan. "This Corlin could be critical to our success. I know how hard this is for you, but it's our best chance to save lives."

Abisina felt the fear hammering in her chest. Would she never be free? Would she always be tied to these people? But if it could save her father, save Watersmeet . . . she had to say yes.

Neiall and several other pale-skinned men—the Vranians ignored the women—had guided the thirty refugees to a clearing close to the dwarf ruin: a ragged group of skinny, unkempt people huddled together, casting fearful eyes toward the trees. The majority were men, with a few women, and some boys between ten and fifteen winters. There were no younger children. No girls.

Abisina barely recognized Corlin as he approached her and Findlay. He had a cut down the right side of his face, his blond hair was matted with dried blood, and he walked with a slight limp.

When he reached them, Findlay spoke first: "You remember Abisina, I think?"

Corlin nodded, without looking at her.

Abisina wanted only to get away, but she had a job to do. "Corlin, my fa—Rueshlan and all of us are here to try and stop Charach. Isn't that what you want?"

"Yes," Corlin said, still without looking at her.

"We need to know everything you know about him—and about the army. Rueshlan—my *father*—" She said it firmly this time.

Corlin's head snapped up. "Your father? You mean—"

"Yes." Abisina persisted. "My father doesn't want to kill Vranians. Charach is our enemy. We need to know if there are other Vranians who would fight against him."

Corlin sighed and touched the wound on the side of his head gingerly. "We didn't see it at first. Not clearly. We—I—" Corlin dropped his head.

Is he ashamed? Abisina wondered.

"I was blinded by his strength and his promises. We thought he was Vran." Corlin glanced toward Abisina then, to see if she understood. She remembered how she had felt when Charach first began to speak at the Ritual. He had described the "bestial" centaurs, the "demonic" fauns, and the "repugnant" dwarves so convincingly, her own stomach had churned in revulsion. For an instant, she too had suffered from Corlin's blindness. Corlin may have seen a glimmer of understanding in her face because he went on. "It got bad very quickly. First the killing of the outcasts, your mother—"

His eyes flitted to hers again, but this time there was no empathy there. "You're not telling me *that* changed people's minds, are you?"

"No," he said quietly. "For a while it even seemed to prove what we all wanted to believe—that Charach could bring us power over our enemies. We thought with Charach we would become what we're supposed to be . . . the Children of Vran." He shuddered as if the words tasted bitter. "He promised us an end to all the suffering—the hunger and disease. He was so sure! How could we not believe him?"

He looked directly at her, pleading.

He wants forgiveness, Abisina realized, and she was thrown into confusion. *He saved me once! Don't I owe him forgiveness? But the rest of them . . .*

He looked away as if he knew her answer.

"My mother didn't believe him," he said dully. "Not even that first day. She actually tried to shelter an outcast. Do you remember Delvyn? For years my mother had been helping her however she could. My mother tried to hide her. But she was discovered. And my mother had to feign happiness at her capture. It almost killed her. She would have died with Delvyn, but she didn't know what would happen to me—"

His blue eyes filled with tears, but he blinked them away. "Sorry," he mumbled. "I haven't told anyone that before." He continued shakily, "It wasn't until Vranians from other villages began to arrive that Charach's plan became clear. We wanted a respite from centaur attacks, more land to farm, but he had a different goal. A few men tried to tell Charach that we didn't want to go east. We never saw any of them again. And we also got our first look at Charach the Worm. He destroyed Vranille that day—all of it. Hundreds were killed. Others fled, but Charach had us hunted down. My mother was caught." Abisina waited for Corlin to pause again, but his voice had gone flat, as if he'd moved beyond emotion. "Charach only spared those who could fight. His army needed more soldiers." Corlin looked toward his companions. "He made sure we suffered, though, for trying to run.

"Soon after that he brought the centaurs in. He'd told us he would lead us against them, and then he *joined* with them—used them to control anyone who he suspected of rebellion. And when the minotaurs came . . ." Corlin shuddered again.

"How did you get away?" Findlay asked.

"We had nothing left to lose. We would slip away in the darkness, during a storm, or on a long march when the men loyal to Charach were too tired to notice. The centaurs were harder to evade, but some of us managed. We met other deserters in the forests, even some of the women who were brought to cook for the army. We've been shadowing them, building followers, hoping to make an attempt on Charach."

"So there are some who will leave him?" Findlay pressed.

Corlin shrugged, his eyes hollow. "As I said, we have nothing to lose anymore. There are some who would leave, but not for you. Not for them." He glanced uneasily toward the trees where he knew the centaur sentries were posted.

"What do you mean?" Abisina challenged Corlin to say it out loud, to call her an outcast, even now.

But he didn't take the challenge. His voice was barely a whisper. "Their homes are destroyed, their families ripped apart. For some of them, Charach and the army are all they've got. They force themselves to believe his promise of power. And even if they would leave—you know what it was like, Abisina." He looked at her again. "You know how the people of Vranille felt about . . . about"—he searched for a word that would not offend— "about the *creatures* of the land. My uncle was killed by a centaur. And, Kabe, do you remember him? The boy who was taken?"

Abisina nodded. The boy who could not be buried in the village burial ground.

"He was my cousin."

Tears threatened Corlin's voice once more, and Abisina spoke more gently. "But Corlin, these centaurs are different." She remembered how angry she had gotten at Haret for saying the same thing. "All that we were taught about dwarves and fauns—and outcasts—it was all lies. Like Charach's promises. . . . We have to convince them of that." She looked toward the knot of exhausted Vranians. "And then they can help us convince those who are still with Charach."

Corlin shook his head. "They won't believe it."

"Corlin, please. We need—*I* need your help. Again."

His brief nod told her that he remembered that last day in Vranille. "I can try to talk to them," he said finally. "It would be better coming from me."

But when Abisina returned several hours later, Corlin had made no headway. As she approached the refugees, one of the

Vranian boys ran toward her, fists raised. Neiall, who was with her this time, caught the boy and held back his hands, but not before he was able to spit in Abisina's face. "Outcast!" he screamed. "We'll never take help from you demons! Never! We're Children of Vran!"

That high, bitter voice, so familiar.

"Lilas?" Abisina gasped. And it *was* her—blonde braid shorn off, a feverish light in her eyes, skinny and grimy, but it was Lilas.

Hearing the shouts, two centaurs galloped from the cover of the trees. Corlin raced toward Lilas, shouting, "Please don't hurt her!"

But one of the centaurs caught up with him and held him back. "Are you okay, Rueshlan's daughter?" the centaur called.

A maniacal laugh filled the air. "Rueshlan's daughter? So the bastard has a father? And such a father! I've heard the truth!" Lilas's voice dropped to a hiss. "Four legs, hooves, and *tail*! Where are yours, Outcast?"

Abisina walked away as Lilas yelled hysterically behind her, "Where are yours? Where are yours?"

Abisina found her father and Kyron inspecting trenchwork by the fairy archers' stand. She needed to be near Rueshlan, to drown out Lilas's laughter ringing in her head. But as she approached them, a fairy leapt from the trees, landing next to Rueshlan.

"What is it, Mahnoa?" he asked, unruffled by the fairy's sudden appearance.

Abisina thought Mahnoa was male—but she was still having trouble understanding fairy gender. Lohring and her closest three or four advisors were often in the Watersmeet camp to talk to Rueshlan, but most of the fairies kept apart.

"We've caught a centaur," Mahnoa reported. "We would like Kyron to take him from our charge."

"Now?" Kyron asked. "I need to finish this inspection."

"He mentioned Icksyon. He may know something."

Rueshlan put a hand on Abisina's arm and said, "I'll go with Kyron."

Mahnoa began to lead them into the trees when Abisina called, "I'm going, too."

Rueshlan stopped. "Abisina, why would you want to—"

"I need to see this centaur, Father."

"Very well," Rueshlan agreed.

Abisina leapt onto Rueshlan's back, but with every step, her conviction grew weaker. She was on the verge of asking her father to let her get down, when a rough voice froze her words.

"My sister's one of his captains! She'll free me soon as she knows I've been taken!"

Drolf.

The brown centaur stood surrounded by five fairies. His chest was covered with hoof-shaped bruises, and he held one hind leg gingerly off the ground. Catching sight of Kyron first, Drolf cried, "Get them away from me! Is this how you treat a brother?"

Kyron spoke quietly, but sternly. "They will leave when we know we can trust you not to run. Do you know Icksyon?"

"'Course I know Icksyon! I'm in his herd! Well—my sister is."

"Where is Icksyon? Where is your sister?"

"They're—well, they're— Hey! I'm not tellin' you! I'm no herd-traitor—no matter what they done to me!"

Rueshlan came forward now, and Drolf stared at him, clearly awed by his size. He still hadn't noticed Abisina.

"Is that what's happened to you? Your herd turned on you?" Rueshlan asked.

The gentleness in his voice surprised Abisina. Could Drolf hear it?

"They didn't turn on me!" Drolf shouted, but he held his hands in front of his chest as if to hide the bruises. "I—I got what I had comin'. I let a faun go. She was young, and cryin' for her ma—but I shouldn't've done that! I should've waited for Surl to come back!"

Abisina couldn't listen anymore. She refused to pity Drolf. She remembered him wiping blood away from her nose when she'd said it was bleeding—but she fought this memory, too. She had faced Drolf to put her fear behind her. But instead she was plunged into more confusion. *Certainly Drolf deserves to be punished! And Lilas!* she told herself, even as doubt settled in.

The next morning, a centaur returned from a reconnaissance ride with a report of Vranian scouts moving through the woods two and a half leagues to the south. The centaur hadn't been able to get a clear shot at them, but this news confirmed what the eagles and the steady flow of refugees had been telling them for days: Charach and his army were very near.

Rueshlan immediately dispatched an embassy of parley. He sent Lohring, Glynholly, Kyron, and Findlay. Findlay confided in Abisina that he was both honored and petrified. Abisina took his hand. She was petrified, too.

As the embassy prepared to leave camp, each carrying an oak branch to symbolize their mission, a faun trotted up with Corlin in tow. "Rueshlan, wait! This refugee wants to go!"

Corlin looked up at Rueshlan, who towered over him in centaur form. "I don't think it will help," Corlin said. "They're mad with hate. But I'm willing to go. Sir."

Rueshlan reached out a hand and laid it on Corlin's thin shoulder. Abisina realized he was only a little younger than Findlay, but years of near starvation had left him much smaller, frailer.

"If—If I don't come back, you'll take care of the others?" Corlin peered back in the direction he had come.

"What do you mean, don't come back from a parley?" Glynholly spoke up, color rising to her cheeks. "They wouldn't dream of touching those who came to parley!"

"It's Charach," Corlin said. "And I'm a deserter."

"Don't you worry," Glynholly replied. "We'll take care of your people—and you."

Abisina watched them walk out of camp—the fluid movements of the fairy, the jouncy trot of the faun, the rhythmic paces of the centaur, the gangly stride of one boy and the halting steps of the other. Were they hopeful? Did they—or Rueshlan—believe this parley had a chance? *Do they really expect Charach to give up without a fight?*

After an interminable hour, the embassy did return—empty-handed—as Abisina expected.

"Charach sent a centaur and two Vranian generals to meet us," Findlay confided in Abisina later. "One of the generals was so insolent in his looks and the way he carried himself that I knew we would get nowhere. But then he saw Lohring! She had been waiting in a tree, and she leapt down. She landed inches from where he was standing. His face went white and he looked like he might run." Findlay chuckled, but then stopped himself. "It's not right to enjoy his fear. We won't get anywhere if we seek revenge!"

Abisina's tension and confusion over the last few days erupted. "He wants you *dead*, Findlay! He's got nothing but hatred for you—and you feel guilty because Lohring scared him? Tomorrow he will try to *kill* us. This—this clemency, this working with the Vranians—it's all a dream! The parley was a waste!"

"Was it?" Rueshlan asked, coming up behind them.

Abisina spun to face her father, chin lifted in defiance, but she faltered under the power of his gaze. Findlay was staring at her, too, and Abisina remembered too late her promise not to take her frustration out on him.

"You understand what we have to do?" Rueshlan continued. "The absurdity of it? We must fight a war to persuade our enemies of our *mercy*. We must convince them to trust us and join with us by holding them at the point of a sword. We have to show them the evil of Charach as he fights *with* them and we fight *against* them. I had no hope the parley would work either, Abisina, but it was not a waste.

"We must do the impossible," he said, "so why even try? Isn't that what you're asking? But what are our choices? To save Watersmeet, should we sacrifice the Motherland? Or to save the Motherland, should we sacrifice the Vranians? That parley may still do some good. Right now, the Vranian forces are mocking me for thinking they would want my clemency. But I hope that offer will be a seed that bears fruit. When Charach is dead, I hope our work with Corlin, our offers of clemency, our conduct on the battlefield will convince the Vranians to join us. If we cannot come together—human, centaur, dwarf, faun, and fairy—some new Charach will rise—lured out of his hole by our hatred. You or your children or your children's children will again stand on this battlefield. So, no, I cannot agree with you. Any parley genuinely offered is not a waste."

"I want you to be right, Father. I want to believe the way you do," Abisina said softly.

"When the time comes, Abisina," Rueshlan said, "you will know what to do."

Abisina touched the necklace around her throat. He spoke Vigar's words.

CHAPTER XIX

ABISINA HAD BEEN STANDING WITH THE ARCHERS ON THE eastern rise since before dawn, her fingers growing stiff and cold against her bow. As the gray light spread across the sky, she could make out the army arrayed to her right: more archers in the vanguard, interspersed with dwarves carrying long, sharp pikes. Behind them, the centaurs stood ready to gallop forward—after the archers had done their work—and break the Vranian line. Humans, fauns, and fairies clustered on either side of the centaurs in order to follow them into the chaos they would create. Hidden somewhere to her left was Neiall and a phalanx of soldiers prepared to strike the Vranian flank. More dwarves manned the trenches dug to protect the high ground and the fairy archers' position in the trees on the other side of the battlefield. Though she could not see the fairies among the branches, she wondered if their fingers, like hers, ached to nock an arrow.

In the low light, Abisina strained to catch sight of Findlay, but she couldn't pick him out in the tightly packed ranks of soldiers. Rueshlan had put him near the back because of his youth, but Abisina knew he would work his way to the front if he could. Haret and Hoysta, with her enormous axe, were somewhere in the trenches below her.

But it was Rueshlan who commanded her attention as he stood as a centaur in the middle of the front line, waiting to give the order for the battle to begin. Next to him stood Corlin, who couldn't bring himself to lift a sword against his countrymen, but who had agreed to advance with one final attempt at parley.

Abisina glanced briefly at Elodie beside her, and wondered if her own face was as drawn and tight.

The first sign of the enemy's advance was a smudge of dust rising from the trees on the far side of the plain. The second sign was several carrion birds wheeling in the sky, their mottled, naked heads contrasting with their graceful flight. And then came the clank of metal and the tramp of feet from Abisina's nightmares, only to be drowned out by the blood rushing in her ears. A wavering black line appeared and grew thicker and thicker until Abisina could distinguish figures of men, row after row marching toward them, with swords and spears and daggers meant for her father, her friends, her new home.

But as she looked closer, Abisina realized it wasn't just men she saw. Behind the first lines came ranks of minotaurs carrying pikes, followed by the hags with their staffs. Along each flank of the regular troops prowled the silver überwolves, and in the rear guard, trolls. As big as boulders, these four scaly behemoths trudged forward, kept in check by chains crisscrossing their chests and arms. And then, a sight that made Abisina's head swim with fear: Icksyon's band of centaurs—with their leader marching in the center, a minotaur on each side. Abisina scanned up and down the line, but she could not find the White Worm.

It was time for Rueshlan to address his troops.

"Watersmeet!" he cried, unsheathing his sword and raising it above his head as he galloped out from the battle lines to face his army.

"Hi-yah!" the army bellowed as one.

"The Motherland!" And again, a deafening "Hi-yah!"

"Watersmeet!"

"Hi-yah!" The cry reverberated against the trees and echoed off the hillside.

"Today, before the sun sets, we will face a test of more than strength or courage. An army approaches, led by Charach!" The name had never sounded so fearsome to Abisina. "They will come at us with hate! They will come at us with rage! But we will not waver, Watersmeet! Because we are descendants of Vigar—"

"Vigar! Hi-yah!" the throng yelled.

"—messengers of the ideals that Watersmeet is built on. Any who join with us will be welcomed! Any who defy

Charach can return to their villages unharmed. But most will fight us—too afraid to defy the White Worm. And we will fight back. As long as Charach stands, Watersmeet and the Motherland will stand against him!"

Abisina had thought the army's cry couldn't get any louder, but then the roar engulfed her. Line upon line of gathered soldiers lifted their voices. Even the fairies joined the cry. Though their lips did not move, a current ran through the air that could have come from nowhere else.

The Vranians kept marching until they were just out of arrow range and then, as one, they halted. Rueshlan and Corlin advanced, Corlin holding the oak bough above his head. A last chance for peace.

"Vranians!" Rueshlan called. "Our quarrel is not with you. We repeat our offer of clemency for all who renounce their support of Charach. This man—Corlin of Vranille—stands before you as proof of our intention. Your villages have been destroyed, and you have been forced to fight a battle that is not your own. Give up now and spare your lives."

As the Watersmeet army waited for a response, Abisina heard a sound she recognized, but before she could name it, there was a sharp crack and a broken arrow lay in the dust at Corlin's feet. It had been snapped in half by a fairy's arrow speeding out of the trees just in time to prevent it from imbedding in Corlin's chest.

One last breath—then the air was full of battle cries as the armies rushed forward.

Abisina missed the first volley of arrows, too stunned to move when Frayda cried, "Loose!" The twang of bowstrings brought her to her senses, and at the next signal, her arrow flew with the rest, angled in the direction she had calculated so many times. As Abisina let her first arrow fly, she thought not of angles and wind direction but of the heart her arrow might find.

She almost missed Frayda's command to shoot at will. *Don't think. Reach for an arrow, nock, pull back, and release. Reach for an arrow, nock, pull back, and release.* Her target was simple and vast—the throng of Vranians pushing to reach the battle line.

Between arrows, she caught glimpses of the fight. Findlay parrying a thrust of horns from a minotaur. Alden and several dwarves running an überwolf through with a pike as it closed in on an injured faun. A Vranian Elder, red sash across his chest, thrusting his sword deep into an archer's chest. Neiall leading his phalanx bristling with pikes into the exposed flank of the Vranian army. An überwolf sinking his teeth into a woman's neck as she removed her sword from a fallen Vranian. A crowd of Watersmeet's centaurs swarming one of the trolls released from its chains, its massive arms swinging as it crushed two centaurs in one blow. The Vranians' terrified faces as the fairies broke cover from the trees like strange birds, leaping into the fray with swords drawn and fury in their light eyes. Kyron and Icksyon rearing up, slashing at each other with hooves and swords. And Rueshlan—everywhere—defending a fallen dwarf, striking a tall Vranian, thrusting his sword into the belly of a minotaur even as he knocked aside an überwolf with his shield.

But where is the White Worm?

Abisina and the archers were ordered to reposition themselves lower on the rise. As the battle lines mingled, they could no longer shoot generally into the Vranian position. Now they needed to seek out specific targets and watch their arrows find their home.

"Let's go!" Elodie called next to her, dropping her bow to her side and following a faun and two men down the slope toward the trenches.

But the Vranians had repositioned their archers, too.

Abisina had begun to follow Elodie when she heard a sickening thud behind her. She wheeled around to see a faun sway at the knees, an arrow sticking out of his throat. She reached out toward him as an arrow struck his right shoulder with another horrible sound. She could only watch as he hit the ground, the life already gone from his eyes.

And then Elodie was there, forcing Abisina to bend double as another arrow whizzed over them.

"Where are they coming from?" Abisina shouted as they ran farther down the slope.

"Over there!" Elodie pointed at a cluster of Vranian archers who now stood in front of the trenches and were raking the hillside with their missiles. Some of the Vranians had crossbows, which meant that they shot fewer arrows but with more power. Abisina knew she had to help stop them as she watched another Watersmeet archer fall.

As Elodie continued downhill, Abisina slowed and pulled an arrow from her quiver. As she put her arrow to the string and drew it back toward her ear, a Vranian man raised his crossbow and aimed directly at her, letting his own arrow fly seconds after she had let hers. She suddenly realized that this stranger, whom she could see quite clearly standing there in the mud, whose name she would never know, was trying to kill her.

And she was trying to kill him.

Abisina knew that the Vranian arrow missed her only because in the next second she was reaching for another one, sighting on a different target without waiting to see where her first arrow ended its flight. From that moment on, her senses sharpened.

Did she kill many? Wound many? Save a dwarf or a fairy by stopping a Vranian sword from descending? Was she right to do so? There was no time to think. Was that scream the scream of a man who had tasted her arrow or her own scream as she watched an ally or a friend fall? Was the nausea she felt from seeing so much blood or from spilling so much herself? And the terrible panic—did it come from seeing the bodies drowned in the mud of the battlefield or from the grip of hands around her own throat, hands that went limp after a sword blow from an unseen savior?

The chaos of that long day of battle, the screams of the

dying, the vicious smell of blood and excrement and mud and sweat, the deadness of limbs moving just so that they might keep on moving—it took over Abisina's body and mind until one unearthly cry penetrated it all and then there was—

Stillness.

She was past the trenches toward the center of the battle-field, though she had no idea how she got there. Immediately to her left lay the body of a dwarf with an arrow through his back; to her right, the twisted body of a hag. Others stood nearby, and they, too, stopped and stared, but Abisina could not make sense of the scene.

All over the battlefield, the fighting had stopped. But in front of her, two hundred paces away, Rueshlan battled Charach: the Centaur and the White Worm.

Abisina stood transfixed, the image that had pursued her through so many nights embodied on the battlefield: the White Worm, black eyes ringing its head, open mouth drip-ping with poison, thick forearms lifting its segmented body from the ground as it searched for Rueshlan.

It spotted him as he galloped in for another blow, sword flashing in the sunlight, and it spun to confront him, razor claws slashing the air.

"No!" Abisina screamed and started to run, her feet pro-pelling her around the fallen bodies, between the soldiers who were falling back. Without stopping Abisina nocked an arrow and watched it fly into one of the monster's eyes.

With a shriek that rent the air, Charach's head swiveled

toward Abisina. The white body came crashing to the earth, knotted forearms pulling it forward as the mouth opened.

Abisina held her ground and nocked her second arrow. But as she planted her feet to take the shot, a blast of the Worm's poisonous breath hit her, forcing her to shut her eyes and gasp for clean air. The smell of rot overwhelmed her, and she waited for the final blow. But before it came, hooves rushed toward her, hands lifted her and carried her away.

She fought to open her streaming eyes, but it was getting harder to draw breath, and she needed all her energy to force the air through her swollen throat.

"Hang on!" Her father's voice.

Abisina tried to answer, but her burning mouth made no sound. And then new hands closed around her.

"Take her to safety!" Rueshlan commanded.

Don't leave me! Abisina screamed in her head. *Don't go back!* She fought and fought, but she was losing consciousness.

"The rest of you, stay away! I can finish this now!" Rueshlan called, but farther off. "And Kyron, take care of my daughter!"

Abisina's head filled with screams as her father's hoofbeats faded.

She couldn't have been out for long because when she came to, Kyron had not yet reached the archers' rise. "Fall back! Fall back at Rueshlan's command!" he called out as he galloped. Abisina felt them start to move uphill and Kyron's steps slowed.

"Is she alive?" It was Frayda's frantic voice. Shaking hands touched her throat, feeling for a heartbeat. "Kyron, let me have her."

"He told me to take care of her!"

"I'm not going to hurt her—"

"I will not let her go!" Kyron's grip tightened around Abisina.

"Water! Give her water!" Coolness splashed Abisina's face. She forced her eyes open and saw blurry outlines. "My father!" she croaked. "What's happening?"

Near them, someone was calling for help, someone else was groaning in pain.

"The Vranians have fallen back, too. Charach and Rueshlan are still in it," Kyron told her. "Rueshlan just landed a blow on the Worm's left side. But the black blood is fuming and Rueshlan must pull back to avoid it. There! He threw his dagger and took out another of the Worm's eyes, and now he approaches again with his sword!"

Abisina's vision was clearing, and she struggled to sit up to see for herself how her father fared. Kyron propped her against his chest, but when Frayda tried to help her down, he resisted, determined to follow his commander's orders.

"Oh!" Abisina cried as the Worm's tail lashed out at Rueshlan. "We have to help him! Find whoever you can! We have to get to him!"

"But he said—"

"He needs us, Kyron!"

The centaur hesitated, then asked. "Can you ride?"

"He told us to fall back!" Frayda yelled, but Abisina and Kyron ignored her as Abisina clambered onto his back.

"There's Brant!" Kyron said, scanning the hillside. "And Morrell—he's hurt. Badly. But Glynholly looks untouched!"

Abisina had to grip Kyron's waist to steady herself, but she urged him, "Go! Go!" And he again galloped toward the battle, calling to those on their feet to follow.

On the other side of the plain, the Vranians had the same idea, and as Kyron, Abisina, and their small force galloped forward, so did a group of Vranians, swords drawn to meet them.

But no one could get close to their champion. Charach's blood and poison soaked the plain, creating an uncrossable barrier. Two Vranians and a centaur fell, overcome with the fumes. Glynholly shot two arrows which incinerated in midair as they neared the Worm, and then she almost succumbed. When Abisina heard the faun cry, "Fall back!" she obeyed. They could not help Rueshlan.

The battle ranged over the field, turning the plain into a morass of mud, poison, and blood. At one point, Rueshlan drove the Worm against the fairies' trees, where its tail struck down several of the tall trunks. From the archers' rise, Abisina watched in horror as three fairies fell to the earth, writhed in the poison, and lay still. But she could spare no more than a moment's grief as Charach rallied and fought against Rueshlan with renewed power, catching her father's shoulder with a claw. Her father staggered under the strength of the blow, but then he regained his balance and fought on, shunting aside a stream of poison with his shield.

It seemed as if the battle would never end. Rueshlan bled from gashes all over his body, and his left arm dangled uselessly at his side. His hooves were worn down to his ankles from exposure to the poisonous mud. He had lost his sword and dagger, leaving only a small dirk for a weapon. His raven hair had fallen out in clumps where he had been struck by Charach's breath.

But Charach was horribly wounded, too. Rueshlan's sword had opened huge rents in the Worm's sides and black blood stained most of its body. Its tail was left twitching on the ground, the tendons severed. And many of its eyes were blinded by arrows.

How can either of them survive one more blow? Abisina thought numbly. She longed to look away, but knew she would never take her eyes from her father while he still stood.

As dusk fell on the field, Rueshlan galloped forward despite his crippled legs. He attacked from the left where most of the Worm's eyes had been taken out. The Worm's head swung desperately around as it sensed Rueshlan's approach, but Rueshlan ducked underneath its chest and drove his dirk deep into the White Worm's soft belly.

At first, the onlookers didn't know what happened.

Rueshlan was racing across the plain, and a cry went up from the Vranians who thought that he was retreating. Their shouts were stopped by the sight of the Worm falling. As Charach struck the ground, black smoke rose, shrouding the Worm's carcass in darkness.

Bellows, shrieks, and howls rose from the Vranian side of the battlefield. Rudderless without their leader, Charach's minions—the minotaurs and hags, the überwolves and trolls—beat a tumultuous retreat to the trees, disappearing into the forest like shadows chased by the light of the morning. The Vranians and centaurs remained, but they looked around the battlefield bewildered.

Abisina hardly noticed the Vranians. Just beyond the billows of noxious smoke, Rueshlan stumbled and fell.

"He's down! He's down! Go, Kyron!" she cried.

They were the first to reach him. Rueshlan lay on his side, his head in the mud, his torn and bloody shoulder hunched over so that Abisina couldn't see his face. She tumbled from Kyron's back onto the ground beside him.

"Father! Father!" She reached a hand toward him, desperate to see his face and yet unwilling to confirm her worst fears.

Then he groaned. "He's alive!" she shouted, and as she pulled his head onto her lap, he transformed from centaur to man. "Help me!" she called. All who were able to walk, or crawl, made their way to their fallen leader.

Abisina's momentary hope turned to despair as he was laid on his back and she could see the extent of his wounds.

"Father! I'm here! Please, Father!"

At her cry, his eyes fluttered open, cloudy, but he tried to focus as she said again, "Father."

"Abisina," he managed. "I'm sorry. I thought I could keep my promise."

"Shhh," she whispered, smoothing back strands of his hair. "It's over now, and you *have* kept your promise. You're here with me, and Charach is dead."

"I couldn't let another one fall, Abisina. Can you understand?"

"Yes," Abisina choked as she wiped her own tears off her father's face. "I understand." She pressed her cheek against his.

As she did, the necklace—of Vigar, of Rueshlan, and of Sina—tumbled forward and caught the last ray of light.

Rueshlan's eyes cleared for a moment as the pendant glittered above him. For another few breaths, he looked at his daughter. Then he was gone.

A high keening broke across the battlefield, echoed in a ululating wail from the fairies descending the trees, carrying the news of Rueshlan's death. Abisina could not bring herself to join the wordless cry, yet it filled her, lifted her, gave voice to the emptiness that had opened inside her.

But the cry of grief soon transformed to a cry of rage, and when Abisina looked at the faces around her, they were twisted with hatred. Swords, axes, and daggers, clotted with blood, were raised toward the sky.

Rage eclipsed her emptiness, giving her something solid to hang onto, rising like a wave that would carry her forward.

"Make them pay!" Across the battlefield, the cry was taken up. The rumble of the centaur; the clear tones of fauns; the multiple timbres of the humans and dwarves; the haunting voices of the fairies: "Make them pay!"

And the words came back to them from across the river of poison dividing the armies. The Vranians, Icksyon, and his band found the purpose that had momentarily eluded them. Their hate-filled screams rang out with the same cry: "Make them pay!"

On both sides, soldiers shook their weapons, the injured ones forced themselves to their feet, Elders and Council members called curses down on the enemy: "Make them pay!"

The words rose in Abisina, who still sat with her father's head in her lap. *Make them pay! For every infant left outside the walls. For every outcast man, woman, and child. For the dwarves, centaurs, fairies, and fauns killed in the name of Vran. For every life lost on this battlefield. But mostly make them pay for Vigar, for Sina, and for Rueshlan.*

Easing her father's head to the ground, Abisina got to her feet. She opened her mouth to join the cacophony—

"Human."

Haret stood, arms crossed, eyebrows lowered. His axe head was broken, his sword was lost, his right arm bled—but he would not let her pass until she heard him. "*You* wear the necklace now."

The necklace.

She felt it again—a weight around her neck.

Abisina grabbed it, ready to yank it off, fling it from her, but as her fingers closed on the cool metal, the screams, the keening, the groans of the dying stilled.

And in the quiet, Vigar spoke: *Charach is everyone's enemy.*

The wearers of the necklace: Vigar, Rueshlan, Sina—*and* Haret. She had forgotten that he, too, had worn the necklace.

She met her friend's eyes.

"Abisina, you know what you must do."

And at last, she did.

She lifted the necklace and held it before her. Though the sun was down and the moon had not yet risen, the pendant began to shine—softly—but with each step, the light grew.

She moved as if in a dream. She stepped through the folk of Watersmeet arrayed against the Vranians. Without hesitation, she entered the murky air rising from the ground around Charach's body.

The fumes parted: her eyes, her breath, her boots untouched by the poison.

The image of Abisina—green eyes blazing, dark hair rippling down her back, a beacon of light in her hands—closed the mouths of Vrania and Watersmeet. Silence spread across the battlefield.

Abisina stopped between the two armies. She held the brilliant necklace over her head so that followers of Vran and of Vigar could see the strands of Obrium twisting into one.

Slowly she turned to each army, the light of the necklace illuminating the many faces she recognized: Findlay, bloodied but standing; Surl, favoring a foreleg; Corlin, clinging to a leafless oak branch; Elodie, with her bow and empty quiver; Elder Theckis, his own pendant missing; Hoysta, supported by her axe; Icksyon, clutching a broken sword; Frayda, grief etched on her face.

Abisina spoke:

"Vrania! Charach is dead! Charach—who destroyed your villages and slaughtered your families! Will you keep fighting for him? Will you carry your hate away from this field and retreat behind your walls, nursing your vengeance until a new Charach rises? Or will you learn from this suffering? Will you join with Watersmeet?

"And Watersmeet, have you forgotten? Rueshlan promised we would fight as long as Charach stands. But Charach lies there!" She pointed to the blackened earth. "This morning Rueshlan reminded us of who we are: *We are descendents of Vigar*. Remember his words, Watersmeet!

"Look at me—Vrania, Watersmeet! You are both part of me: my mother was Vranian; my father, the Keeper of Watersmeet, was a man and a centaur. I, too, have heard the call of fear, vengeance, and hate. But look around you! This is where that path leads."

On either side, weapons were lowered by some while others clutched theirs tighter. As Abisina continued to turn and turn and turn, flooding the plain with the necklace's light, she dared to hope. There were other Charachs. But right now, this one was defeated. And she was the daughter of Rueshlan and Sina. They both had spent their lives fighting Charach in their own ways. She could do the same.

She would use whatever gifts she had inherited from them so that she, too, deserved to wear the necklace.

Abisina lifted the necklace higher, light spilling before her, showing her the way.

EPILOGUE

The Green Man had not been seen on either side of the Obrun Mountains for countless generations. There was no record of him in Watersmeet's library; he had even passed out of stories and legends. But he had been in this land before, and he returned to pay his respects to Rueshlan.

The grieving folk of Watersmeet had watched and wept as Rueshlan's funeral pyre burned for three days. They were joined by refugees from the southern lands and a handful of Vranians who had responded to Rueshlan's call for peace and unity. Just before dawn on the third morning, the pyre was no more than a smoldering pile of ash and all eyes were on Abisina. She stood—Haret at her side—watching the dwindling flames, holding her father's necklace as she had since the first spark had been touched to the tower of wood. The folk waited for Rueshlan's daughter to lead them home.

But before the last flame went out, the Green Man was there:

a giant of a man with green skin, eyes, and lips. His body and head were covered with leaves. Vines snaked from his mouth toward the ground and took root. Although none could name him, they knew what he was: the patron of all that grows, dies, and is reborn.

The crowd fell back as the Green Man approached the pyre. Abisina did not stir until he knelt beside her and laid a hand on her shoulder. Slowly, slowly she lifted her eyes to his. Some say he spoke with words, others that she understood him without speech. The Green Man then reached into the remains of the fire, filled his cupped hands with ash, and brought them to his lips. He blew the ash first to the south and then to the north, creating two great, churning clouds. For a moment, the twin thunderheads glowered down on the gathered folk, but as the sun broke over the horizon, the gray turned to gold. With another breath, the Green Man sent the glittering ash spinning away.

Dazzled by the sparkling clouds, few saw the Green Man brush the last bit of ash from his hands and onto the ground at his feet. But Abisina saw it—saw a golden tendril sprout from the trampled soil and begin to grow. When the folk pulled their eyes away from the now distant ash-glow, a tree with golden leaves and white luminescent bark had reached the Green Man's waist. When it brushed his chin, golden leaves trailing gracefully toward the ground, the Green Man spoke in a deep, rumbling voice that made the leaves covering his body whisper beneath his words: "I give this land the Seldar tree, born of great pain. Watersmeet, Vrania, fairies, folk of the north and the south, attend the lesson it holds for you."

Without another word, he turned away and strode north.

*A miracle awaited both armies as they made their way home.
Seldar groves dotted the landscape, white bark and golden leaves
shining through even the darkest foliage, easing the load of grief so
many carried from the battlefield.*

*The folk of Watersmeet and the fairies found a second miracle.
As they reached the place where they would begin the climb to the
Low Col, they were met instead by a deep cut chiseled through
the mountain range, forming a road broad enough for twenty centaurs to walk abreast. Sheer walls stretched up from the road into
the sky, blocking the sun except at high noon.*

*Both miracles brought the possibility of unity to the divided
land: the road promised contact and communication between the
north and south as never before. And no one could look at a Seldar
and not be moved. From these trees, the land took a new name: Seldara. But though the barrier of the Obruns was breached, and
though the people were united in their love of the Seldar, Vigar's—
and Rueshlan's—vision of true unity had not yet been realized. . . .*